AN OPAL IN THE WEST

Sally Harper Bates

A debt of gratitude is owed the following people
for their encouragement, and for reading
through this novel with me, and for me:
Matt Bates, Heidi Thomas, John Rust, Brenda Whiteside

Of course,
To my husband Pat who never fails to tolerate my
middle-of-the-night stints at the computer.

To, Mike Capron for allowing me to use
some of his, oh so perfect drawings to
brighten the pages and the story.

Especially to Lynn Brown whose cover
artwork is so appreciated.

Other illustrations are drawn from
antique catalogs and linens.

COPYRIGHTED BY
Sally Harper Bates © January 2015
For Arizona Cowboy Connection
ALL RIGHTS reserved.
ISBN # 978-0-9895085-3-7

Cover artwork copyrighted © by Lynn Brown
Bluffdale, Texas.
Mike Capron holds © on his illustrations.

INTRODUCTION

Human nature itself dictates there are no innocents in life, only some 'bystanders' who might claim that to be so.

This story is loosely based on several incidents that happened in the West, somewhere in New Mexico, Arizona, Texas or maybe even California. The names in my story have been changed to protect the "innocent"- if in fact there is such a thing.

Within each incident this story might bring to mind, there are many points of view and in each of those are facets that no-one sees, not even the ones who are living the events that unfold. We cannot see farther than what our eyes will absorb, our mind will open to, and our hearts allow.

They say hindsight is 20-20. My granny used to tell me that one should believe only half of what they see and none of what they hear.

So, it's safe to say there will be those of you who read this story and think you know exactly who it's about, when and where it happened, and have a different version of the "reality" that unfolded. But it's only a story . . . of life in the West for oh, so many who settled throughout the breaks of her bosom.

Just a note . . . Crusty old cowboys don't say "aw shucks". If you have rather "tender ears", there are a few pages that may be a little "hot" for you. Just skip over those lines.

***

Early morning sun lit the tips of the apache plume brush along the ranch road, causing them to appear as though white fire dripped from murky green stems. Opal Redding sat alone on the bench of her buckboard, humming an old Irish tune birthed in her brain by her maternal grandmother. She fancied the buckboard creaked and the wheels rumbled to the tune she was humming, so she continued the melody until the buildings near town loomed ahead.

She pulled onto the main street, headed for the general store and turned her attention to her horses, until she noticed Will Martin on the boardwalk in front of the small café. He was in the midst of a heated discussion with a man who appeared to be inebriated and was certainly being obnoxious.

She started to rein in the team as she watched the older man poke Will in the chest with his finger, his voice rose to a level of anger that made her nervous as she drew near enough to catch the tone of his voice. Her lips tightened and her face flushed. She wanted to dismount and run to Will's defense, but she knew better. That would not be seemly and neither of the men would appreciate a girl in the mix. She let out a heavy sigh. *Why wasn't I born a man? Life would sure be easier.*

She continued to the general store, watching over her shoulder to see Will address the older man, then step to his horse and in one graceful, smooth motion, mounted. He sat still, watching his adversary for a few moments, then turned and trotted out of town.

Opal pulled the horses to a halt near the front of the little store, jumped lightly from her perch and bounced through the door. Even at her age she found the contents of the old mercantile fascinating. Handing the man behind the counter her written order, she took time to walk around the room seeking satisfaction for her curiosity.

For several moments she gazed at a collection of hats on the wall, taking notice of a fluffy women's chapeau with too many feathers and flowers, wondering who would wear a hat like that. *What in the world is that geegaw for, anyway?* Would she ever have need of a pair of shoes such as those on the shelf? She smiled, looked down at the scuffed boots pok-ing out from under a man's breeches. Her mother wouldn't be caught dead in anything but a skirt or dress, but Opal found it uncomfortable to work in the garden or mount to ride in skirts that hindered her freedom. She wondered how many rounds had she fought with her mother over that one.

Opal's reputation as a tomboy and scoundrel throughout the community didn't bother her all that much. She was considered a rebel and most of the older ladies looked at her with a mixture of disgust and repulsion. But the younger women had begun to watch her with a completely different mixture of expressions. It wasn't her intent to cause others to be as impertinent of social niceities, but she wasn't willing to back up from what she knew was right for her own life.

There were times she wondered if her tomboy ways would cost her the respect and commitment of a certain young cowboy, specifically the one she had just witnessed in an altercation on the boardwalk. But she had decided much earlier that as long as she could ride, that would be a higher priority than frills and lace. She hoped that would be true of that cowboy she had in mind.

Gathering filled boxes from the counter she loaded them in the buckboard. For a moment she questioned why Mr. Bradden didn't offer to load them for her, the way he would have if she'd been wearing a big feathery hat and waving a lacey umbrella. Or, if she'd been in a surrey instead of the ranch buckboard. It didn't take long to dismiss those thoughts and load herself into the rig to head for home.

She wondered if she would find Will along the road somewhere, or if maybe he would go out of his way again to stop by to visit her family. The hopeful thought caused her to swat the horses on the rump with her reins and they moved easily into a trot, pulling hard on the buckboard to speed things along. She smiled as one tossed his head around and snorted his displeasure. As they rolled past the local café she pondered what Will had been dis-cussing earlier with an obvious adversary.

It wasn't a short journey to her home, so she watched the scenery slowly pass, firmly holding the double set of reins, responding when she felt a tug that indicated they were changing their pace. She held them to an even trot as she let her mind drift. She'd traveled this road numerous times, yet still there was always something that gathered her interest like a dust-devil on the plains pulling loose remnants into its vacuum. She day-dreamed of horses, and of a world somewhere over that far horizon. Wondered at how little she knew of what lay far beyond the purple hills. She really wasn't interested in "all that." At least not enough so to warrant leaving her home and the familiarity of friends and family.

She began to wander back in thoughts to her early years with Will. She had taken notice of him as soon as the door to the school house opened to his lanky frame. His worn cowboy hat drew the attention of every child in the room. He'd been so quiet when he walked in that first morning and took a seat in the back of the room. Asked if he would like to move a little closer, Will shook his head and fussed with the edge of his desk. He didn't come to school every day, only now and then when his chores and work made a place for free time.

For several days, Will used his lunch break to locate a seat where his solitude allowed him complete privacy. The only person who encroached upon this realm was his friend, Matthew Baker. During free time, or lunch, Opal mustered up enough courage to sit nearby. She would ask if he would like to share her basket lunch. He never accepted, but always thanked her kindly.

Her proximity gradually drew closer to his perch in the shade of the massive oak that sheltered the side wall of the small country school house. Through those early years, their grade school friendship grew strong and rich. Their trails seemed to cross frequently and the friendship began to develop into a deeper bond. As they reached their teen years they began to understand their lives would always intertwine and they drew closer as the moon changed its face month after month.

They were frequently seen together, and as they passed puberty with little notice, their parents began to restrict the hours and miles they would spend together. But they were so engulfed in their love of horses, of the land and the freedom they moved in, that only on rare occasions would the rising tide of maturity catch their attention. Theirs was the simplest form of love, that of a deep and abiding friendship.

She watched for him constantly, hoping to hear the ring of shod hooves on the dirt road below her home, and always her heart would pound when she recognized his dirty grey hat. She smiled to herself as she remembered that no matter how dirty that hat was, he always found a way to keep it creased "just so." She swatted the horses again as the buckboard rounded the final curve in the road before her home came into sight. Will's horse was tied to the rail near the porch, which brought a smile and a quickening of her pulse. She adeptly pulled the buckboard parallel to the porch, whoa'd the horses and began to unload the supplies onto the nearby boards.

Will came through the doorway of her home, moved toward her and she heard his soft, mellow voice asking, "Can I help you with that pile of loot?"

She stopped, resting her left hand on her hip, and flippantly responded with a big grin, "I'd take that right kindly, sir."

They chuckled easy-like and chatted about little things as they finished the chore. Before moving into the house to join her family for an evening meal he reached to pull his hat from his moist, curly locks and pulled one of his usual gathered flowers from the hat band.

He bowed slightly, waved the flower in front of her nose, and whispered, "For the lovely lady."

"Goober! I'm a long way from bein' a lady," she whispered back.

"Not to me." His voice returned to normal, he took her by the elbow and escorted her into the kitchen. They sat at the table and visited with Opal's parents. Maxwell and Lily always made Will welcome at their table, or in their home. They'd become accustomed to his frequent visits.

They all sat down to beans cooked down with a shank of ham hock, cornbread, and for a treat some home-grown, canned green beans mixed in with store-bought canned tomatoes, salted and peppered with a few flakes of dried parsley. Surely, Will would consider this to be a fancy meal. Home-cooking with a woman's touch was a treat to men who ate beef and beans and an occasional potato in the bunkhouses around local ranches.

The meal wasn't as important as the company and the visiting that commenced over the table. She listened intently while Will filled them in on the confrontation in town earlier. The young cowboy played with the handle of his coffee mug, revealing slowly and carefully the chain of events he had walked through for the past several weeks.

"Months ago, Matt and I started keeping an eye out for a small place we could lease or buy. We had some plans that didn't seem to be working out until ol' man Danner's son, Pake, contacted us. He heard we were looking to lease something, so he offered us their place over near Bull Canyon. It's not much, and there are no buildings, but the fences aren't in too bad a' repair and there's grass and browse in all the canyons with springs running out of a couple of rocky ledges."

Opal's father stood to turn his chair around using the back as a rest for his forearms and elbows, watching Will carefully, listening to more than his words.

"Pake and Matthew set the deal up, and I signed off on the lease, but we weren't sure where, or even if, we would find cattle to run on the lease. We started snoopin' around trying to figure out when we'd be able to buy a few head to put on the place for a starter herd. Then this young Mexican boy came into town a few weeks ago and said his father had an accident and needed a doctor. The doc was tellin' some of the hands in town the pair had a pretty good sized herd of sheep they needed to sell so the boy could take his dad back to Mexico. So, me and Matt rode out and cut a deal with the Mex for his herd of sheep. We figured a couple of years would give us a jump start toward a herd of cattle and some good bulls, so we sort of went for it."

Opal started as her father sat straight up in his chair and the front legs banged on the floor. He nearly jumped out of his seat saying

"You bought *sheep?*"

"Yes, sir." Will swallowed hard.

"What'n hell were you thinking, boy? You ever been around sheep before? You know how to drive 'em and deal with the dirty things?" Surprise and anger tainted his voice.

"No sir, not entirely, but we're learning, and we hired an old Mex from over near Animas and he's gonna stay out there with 'em . . . him and a good dog."

Will stuttered slightly through the explanation, and his voice quivered. Somewhere down deep he must have been feeling some resentment surge, as his voice changed and he became somewhat nervous. Opal was torn between being aggravated at her father's reaction, but her own surprise at what Will had gotten himself into was pushing her emotions around causing her pulse to accelerate.

"You know every cattle rancher in the territory is going to be fit to be tied over that, don't you?" Maxwell demanded.

"Well, we were hopin' different, sir," Will answered in a low and tentative voice. "But we intend to keep the sheep on our own lease and we've checked all the fences, so they won't be driftin' over on anyone's spread messin' with cattle and grazin' off our own allotment. But that ain't the worst of it. Ol' man Danner is the one who's cranked up about the whole deal, and since he suddenly wants to sell that land, he's just plumb ticked off about us havin' it leased at all, and the sheep are just addin' fuel to his fit."

Her father sat quietly for a few minutes taking a couple of sips of what had become cold coffee. He lifted smoky eyes to gaze intently into the younger brown eyes looking straight back at him. Shaking his head, he drank around the dregs in the mug then stood and walked to the dish pan to set the cup down.

"Well . . ." he turned and leaned against the edge of a butcher block table. "Guess you'll have to finish whatever comes now. But I don't want Opal mixed up in any of this, ya hear? She thinks she's pretty big stuff these days, but age don't mean smarts and she ain't got much of those at times."

Opal stiffened and felt the blood come to her face as the words poured from what right now seemed to be a big round hole under her father's nose.

"I'm sittin' right here, Dad," she said quietly. She pushed away from the table, agitated, and walked out the front door onto the steps. Suddenly she realized she'd left the horses and the buckboard untended. *No wonder Dad said I didn't have too much in the smarts department.* She jumped onto the buckboard and speaking softly to the horses, headed for the barn and corrals.

What the men continued to discuss wasn't of interest to Opal, so she unhitched the team and set things to right at the barn before she headed for the house. Will and her dad were standing on the porch as she rounded the corner, but Will walked down the steps as soon as he saw her. "I best be goin' on back to the ranch, but I'll come back by when I can." His voice was low and soft, tainted with a hint of sadness.

Will's spurs sounded like little bells far off on the wind as he walked to the hitchin' rail and prepared to mount. Just before he lifted his left foot to set it into a stirrup, he glanced over his shoulder and the corners of his mouth turned up just a bit as he winked at Opal. She smiled back and waved from her hip, then watched with her dad as he rode off. She turned to move into the

house when her dad reached out a hand to stop her.

"I like Will, Opal, but he and Matt have maybe built themselves a hangin' rack and I don't want to see you hurt if that comes to pass. You know folks are gonna be ticked off, and you bein' in the mix is asking for sour talkin' around town."

"I know." She stood for a moment with her dad's hand on her arm, watching Will disappear in the dust.

Mr. Mitchell was a kind man with an eye of favor for Will and Matthew. Well aware of the potential predicament they had bought into, he met Will at the door to the bunkhouse as he unsaddled to put his mount away for the night.

"I want to visit with you a little bit, Will. Would you gather Matt up and come to the house for a bit?"

"Sure thing. Any trouble?" Will stopped and looked over his shoulder, one eyebrow up.

"No, just want to visit a few minutes, nothin' to worry about, yet."

As Mitchell returned to his home to wait, he played with memories of the pair. Will and Matt had signed on for his spring branding crew when they were barely into the years they could write two numbers for their age. Neighbors for most of their lives, they grew up in the breaks of New Mexico territory when she herself was struggling with her own growing pains. They spent every spring for many years signed on to the branding crew and while they were given opportunities to be horse-back and swing a rope, most of the time they were on the ground crew breathing dust and smoke.

They understood fully there were "dues to pay" as they entered the brotherhood known as the cowboy nation. For years they wiped the smoke of a branding iron from their eyes, cleaned cow manure from under their lower lips and rolled in the dirt beneath the hooves of a mama cow defending her young from what she didn't understand.

Mitchell was born in Texas and came to New Mexico with his parents in a covered wagon, walking much of the way in spite of being barely past boyhood. He would watch enviously from the ground as four riders moved a small bunch of cows and two good bulls along the trail with the wagons. He grew tired of breathing dust and kicking rocks aside, wishing his father would give him a mount and let him ride with the others. What became their family ranch was now his to manage and develop into his father's dream. But it was his dream as well, and he tended it with a sense of duty.

Will and Matthew had become almost a part of Mitchell's family as he watched them mature both physically and in the prowess of the working cowboy element. Strong men, found in New Mexico just past the turn of the century. Straight-forward young men with dreams of a future and an eye for the past, they held fast to the old-school methods of dealing with cattle in the canyons and breaks of a tough country that gave little and required much.

Mitchell knew Will had a long held dream . . . to own a small ranch where cattle and horses would be the mainstay with a lot of day work and side jobs to give the ranch a solid financial under-girding. He and Matt were long on dream and short on what it took to make one come true, but that didn't seem to slow them down much. With the recent signing of that infamous lease, things were starting to slide into place, but not without complications. Mitchell shook his head as he checked the coffee to see if it was boiling.

That small, unused piece of ground suddenly seemed to have become quite valuable to Danner, who had completely ignored the property for several years. In the past, he had been a respected rancher and lawman, but had become a heavy gambler and spent long hours drinking with men who called him friend as long as he was buying drinks. The man's family had been forced to re-locate to another town in order to avoid the gossip and hardships placed on them with his additional bad habit of visiting the business of a local "soiled dove".

His son, Pake, had become caretaker of the father, trying to keep the family holdings together and meet the needs of his sisters and mother who now lived with her aging parents far from the spicy tongues of locals. None of which was an easy task, but Pake was apparently still of a mind to work things out with Will and Matt, to string along with what was unfolding with this herd of sheep. So, the days unfurled in dust and duty while two young cowboys faced an uncertain future, and a very certain present.

Mitchell moved the coffee pot to the front of a wood stove and threw a stick of wood through its door, then answered the knock he was expecting. Welcoming the two young men into his kitchen, he poured coffee, asked how their day had gone, then settled into a worn chair with no padding. From there, the conversation became short and to the point.

"You boys are workin' up to a fight, looks like. What's on your mind with this lease and the sheep?"

Will straightened up in his chair, wrapped both hands around his coffee cup and responded quietly. "A fight sure wasn't our intent, Mr. Mitchell, we're just lookin' for a couple o' years hard work and then turnin' this sheep herd into cattle." He didn't raise his eyes from the circle of dark brown muddy liquid in his hands but his face burned hot with a red flush.

Matt raised up, set his elbows on the edge of the table and leaned forward. His expression was tense as he filled the conversation with expletives where the Danner family was concerned.

The old rancher listened quietly as he drank his coffee and watched the expression on Will's face. Matt was an outgoing youngster with a hot temper. Will just the opposite, quiet and with a great deal of composure and self-confidence.

Mitchell remembered several years back when Will brought two cattle thieves to his front door with nothing more than his guts and an old pistol that may or may not have fired when the trigger was pulled. He'd caught them branding a long-eared calf under the rim of the mesa in a thick growth of oak brush, snuck up on them and quietly, calmly ran a bluff on them and carried it out until he got them to the ranch headquarters.

He listened intently as Matt finished a heated explanation of how the pair ended up with a herd of sheep and a leased ranch with an angry owner. His mouth tightened, but his heart softened substantially. He was a little irritated that Matt had taken on the bulk of the conversation while Will sat quietly watching.

I can't help it, I like these boys . . . they've been like my own kids since they were hair-brained youngsters looking for a job. Any job! Pride rose inside his chest, realizing they had grown into the cowboys he sat with at that moment. *I have to keep trying to help them see they've painted themselves into a corner and there is only one way out.*

"I want both of you to stay on here for some day work, keep your bed and board. And I am willing to give you time off to deal with that herd of sheep, but only when you can take off without leaving others here to take up slack for you." Mitchell searched the faces of the younger men, looking for signs of acknowledgement and understanding. "I guess for now I'll even encourage you to do what you've set out to do, get the job done and over with. But if this turns into a heated confrontation and the anger with my neighbors runs over into my front porch, I won't back you and I won't let my men get drug into the fray. Understood?"

"Yes sir," came from the lips of both young men simultaneously as they rose to empty coffee dregs into a bowl near the sink kept for the garden.

Will stood for a moment looking at the broken egg shells mixed with the coffee, and suddenly realized he'd mixed farming and ranching in a way that could lead to a broken relationship with this old rancher he loved and respected more than most anyone in his life. For the third time, he found himself regretting the decision to move forward with the lease.

He and Matt shook hands with their boss and silently walked to the bunkhouse where Matt joined a hot card game, but Will declined the invitation to join in. Sleep came hard for him that night. More than once he returned to the moment he and Matt signed that lease, thinking they were moving toward a cattle ranch and new beginnings. *Dam' sheep. . . Dam'dable sheep!* Eventually he slipped into a fitful sleep filled with visions and murmurings.

Early the next day he watched as the morning came softly across the roof of the barn and spread through the yard and across the porch. Waiting for the cook to serve up breakfast, he'd already saddled a horse for himself, and had Matt's day horse hobbled and waiting to be saddled. They stomped to interrupt the bite of flies and nipped at each other. They nodded their heads up and down, their manes catching the sun just right to light up their ears and shoulders like fire dancing along a ridge.

It didn't take long for the crew to down the oatmeal and pancakes with a side of bacon. Cowboys chewed with their mouths open and talked with their mouths full. Plates became empty and coffee cups filled for the third time as they all listen for orders from the foreman. Will was very familiar with each of his peers, and he sat comfortably with them around the long boards of an ancient table. The day held more dust and duty, but all the men would meet it head on, joking and poking fun at each other. He joined the group as they filed out the door of the bunkhouse leaving the cook and a hired kid to clean up.

As Will walked to the left shoulder of his horse and reached to untie the neck-rein, the short legged sorrel shied and blew warm breath through flared nostrils, pointing his ears at him. Will spoke to him, then raised his hand to gently, slowly scratch the soft ears around the bridle path.

"Sorry, pard," he murmured as he gathered a fist full of mane with

his reins and slid the toe of his dusty boot through the stirrup. Swinging his right leg over the cantle of an old, freshly oiled saddle, he settled and gave the young horse a minute to adjust to the weight. He and Matt circled their horses and rode out at a walk until they'd passed the corral then moved into an easy lope and made a concentrated effort to catch up with the crew.

The day wore on as it always does for a cowboy - dusty, dry, hot, and full of the smell of manure and sweat. Will's mind was filled with questions and few answers regarding the lease and the sheep herd, as well as the obvious animosity building over their situation. He found his heart heavy, and a sense of foreboding wore at his soul throughout the day as he wrestled between "get out now" and "get the job done and over with."

Mixed into the whirlwind of thoughts and visions appeared a soft little face framed with hair the color of mud and eyes watching him like a hawk out for his breakfast. As always, thoughts of her made the corners of his mouth turn up and his heart lighter.

As sure as he was about her love for him, he was just as unsure how their relationship would fare in the light of what waited ahead for him and Matt. The day wore on as mental debris swirled through his brain, making it hard to concentrate.

Pake Danner stood in the doorway watching his drunken father with a fusion of anger and pity. He remembered a different man buried somewhere beneath the third button on that wrinkled, dirty shirt that wrapped his father in a stench Pake had become accustomed to. Sonny's fall from "grace" had been similar to riding a horse full speed off a twenty foot cliff; it had come hard and fast.

He eyed Sonny, who stood sulled up at the bar with a warm beer in his hands, his smoldering large enough to draw attention from most in the room. He spoke to himself under his breath, grousing and wiping the hair out of his eyes as he emptied the glass and ordered another with a shot on the side. The bartender slid the beer across the counter, deliberately trying to ignore the second half of the order, but reproach followed quickly from the angry lips of the old man.

A kinder, softer, easier-to-get-along-with man had raised Pake. One minus the seething hatred that embroiled this older version. He'd been a buffalo hunter, guide, cowboy, peace officer, father, husband, son of someone, somewhere. The figure from past years had been a different sort of man. Drinking and gambling followed the loss of a job that wrapped his identity too tightly, and from there to the back door of a house of ill repute and eventual loss of wife and family. The respect he held as a younger person was gone, faded with years of bad choices and opinions mixed with the kind of men that cared not a whit about their reputation.

Pake remembered when his father had managed to buy some land here and there at a time when he was better heeled and more careful with his jingle. Lately he'd been short on cash and wanting to sell part of his holdings. Among which was the half-baked ranch his son had leased to a couple of what his father considered to be dam' worthless cowboys who were planting stinkin' sheep all over the range.

As Pake fussed around his thoughts, they built an invisible mushroom over his head that hung there like a ripe cloud of juniper dust. Just before it exploded, Pake pushed his way

through the doors and stepped to his father's side, reaching easy-like to touch the arm of his coat. His father took a swing at him, staggering away from the bar with a bellow and curse, but Pake continued to talk to him in a low tone of voice until they meandered and staggered onto the boardwalk.

Pake glanced back to smile at the bartender who watched them leave shaking his head and wiping the bar where booze had been slopped on the polished wood.

Pake and Sonny found their way to the front porch of the rooming house where Sonny rented a room for his days in town. He shook his son loose, then plopped himself down in a straight backed chair. Pake continued to talk to the older man in low tones and soft words, but before long his patience ran short.

"I want those dam' boys and their stinkin' sheep off my land." Sonny was belligerent, surly and his voice was loud enough to draw the landlady from her work to draw near a doorway close by.

"They'll be off soon enough, but you need to leave 'em alone until we get things lined out. I told you I have a buyer for the land, and he's talkin' like he'll buy the sheep along with it and ship them himself. Can't you just give it time to cool down? He'll be here the end of the month, so stop pushing, Dad."

"Dam' yer hide, what'n hell did you lease that place to them for anyhow?" His voice slurred, sounding like a wind-up phonograph just about out of juice. "Because we needed the money." Pake stopped, stared at this slight resemblance to a man he knew in his youth. His inner man swung hard from being angry enough to sock his father in the jaw to being fed up and simply wanting to be somewhere else. "Mother is ill and Betts can't make enough working in the mercantile to keep them both, so she sent word for help. I can't turn her down and you shouldn't either."

Pake reached for his father's shoulder as he made an effort to rise from the chair, only to stagger a little more, and fall back in his chair. Pake's ire was reaching a boiling point. *Dammit, I gotta get him to bed.*

17

"Aw hell . . . if she'd stayed here where she belongs she wouldn't be in that fix."

"Yeah . . . she'd be livin' in a house filled with fear and hate and you'd be drunk all the time and she'd be embarrassed to even go shopping. Come on Sonny, when are you ever going to stand up and take responsibility for what you've done?" The words spewed forth, rather than finding their way past pinched lips.

"Go to hell," the older man yelled as he raised himself up and staggered into the open doorway behind him.

His landlady stepped aside as though she knew what would follow if she stayed within arm's reach of his anger. She moved onto the porch after he'd made his way to the room under the stairs and waited to speak to Pake. "I remember such a different man, Pake. He's hurting and lost."

"Yeah, I know. I'm just getting fed up with it." He turned to walk outside, and found his way back to the main street.

Thoughts seemed to come in a perfect rhythm with his footsteps. He'd grown up on those streets when his father and mother owned a small store and his father worked as a cattle broker in the fall. He knew everyone who'd been there for more than a couple of decades including the two young men he'd leased his father's ranch to.

We grew up together, sat in the same schoolroom together as kids, fought with each other and made up. His thoughts returned to happier days when they romped and rode through the hills when they had precious little free time. They were his friends, at least they had been, and he hoped they stayed that way after all this mess was settled. But he knew if Sonny kept up his tirades, there was no tellin' what would come.

Will and Matt won't put up with it forever, he thought. And he couldn't blame them. His shoulders tensed, pulling up toward his ears. He regretted leasing the ranch after he found out they'd bought those sheep from the injured old Mexican. But he had no choice, there was no other way to pull together enough money to send his mother and sister, and he couldn't stand by and let them suffer any more than his father's actions had already produced. He spit on the ground, hard. *Dammit, just dammit.*

***

Opal spent the next few weeks riding with her father and working with a couple of young horses he was getting ready to sell. Her heart was always lighter when she was horse-back, but with good reason her thoughts were troubled now, and her mind bounced from herself, to her horses, to Will and Matt, then the Danners.

A young girl long into her teens, she was talented and well trained when it came to being horseback and working with young colts. She had a knack for knowing what a horse was thinking and what he might do before he made up his own mind. Sometimes she could ease them out of it before they   realized what happened, but she'd been bedded down in the   dirt enough times to be able to say she would rather talk a horse out of bucking than put on a ride till he quit.

From the day she was old enough to climb on the fence and coax her Dad's mare close enough to slip a leg over, she'd been found on the back of a horse. She rode to school, rode to town, and rode for the sunset like a mad-woman as the years brought maturity on too soon. She never wanted to leave this valley, never intended to leave her home, and had no thought as to what she might do instead as she grew into womanhood. But she moved in the full realization that whatever it was, it better include being found astraddle of a horse.

Dependent upon her father for her care and keeping, she knew that wasn't going to last forever, even though she wanted it to . . . forever. . . and ever. As long as she was there, horses were hers to ride and touch. Her father had a good herd of brood mares and a fine strong blood bay stud horse that threw hardy ranch horses. Each year ranchers for hundreds of miles around would send a rep to pick out a couple of young horses for their own remuda.

The touch of them was like warm water flowing over her heart. Every time she was near one she indulged herself in the smell of the curve where their neck rose into the shoulder muscle. Their eyes were nothing shy of wonderful and intriguing. deep as a pool of clear water with a rocky bottom waiting for a person to dip their toe into the stillness. Their breath moved warm and gentle when their nostrils drew close to her cheek and as they breathed softly, her hair moved with the outflow of their breath. She felt easy in her soul when their presence filled her space.

Her father had given her the first foal when one of the older mares gave birth and wasn't producing enough milk to feed the baby. She fed him cow's milk and nurtured him through his early months, then she and the little spindly-leg thing had romped and played together as their hearts enlarged. Their tracks merged constantly, and the direction her life would take became cemented. She became as connected to the leggy little creature as to her own mother and father. She rode the old mare and gave her as much love as time afforded, mostly because she was thankful to the mare for giving life to the foal.

What had begun as a small homestead with 160 acres had grown to what became her father's ranch. Large enough to warrant hiring an old cowboy who stayed on for years, and now and then a couple of younger men to work during spring and fall works. Cattle and horses were the mainstay of their ranching endeavors, but her mother made sure their table was filled with eggs, chicken and ham steaks when the call for beef went dry.

This particular morning her mind was swirling with words and fear all muddled together. She rode alongside her father, and asked a question that had rumbled around in her since Will's supper in their home. She knew there was a snake in the grass, watching, waiting. His name was Sonny Danner. "Have you known old man Danner for a long time, Dad?"

Her father's eyes narrowed and his countenance changed from the stifled smile that spread over his face as she rode up. "He's not old man Danner to you, young lady. It's Mr. Danner, and yes, I've known him for many years."

She realized she'd been rude, so tried to take the conversation a little different route. "I remember Pake from school, but he was always pushy and acted tougher than he was. He ran with Will and Matt sometimes, but seemed like he spent more time in town messin' around than doin' anything very productive. You reckon he's gonna be the cause of problems for them or will it be old . . . I mean . . . Mr. Danner?"

She cringed as his voice became terse, and the muscles on his neck tightened as he responded. "What trouble comes of the sheep bein' on that ranch are the makin' of Will and Matt themselves. They been in this part of the country long enough to know what that will breed."

Then his voice softened as he remembered how close his daughter had become to the young Will. "But, I understand that sometimes it takes a reckless gamble to put a man over the top of what he's wanting to accomplish, so I can't hold hard feelings toward either of em. I worry about the Danners, both the young and the older. That family's been settled between a rock and a hard place for a lot of years and the more drinkin' goes on the worse the outcome will be for everyone."

Opal felt a stinging sensation in both her elbows at the words her father spoke, and her stomach felt queasy. "What do you think will happen?"

"For Will's sake, I hope Danner will just stay in town and stay drunk, leavin' those boys alone until they can get a crop of young sheep on the ground and get them sold. But honestly, Opal, I just can't tell you for sure. Sonny has never been a man to set back and let things happen, he likes *to make things happen* and especially if it's what he wants over what's best for everyone."

He paused, pulled up his horse and looked at Opal. "He's been known to pull a gun on more than one man, and I heard he's killed a couple in the past. One was unarmed and just standin' on his porch. But, he was a wanted man with a price on his head, and Danner's actions were somewhat warranted. It sure didn't make him no friends though, and after that he lost a lot of respect from those who were around him much."

"Do you think he'd kill Will or Matt?" Her tongue nearly stuck to the roof of her mouth and she felt like she was talking around a ball of cotton.

"I wouldn't put it past him, Opal . . . that's why I don't want you mixed up in any of this no matter how much you care about Will. I couldn't bear it if somethin' happened to you and your mother would never get over it. You stay away from either of those Danners and do everything you can to stay out of the mix when any of those men come in contact with each other, you hear?"

All she could do was nod her head up and down and blink back warm rivulets searching for a path through dusty cheeks. A wisp of her hair stuck to the corner of her eye, she wiped it away with the back of a dirty hand.

The following Sunday morning as her dad hitched up the buckboard for her mom to drive into the local church meeting, Opal didn't argue about going along. She had dressed quickly into one of two rarely worn dresses and searched her room for the little hand-held Bible her mother gave her as a child. This morning, she had a purpose in joining her neighbors in the old school house with a heartfelt prayer.

As they made their way along the dusty road toward town and the old schoolhouse and church building, her mind drifted back to childhood days. She, Will and Matt spent many hours together growing up with no desire to exchange their childhood freedom for responsibility and adulthood. Opal smiled as she thought about the day Matt had tried to coax Will into riding their horses into the school house.

"Come on . . . let's give that ol' coot something to talk about besides history!" Matt challenged.

Will relentlessly tried to talk him out of it, but it was only a couple of days before Matt Baker rode his horse right up the three steps leading into the narrow doorway, reached down and flipped the latch, shoved the door open with his foot and drove his horse hard through the door and right up to Mr. Roer's desk. The children screamed and laughed, cheering the antic. Roer yelled and cursed, Matt "hoorahed" until the hell that broke loose was in full bloom, then rode for the door.

As he left the school house Will and Opal watched aghast that he'd actually done the deed. In the weeks that followed Matt refused to attend the small school, and it wasn't until at least two months later he returned to take a seat in the back of the room as though nothing had ever happened.

Mr. Roer had lectured the entire class as soon as they were settled again. "You kids need to go to finishing schools and military schools and learn manners and etiquette. You should want to see what lies out there beyond the dust and desolation of this place! You have no idea the opportunities that lie in waiting out there beyond that farthest purple peak on the eastern horizon. You could really be someone if you just gave up being rude and unkempt and just tried a little bit."

She remembered Will's slow drawl as he answered, "Ain't nothin back there we want, Mr. Roer, we like it just fine right here where we are."

As Will grew out of school and boyhood, he had signed on different ranches for day work, or spring branding and fall shipping. Their lives began to drift apart somewhat.

It was in that passing of time they would each realize just how deeply ingrained their lives had become, how frequent faces would leap across the miles to appear, and how much they meant to each other. Somewhere among the days and hours they began to see their future merging.

When Opal found herself watching the men who lived and worked in the valley, the only ones she gave a second glance were the ones who rode to cattle— like Will and Matthew.

Will rode easy in his saddle, sitting like he was born to it. When he rode, she imagined that kind of ease must be what a king looked like as he ruled from some kind of throne. He'd been horseback from the time he found a way to sling a leg over the withers of a four legged friend or foe. At a very young age he began helping neighbors with horseback chores, earning what little cash money was available in those days. Most of the time it was working a few weeks for short pay that included a good meal and a good horse to ride.

Will was one of only a few people on the face of the earth who could draw her attention away from horses. When he stopped by their ranch coming or going to town, her heart beat a little stronger, her mouth would be a little dry, and she found it hard to find a subject worthy of mention. But then they'd speak of horses and all was calm, and she content.

As the months dropped off the calendar, she found herself watching for him more earnestly, and he rode their way a little more frequently than before. She wondered if he fell asleep at night with her face in his mind the way she did with his.

Beside her bed, on the night stand, was a small hanky with her initials embroidered on the corner, a gift from her mother. Folded within were a dried collection of flowers he always found along the road somewhere. He would tuck them in the band of his hat and present them to her with a silly flourish as he came to call. Manzanita bells and wild cliff roses in the early spring. Wild daisies a little later, and mariposa lilies in early summer. Fall would bring the wispy branches of the bonnie bells along the creeks . . . but what she loved best were the fiery Indian paint brush.

**

Sonny Danner didn't soften; as the days progressed his anger and animosity accelerated, noticeably causing people to avoid contact with him. Pake spent hours with him, trying to work through their issues and assuring his father the situation with the ranch and the sheep would be handled within a few months. He continually asked him to "leave it alone," which Sonny ignored completely and he continued to press the young cowboys he viewed as enemies.

Sonny sat on a stool near the front door of the little building where a sign advertised haircuts and tobacco products, and watched Matthew Baker ride up the dirt road. Matt stopped

24

at a nearby shop and tie his horse to the rail. Sonny's lips tightened, and his thoughts ran first to sidestepping any contact, but his guts wrapped around his brain and he decided if it was a confrontation that was due to happen, it may as well be now as later. His gaze was steadfast as Matt stepped onto the boardwalk just up the way.

Matt stepped lightly and whistling nervously as he approached. Danner's hatred and resentment seethed through every fiber of his being. Like a silent rattler he waited, tightened, and gathered himself. When Matt was within the sound of his voice, he raised himself up, tensed, and began to mock him.

"Hey sheepherder! Did you suckle yet this morning?" His words were followed by a forced, haunting snigger. His malice was encased in words of hate and contempt, spewing profanity in waves. It was as though his intelligence left him completely, and all he knew were swear words, repeating them time after time.

Matt stopped mid-stride and set his boots down carefully, positioned one foot slightly behind the other, leaning forward as if to brace against a hard wind.

"Hold on, Danner." Matt raised a flat hand shoulder high toward the approaching dissention. His words fell on deaf ears as Sonny kept walking, adding insult to mockery, and slowly moving within touching distance. Deliberately, before Matt realized what happened, Sonny reached out and poked him in the chest with a stiff forefinger, intending to push him backward and put him on the defensive. His inebriated brain moved him to push harder, again and again.

To his ultimate shock, Matt struck back, hard, straight to the nose. Sonny staggered backward holding his face as blood flowed from his flared nostrils. Bellowing words that passed discernment, he leaped for Matt with both hands outreached with claw-like presentation. He tripped, catching his foot on the corner of a bench near the door, falling. He caught himself on the nearby stool, rolling sideways he fell onto his back. He drew himself up to his knees, realized he was gushing blood and stayed there, watching thick red liquid fill his opened hand. His face became as sharp and cold as a hilted blade.

25

He sensed that several people had gathered near the windows, and a couple of men had stepped out of the barber shop with towels still draped around their shoulders. One older man pulled the towel away from his shirt, throwing it to the ground near Danner and stepped between the two.

"Hey now . . . hold on there."

Matt turned on his heel, leaving Danner's blood to his own resources. He walked away with fists clenched tight and his head spinning with what had just happened. He found himself in front of the Sheriff's office within a matter of moments. Pushing the heavy wooden door open he stepped in and waited for the man behind the desk to lift his gaze.

"I just poked Danner in the nose . . . he's over there by the barber shop bleedin' like stuck hog. He'll probably come huntin' you pretty quick." The words rushed out, nerves and anger pushing them from depths uncharted.

"What happened, Matt?" the officer replied tersely, rising from his chair to lean across the desk. He appeared to be more than a little amused, and it showed in his expression even though he acted serious about the incident. It was clearly known that Danner was a pain in his backside and it probably wouldn't really bother him much that Matt had planted him in the dirt with a little blood induced.

"I've had all his crap I can take," Matt continued. "He's pushed and prodded and when he poked me in the chest yellin' all his trash I just let him have it. I wasn't thinkin', I just did it. Now I'm goin' back to the ranch. You know where to find me."

He turned to the door, and walked quickly to the rail where his horse was tied. Mounting, he rode out of town without looking back. His breath came fast, and his head was buzzing with what might follow. He needed to find Will. He leaned forward and clicked his tongue to the horse beneath him, stayed standing in his stirrups as the horse broke into a trot. He eased back into the saddle to the feel of an easy lope. By the time he got to the ranch and unsaddled, the blood had stopped racing through his veins.

Will wasn't around, so he wandered back to the bunkhouse and poured a cup of cold coffee then settled onto a stump in the corner of the porch, watching for his friend of old to ride in. He tried to think just what it was that set him off so fast. *It was the way he came at me. He was gonna' hit me if he got the chance.* Swallowing another sip of the cold, muddy liquid, he stood to his feet as he saw Will and a couple of the boys riding across the horse pasture. Tension returned to his shoulders and the muscles along his jaw tightened. Tossing the rest of his drink in the dirt he headed for the saddle house.

"What's up?" asked Will as soon as he saw Matt's face. "You look like the dark cloud of doom, buddy!" He slid out of the saddle and turned toward Matt, draping the reins across his forearm.

"Yeah, well there's a good reason for that," replied Matt. "You better unsaddle and I'll meet you over by the horse trough." Turning abruptly away he walked to the drinker in the corner of the corral and waited with one boot heel stuck against the bottom rail. Before they returned to the bunkhouse, Matt gave a full account of the incident.

"Hell's bells," mumbled Will. "Is he ever gonna quit this crap? That old man's gonna be the death of somebody sooner or later."

***

Will rode into town with Matt early the next morning, moving straight to the sheriff's office. They needed to find out what had happened after Matt pulled out, and if any charges had been filed. The door was locked, so they headed toward the small café across the street where they found the lawman eating breakfast.

"Coffee?" he asked as they approached.

"Yeah, thanks," replied Will. The pair sat down at the table as the sheriff held up a hand to signal the waitress.

An older woman, a little too plump and a little too frazzled, brought mugs and a coffee pot to the table. "Mornin' you two, a little mud this morning?"

"Sure," the pair spoke simultaneously.

The sheriff chuckled, then set them at ease. "You're off the hook, Matt. Danner never even came by my office, just went straight home and cleaned up, then went to the saloon and nursed his nose. He's been a little subdued to say the least."

"So what now?" asked Matt, brows furrowed deep. "That man's off his dam' rocker."

"Avoid him at all cost," was the reply from the sheriff. "You boys bought into this, and for now all I can do is warn him not to start anything . . . which is what I'm tellin' you right now."

He stood up and put his dirty hat over his dark hair, pulling it down snug over his forehead. Smiling at them he told the wait-ress, "Bring these two a piece of pie and put it on my bill." He gave them a stilted salute from the side of his hat and walked out the door.

"Well, guess that's all of that for now. We better just stay out of town as much as we can and keep off the same side of the street he's on." Will fiddled with the handle of his mug and picked up a fork, waiting as the waitress set down a plate filled with apples and a thick crust.

"That's gonna' be dam' hard to do, my friend . . . he's comin' across the street headed this way right now." Matt set his cup down, scooted his chair back and readied himself for another confront-ation.

Will shook his head at Matt. They picked up their hats from beneath their chairs and stood quietly watching to see if this nemesis would approach. Danner stood at the door, then turned away as they heard the familiar voice of the sheriff address him before his hand reached the knob.

"Goin' in for breakfast?" asked the lawman. Will breathed a sigh of relief, knowing the sheriff was helping to avoid any conflict.

"Maybe. Mostly coffee," came the terse reply.

"I'd like to hear your version of what happened between you and young Matt if you could come over to my office for a few minutes,

Sonny. Coffee pot's on over there."

Will's face was flushed and Matt was visibly irritated as they waited until the two men crossed the street and went into the lawman's office. It didn't seem right, standing there with hats in hand watching like a couple of scared kids being hounded by some bully.

"This ain't settin' well with me, Will. I'm sick of actin' like we done somethin' wrong every time we have to deal with him or Pake." Matt slapped his hat on his head and throwing some change on the table for a tip he walked out the door in a huff. To his surprise, he nearly ran square into Pake Danner as he stepped through the opening.

"Mornin', Matt." The younger Danner reached out his hand as if to shake, then withdrew it as he realized the reach wasn't being reciprocated. "Got time to talk, you and Will?"

"Maybe. If this is about what happened yesterday I ain't up for it though," replied a heated Matthew.

"I have some news about the lease I need to fill you in on." Pake went on as though nothing had happened the day before, or any other day recently. All three returned to the table that still held half eaten pie and not-so-empty coffee mugs. The waitress came back with a fresh pot of hot coffee and a new cup, watching each face intently as she poured.

"You boys okay this mornin'?" She seemed more than just a little concerned about what this meeting might turn into, so she stood quietly waiting for an answer.

"We're good," replied Pake. "We're good." He glanced at the other two with a hint of a smile on his face as he rubbed the back of his neck with the flat of his hand.

"You two want that piece of pie you just walked out on?" she asked as she reached for the leavin's of the slices they left on the table.

"No thanks. We're good," replied Matthew. She lifted the dishes and walked away abruptly.

29

"So what's up?" asked Will. *Darn that pie was good. Matt should speak for himself.*

"We have a buyer interested in the property you guys have leased." Pake leaned forward and put both hands deliberately on each side of his cup. "He's from Oklahoma, and from what he says he's even interested in buying the sheep. I'm guessing he'll ship them all to farms back east once they're gathered and off the ranch. The catch is that you'll have to be willing to sell, and willing to gather and ship the dam' things." He flinched and squinted as he turned his face toward the sun. "Sorry, but that's the best he would do."

"So how much time do we have?" asked Will.

"He's coming in about the middle of next week, or maybe the end of this week. He'll send me a wire when he knows for sure. Dad wants to take him out to the place and show him around himself, so it might be best you guys aren't around out there. I guess what I need to know is if you're okay with the deal and if you'll let us out of the lease."

Will and Matt sat quietly, watching each other, waiting for some hint of what the other was thinking. Will seemed to hear his dream drifting past the heavy curtains on the window with the loss of the lease. *Aw hell, that dream was already dried up and blowed away anyhow.*

Matt looked up and said quietly, "It's up to Will. I'm sick of the whole deal and just want to get back to workin' for Mr. Mitchell and feelin' like somethin' common is happening in my life."

"Same here," said Will. "Let us know what we can do and when, Pake." He reached out to shake hands with his old school mate, gripping firmly the hand that came to meet his. They stood for a moment, looking into each other's face, seeing sadness in the eyes that locked. Matt nodded and pulled his hat on as he stood and slid his chair under the table.

Reaching their tied horses at the same time, they swung into their saddles nearly in perfect synchronization. Will smiled for the first time that morning, *That's what comes of being practically tied at the hip most of your lives.* Riding out of town side by side, Will sensed a flood of relief pouring over their shoulders, tainted slightly with disappointment.

The morning was beautiful, the air smelled like a little rain might blow in later, which should have been a balm to their souls. "This dam' dry wind is killin' everything." Will commented to his riding pardner quietly.

"It'll rain . . . someday, it always does," came the terse reply, followed quickly by, "Hell Will, we won't let all this come between us, will we?"

Will pulled up his horse, sat listening to the wind, the flitting birds through the bushes and watched the clouds move slowly across his big sky. "Nah . . . nothin' could come between us, Matt."

They laughed, spurred their horses into a lope and moved toward the ranch and some hard work. Tension eased as they rode into the ranch yard where they would have to find busy work around the place to make up for being gone most of the day. For two men with better work ethics, just keeping busy wasn't settin' too well.

"I'll ride out in a couple of days and check on the mex at the ranch," Will dismounted, and loosened his cinch. "You stick close to the job and maybe you could pitch in a little more around the bunkhouse so we don't get fired here pretty pronto."

***

Two full days passed before Will rode to the lease to find the old Mexican herder and his dog walking the hills, checking babies and water. He stepped off his horse and reached to shake hands with this competent and dedicated old gentleman from below the border. He'd grown to have a great deal of respect for these herders of sheep through the years as he watched what one or two men and a handful of good dogs could produce.

"How are you, Manuel?" he asked. "I brought you some bacon and flour, some canned peaches and tomatoes, and a little sugar this morning. I left them in the wagon at camp when I came through. Do you need anything else next time I come back?"

"No, señor Will, we are fine, me an' my freen." He smiled from under the wide brim of an old straw hat and whistled for the dog to return and lie down beside him.

Will explained what was going to happen to the ranch in coming weeks as the gray-haired man listened intently trying to understand Will's Spanish. His expressions changed from concern to a smile, then sometimes confusion. Will noted the heavy life-tracks embedded deeply into his complexion as he spoke in mixed English and what little Mexican he knew. He was pretty sure the old man understood.

"How many sheep?" asked Will. *"Quanto mas ovejas?"*

He struggled to find the right words, hoping the old man would figure out what he wanted to know.

"Possiblé trescientos, chancé mas."

Will was staggered. *Three hundred, maybe more. I thought there were only about two hundred when we bought them. This is good news.*

"Quanto mas pequeños?" Will asked about the babies and little ones. Some of those sheep must have been heavy with lambs when they bought them for there to be this many already.

"Uh . . . chancé cien, possiblé . . . poquito mas."

Will nodded and shook hands with the old gent. *Three hundred sheep and about a hundred more are babies.* He was anxious to tell Matthew the news. The old herder wasn't sure so there was no way to get an absolute number until they gathered everything. *All I can say is I'm glad we don't have to brand the dam' things.*

He mounted and waved as he rode through the mesquite, noticing how many beans were hanging on the shrubs. *Good feed for cattle . . . too bad there won't be a herd on this country for a while.* Maybe all this was worthwhile after all. His heart was a little lighter as he made his way back to the head-quarters of his "home ranch" of many years.

***

Charles Strickland made most of his money in railroad investments, but raising livestock for food was a good backup income to his way of thinking. He was never sure what brought about the desire to purchase ranches in the west, but perhaps it could be traced back to hearing stories of the big trail drives and the cowboys of the far western states.

Advertising in small town newspapers had paid off and he'd purchased three ranches in Colorado and New Mexico in recent months. Pursuing a new endeavor, he sat in a train watching the scenery of the west slide past in what sounded like three quarter time played on an old honkytonk piano as wheels pounded the rails. Not many riders on this trip had made for a boring journey, his mind wandered easily, and the newspapers on board held trivial information.

This time, this town, he would be meeting an old lawman and buffalo hunter of the west, and he was anxious to do more than just take a look at the ranch he wanted to purchase. As ranches go, this was a small one, no improvements and not much to look at, but the history of its owner was worth the price of the ranch. He drummed his fingers on the arm of his seat, fidgeting with a newspaper in his lap. He watched the miles be eaten up by this monstrosity breathing smoke while he wondered what this old man would have to tell. What stories of the old west and riding to herds of buffalo with his old gun held steady over the back of a saddled horse. Or did he ride to the chase like the Indians, firing on the fly?

As the train slowed and smoked into the little station he stood and procured his valise from the seat across from his. He walked through the narrow aisle, stepped out onto the platform of the rail

33

car, and put one foot on the stairs as though ready to leap into the dust that was boiling up from the wind of the train's passing.

No one waited for him at the station, and the man in the small room where baggage was being unloaded hadn't seen anyone asking for him. Disappointed, he decided to take the short walk to the rooming house he could see from the station. A little of his earlier excitement returned as he found himself walking through the dust imagining some outlaw had walked these streets. Some lawman had been in a quick draw with an upstart, or perhaps even a cattle drive meandered through this small town in the not too distant past. His thoughts were locked in on what might have been, not realizing that the not too distant past could be as recent as yesterday with little stretch of the imagination.

His eastern view of what was unfolding in the west was limited to reports and stories through the pen and page of writers who found the west fodder for the vivid imagination. Some were children with big dreams, others old men who missed an opportunity to live their own dreams. He was no exception.

He spoke to a woman near the stairs as he entered the front door of the rooming house. "I'd like a room for a few nights. I believe a Sonny Danner made arrangements?"

She leaned her broom against the doorpost that led down a short hall and smiled at the newcomer. "Well, I don't recollect Sonny sayin' anything about your comin' here, but his son Pake had me keep a room ready for you. He wasn't sure when you would arrive, but it's sure and certain I don't have an overload of residents." The stocky woman wasn't unpleasant, but abrupt in her dealings. Not hard to look at, she wore signs of a hard life that left her shoulders slouched and her eyes tired.

"Sonny is my best customer, so you'll be able to meet him soon." She stepped to the corner of a small roll-top desk, which was missing the roll top. Stacks of papers covered the writing area. She pulled a small receipt book from the drawer with a pen and set it on top of the desk, looking up at her customer.

Charles dusted himself off and stepped to the desk, pulling a leather pouch from his inside pocket. He flourished a pair of

34

twenty dollar bills as he took them from the slot, making much of being sure the lady behind the desk was aware of the amount of money he was flashing. He couldn't help himself, he just liked the fact that he was well heeled and didn't mind showing it off. Likewise he couldn't help thinking, *Just wait until I roll out some hard cash to pay for the ranch.* He was quite impressed with himself, when one just got right down to it.

"Any place I can get a bite to eat?" he asked the woman.

"Uh huh. There's a café across from the sheriff's office. They serve good food and the coffee's okay. You get coffee here in the morning with your room, there'll be a pot on the stove, you can help yourself." Handing him a key she went back to her broom and continued sweeping the hall that led to four rental rooms.

Charles discovered quickly the key was simply a formality. The door to his room had been 'jimmied' at some time and would open readily without using the key. He stashed his valise under the bed, secured a well-worn money belt around his heavy mid-section and began to concern himself with a meal. He hadn't notice any sign of a bank in the little town, but maybe the telegraph office had a safe he could stash this belt in. Wishing it wasn't quite so late in the day, he glanced around the room searching for a hiding place for when he returned.

Within a few minutes he found himself seated alone in the café as the sun lowered itself into the horizon. He ate alone, steak with fried potatoes and sliced peaches. He'd eaten fancier food back east, but the steak was much to his liking. Charred on the outside with just a hint of pink in the middle. He couldn't remember ever eating canned peaches laid on a plate.

The waitress returned with a refill for his coffee, so he asked if she knew where he could find Sonny Danner.

"Why would you want to find that old crank?" she asked through a stilted smile.

"I got into town a few hours ago and haven't been able to locate either Sonny or his son. Any idea where they might be?" She stood holding the pot with her right hand and a folded towel under the bottom of the pot "You check the saloon over there? Just about

35

most of his waking hours are spent standing with his foot on the rail and a glass in his hands." She walked away muttering, "It's a cryin' shame is what it is, just a cryin' shame."

Charles finished his coffee and stepped outside to look around for the saloon, which was just up the street a short way. He walked slowly, drinking in the sights and sounds of this western town, once again imagining what might have happened just months or years ago. The aroma of fried meat followed him out the door, and just a hint of dried weeds of some kind blew in on the breeze. He smelled the whiskey wafting over the dirt road from the open doors of the saloon. Stepping over piles of dried horse manure he made his way to the salon where he hoped to find the old buffalo hunter. *I waited my whole life to walk through streets like this, watching for a friend I've yet to meet, searching for a place I could fit in. Wonder if this is where home is for me.*

He walked through the door of the saloon and stood for a moment to allow his eyes to adjust to the change of light, then stepped to the bar and asked for Sonny Danner. The bartender nodded his head toward a man seated at a round table near the window, but Charles hesitated a moment and asked for a whiskey neat before he approached Danner.

"I'm Charles Strickland, Mr. Danner." He reached a hand out and cringed slightly as Sonny's grip connected. "I came in this afternoon on the train and just finished my supper. Can we talk now or should I meet you in the morning?" He wasn't too interested in doing business with a man who'd been drinking, no matter what the circumstances. "Is your son Pake around?"

"We can talk now," responded Danner. "Pake should be around tomorrow, but we didn't think you'd be here for a few days." He spoke sternly, words slightly slurred as he tried to sit up straight.

"My business concluded in Oklahoma so I was able to catch an earlier train. I wanted to have more time to look around and get acquainted with the area. I have no problem waiting until tomorrow morning if you prefer."

"Suit yourself," replied Danner. He lifted a glass briefly to Charles and downed a swallow.

"Maybe we could talk about something besides business this evening," suggested Charles, hoping to draw out some of the older man's lifetime of experiences in the west. He'd heard of his exploits as a buffalo hunter and tracker in his younger years, and even a few rumblings that he'd killed more than one person. While it was intriguing, Charles wasn't sure this was the time or place to open that discussion. Looking at the grizzled, unshaven old man across from him he decided he was ready to settle down on the porch of his rooming house and deal with the Danners under a fresh morning sun.

"Sure," replied Danner. Then flipping the subject, he asked Charles why he was interested in a ranch and moved the conversation immediately toward the business arrangements.

Disappointed in the turn of the conversation, Strickland answered courteously, but couldn't hide his frustration at being pushed into this line of conversation. He really did not want to discuss any business with an inebriated; smelly man who slurred his lines to the point Charles wasn't sure he even understood what was being discussed.

The two continued to visit long past sunset over a couple more drinks and a flickering coal oil lantern on the edge of the table. Eventually Danner began to reveal his earlier exploits in life, which pleased Charles and he listened with deep interest and fascination. He asked questions about the buffalo which led to stories of Danner's past. The old man grew excited as he bragged on the hunts and the kill. Trails drives of his youth seeped into the conversation and Strickland absorbed the stories like a child at the feet of a visiting friend. He was disappointed when Pake came searching for his father, surprised to find him openly conversing with a well-dressed stranger. An introduction was quick and short, the elder Danner seemingly wanting to get back to his braggadocio since he had an avid listener.

Pake tried to bring them to terms of involvement for the morrow, but was interrupted frequently by his father. Strickland answered and asked questions, until the conversation turned to the fact the ranch held a herd of sheep and was currently leased to a pair of young cowboys. In spite of Strickland's reluctance to discuss business under those circumstances, he responded to Pake and began to discuss the terms of the purchase conditional upon the sheep being gathered and ready to be shipped back east.

"As I mentioned in my communication earlier, I would be willing to purchase two hundred head of sheep with the ranch as I believe I can market them pretty quickly, but my plan is to see cattle on the ranch before long. Have you had a chance to ask if these two young cowboys be willing to gather and ship them once the land transfer is made?"

"I'll meet with them tomorrow and Dad can take you to the ranch. Hopefully I will have some kind of an answer by evening if Will and Matt are where I can find them," promised young Danner.

***

Sunrise found Pake riding to the Matthews ranch hoping to catch Will and Matt before they left for the day. He trotted and loped intermittently until he pulled his horse up near the bunkhouse where he caught the crew between the house and the corral. They all stopped to watch him ride up, saying their "howdys", and Will stepped over to ask what he needed.

"Got a minute?" asked Pake.

"Sure . . . what's up?" asked Will as Matthew walked up and shook hands with Pake.

Pake carefully explained the terms of the purchase and transfer, careful to include numbers and requirements. "You two still interested?"

"Hell, yes," replied Matt. His eyes flashed and a smile began to work its way out from under the heavy brown moustache on his upper lip. Apparently he was ready to be done with all the conflict of the lease and move on.

Will, on the other hand, wasn't so quick to answer. He stood for a minute looking at the ground before he responded to Pake. "Manuel says three hundred is a lot closer to the numbers. Where would we go with the other hundred head? Any chance he'd go for takin' the whole bunch?"

Pake sat musing for a few minutes, fussing with the reins as he focused on the top of his saddle horn. "Not sure. He said two hundred. I'll have to head back to town and find out. This is gonna jam up the works, Will."

"I know." Will's voice came strong as he stepped away from the shoulder of Pake's horse.

Will and Matt stood quietly until the rider had passed from sight. Matt looked at Will and shook his head before he turned and went to the corral to catch a mount. Will noticed Mr. Mitchell had been standing at the corner of the barn and now watched to see what would follow.

Matt turned on Will for the first time in his life. "I'll tell you what I'm gonna do." He yanked his hat off his head and spun around to face his friend. "I'm so fed up with this crap. You're the one that stands to gain the most off'n this deal since you're the one lookin' for a home and long term relationship. If that guy don't take all those sheep, I'm gonna' shoot what's left and leave em for the dam' buzzards!"

Will stopped. "Com'on Matt, you ain't gonna go shoot a hundred head of sheep and their babies and leave em out there to rot. I know you're mad as hell and so am I, but you don't need to come at me over this." Will tried to control his anger, but the words fell from his mouth before he had a chance to think them through. "And, come to think of it, who was the one who come boilin' in tellin' me they found all those cussed beasts and we should run right out an' buy em? Who did that, huh, Matt?"

"Well I'll tell you what I WILL do," Matt yelled back. "I'll just make a gift of the dam' things to you! Whatever's left over after that dummy buys them sheep, they're yourn. How 'bout them chiggers?"

"Knock it off, Matt."

From the corner of his eye Will saw Mitchell step away from the barn and walk quickly to the pair. Stepping between them he putt a hand on Will's shoulder. Nobody spoke; they all just stood quiet and solemn.

Emotions played out a different dance on ruddy faces with eyes flashing like the notes of a hard played fiddle tune. Sorrow began to rise up in two of the men, but only anger stirred the countenance of the third.

***

Will and Matt rode into town early the next morning together, but nary a word had passed between them since the day before. It was pushing Will's emotions in a direction he'd never had to deal with where Matt was concerned. He found his thoughts embroiled in a war of words that would never be spoken to his friend. They bounced from anger and resentment to ping off the other side of the table in regret and confusion, then somewhere off the corner pocket into explanations and opinions. Before long, his thoughts moved on to cattle, horses, gathering sheep, where to find Mr. Strickland and how to deal with Sonny if things went sour.

Yet, right before his eyes for prolonged moments the world had presented one of the most magnificent sunrises he'd ever seen. It hadn't gone unnoticed by either him or Matt. They pulled up their horses in the same moment to watch the clouds turn to scarlet and gold as they moved slowly across the horizon. His soul began to soften, and watching the expression on Matt's face he was pretty sure there were some changes taking place behind that sour attitude. He actually caught Matt looking sideways at him with just a hint of a smile.

Continuing the journey, the conversation began to break through the silence in brief spurts of short sentences. As their minds quieted, hearts turned back to friendship, and while words were unnecessary to either, the bond between them remained unbroken, though tested. Mother Nature again dealt generously in the connection she'd had with them since their introduction to her wiles and ways, her beauty and her belligerence.

Their horses moved at a slow trot when they entered the edge of town and found a hitching rail. They stood silently for several minutes watching for sign of either Pake or Strickland before they headed to the café. Coffee sounded good and perhaps one of the Danners would be about his morning affairs. They opened the doors to a nearly empty room, chose a window table and shortly afterward ordered breakfast with coffee. It was about three minutes after their food was delivered Matt looked out the window and took a deep breath.

"Here comes Danner."

"Which one?" asked Will, without raising his eyes or moving his head.

"Aw hell, which one do you think?" replied Matt.

Both men tensed and waited thoughtfully for a moment. Sonny Danner would be hung-over and cranky this early in the morning. Hopefully wanting coffee more than a fight, but then either one would possibly suit him. Both Will and Matt reached for their hats and pulled cash out of their pockets, rising to pay for the meal with every intention of leaving the building. It didn't work out that way.

"Well, well, well . . ." Danner spit at the two as soon as his head entered the doorway. "If it ain't the sheepherders! Did you milk the ewes and feed the titty babies yet this morning?"

Will tried to stop Matt before he spoke, but was a hair slow and heard his pardner say, "Hell no . . . you had your first shot of booze for the mornin' yet, Danner? Might help your attitude a mite."

"You little dipwad!" spat the old man. "I oughta just pound the crap outa you right here." His face began to screw itself in-to a snarl, and his eyes narrowed to reveal a hatred that neither of the young men had ever experienced before Sonny Danner was thrust into their realm of existence.

Will stepped between the two and tried to calm them down, but his actions seemed to agitate Sonny even more. He turned his tirade toward Will, yelling at the top of his lungs "An' you too, you stinkin' sorry little piece of chicken crap! If I was packin' I'd just shoot both of you and be done with it."

Will grabbed Matt's arm and pushed him toward the door but anger kicked in, and Matt pulled away, shoving Will to the side. Danner exploded in a verbal tirade that brought both the waitress and the cook from the kitchen, eyes were wide with fear of a fist fight that could destroy the room. Will pushed Matt to the door, insisting they leave the old man alone to stew in his animosity.

Before they were fully past the door and into the street they saw Pake coming down the dusty road at a fast pace, and waited as he jumped onto the boardwalk.

"What the hell gives?" Pake paused for a few steps with a puzzled expression.

"Just deal with him and we'll see you later." Will, slung his head toward the door. Moving through the door toward their horses, he and Matt stood for several minutes then found a bench near their horses and sat waiting for close to an hour.

They watched as Mr. Strickland left the rooming house, stretched and meandered down the road to the café, then waited another half hour before the three men re-entered the street.

**

Pake's eyes searched both sides of the dirt road before he located the young cowboys, then he lifted a hand to show he saw where they waited. He spoke to his father and the easterner before moving toward the livery stable and blacksmith shop at the end of town. About a quarter of an hour passed again before he drove a buckboard with a pair of large draft horses up the road and delivered it to his father and Strickland. They climbed into the wagon and Sonny lifted the reins, slapping the horses on the rump with a smack and headed for the ranch.

Pake cringed as he watched his father glare at the two cowboys on the boardwalk as he drove by, chewing on the stub of a cigar as he smacked the horses again. Strickland didn't seem to be completely oblivious to the exchange, but apparently tried to change the subject by asking questions about the town.

Pake walked toward the two waiting on the boardwalk, his eyes toward the ground. He carried a burden that had become too heavy for his young shoulders. None of these three were far enough into the second decade of their lives to be embroiled in the kind of hostility they found themselves experiencing. Certainly none were adept at dealing with the older Danner and his ire. Pake was running low on patience, as were Will and Matt. All three were wearing thin with the animosity that raged through the guts and out the gritted teeth of the old man.

"Well, Strickland is only interested in 200 head of the sheep." Pake stepped onto the boardwalk. He didn't waste any time getting to the grist of the matter. "I can't tell you any more than that. He and Pop are headed to the ranch to look it over and I'll know more tonight, but till then could you two just steer clear of either one of them?"

"Gladly," responded Will.

Matt, on the other hand, wasn't as willing to be told what to do by his old school mate, and reared up at Pake immediately.

"Tell you what, Pake, you tend to your old man and we'll tend to our own business. Sonny is a dam' drunk and he's a pain in the butt. So you keep him out of our way and we'll all get along better."

He turned off before either Pake or Will could respond, pulled his reins from the railing, mounted and rode out of town at a slow lope. Pake's anger welled up momentarily. Sonny Danner was, after all, his father and he could think what he wanted to about the old man, but hearing the words from the lips of an old schoolmate grated hard at his guts.

Will turned to Pake and stood looking him in the eyes for a few moments before speaking. "Pake, we want out of this deal as bad as you and your dad, but I got no idea what to do with a hun'erd head of sheep and until I can figure that out, this deal is not going to pan out. You're gonna have to deal with Sonny, Strickland, and whoever else gets involved in this deal until something breaks loose." He stopped, watching Pake carefully. "An' if you've got any ideas how to shake this thing out any different, just let me know." He turned and stepped to the side of his horse, reaching up with a right hand he rested it on the saddle horn and turned back toward Pake. "Sorry. . . this isn't what we wanted to have happen here, you know?"

Pake nodded and replied tersely, "Yeah, I know. But it did and now we're all in it up to our necks. Figure it out, Will."   He turned and walked away as Will stood biting his lip for a moment before he gathered his reins and pulled himself into the stirrup.

***

As Will trotted and loped intermittently toward Opal and the quiet rest of her home, he realized he could use some advice. Her father had been a good friend and mentor through the years. *Maybe he'll have some words that aren't so rattled, an' could bring some sense into this entire escapade.*

He noticed her usual ease around him was gone as they sat on the porch waiting for her father to finish his chores and come back to the house for the evening. Both were tense, quiet, with little desire for the usual flirtatious remarks and glances. They watched Maxwell Redding walking toward the house with a headstall draped over his arm. She nervously slid her arm through Will's and squeezed gently. He put his hand over hers and played with her thumb, letting her know he felt her presence.

As Maxwell stepped onto the porch, Will stood and shook his hand in the usual western greeting. "How are you, sir?" He was hesitant to begin the conversation he'd come for, but it had been boilin' in his brain long enough he just wanted to get it over with. "I was hoping you had some time to talk to me this evening. I'm in need of some solid advice."

"Come on in and sit," Maxwell responded. "You wanna stay for supper?"

"I'd like to sir, but mostly I came for a talk." He was always glad for an invitation to eat good food, but he wanted Maxwell to know he mostly needed the talk.

"Stay to eat, and we'll visit while Lily gets supper on." Maxwell turned and walked through the door of the small kitchen. He found his tiny ranch wife cutting potatoes and throwing them in a big cast iron pot on the back of an ornate wood stove.

"Got one more for supper m'love." He kissed her gently on top of her curly hair, damp from the sweat of a hot stove and small kitchen.

"I figgered as much," she responded, then smiled up at her giant of a husband. "One more tater in the pot. Opal, get your-self in here and help me out while your dad talks to Will."

Will and Maxwell remained on the porch while the women-folk bustled about the kitchen preparing the meal . The old rancher sat listening attentively.

"I got myself all fouled up, Mr. Maxwell," Will began. "Sheep, leases, my job's on the line here and, well . . . I could get myself killed or get Matt killed from the looks of things today." Sweat beaded and formed rivulets from his sideburns. Anxiously he tried to find a way to say what he need to. It was not coming easy.

Maxwell leaned forward, listened intently as Will gave him a blow by blow description of what happened earlier with the Danners.

"Dam' his hide!" blurted Maxwell. "Sometimes I'd like to give him a taste of his own medicine."

Will felt someone vindicated with that statement. At least he wouldn't have to convince Maxwell that Danner was the aggressor in the situation.

When Will finished his explanation, Maxwell sat quietly for a long time. "So you can sell two hundred head with the ranch?"

"Yes, sir."

"You got a deal on the sheep to begin with and you think you bought about two hundred head originally?"

"Yes, sir."

"So the other hundred or so holds what profit you're going to make when you finally get them all sold, regardless of who you sell them to?"

Will simply nodded.

Maxwell's face lit up with a wry grin. "And Matt's willing to kill all the sheep Strickland doesn't take just to get out of the deal?" He shook his head and chuckled in his usual dry sense of humor.

"Well . . . I don't think he'd actually do that, and if we did lose all the rest there'd come a day he'd be madder'n he'd like to admit right now that we didn't make any money after all this trouble."

Will suddenly realized Maxwell was razzing him, and chuckled as the tension eased somewhat.

"I guess what I'm askin' is if you'd both be willing to sell the rest of the sheep for just anything you could get for them to get out'a this deal."

"Yes sir, I think we would."

"Then split the herd now, leave two hundred head or so on the ranch and take the rest of them south to Mexico and sell them to anyone that'll buy 'em. Sell them in bunches of ten if you have to, but get them south and in the hands of someone who needs 'em. Then when you get back you can gather the rest for Strickland and ship them off to wherever he's thinkin' they'll sell. That's what I'd do if I was in your shoes."

"Yes sir. I thought of that, but there's a few problems with that plan I can't figure out how to get around. It could take us several weeks to get that accomplished and Danner's buyer wants the ones he's buyin' off the ranch before he takes possession. It's the time frame that stumps me here . . . but I guess we'll know more after tomorrow. Pake's trying to get something lined out. I have to take another day off work and I think Mr. Mitchell is about fed up with me and Matt bein' part time employees."

"Then do it the other way around. Gather the two hundred head and ship them for Strickland, then cut a deal with Pake to move the rest south as soon as you can."

"Strickland wants them off before he takes possession so he can load it up with cattle right away. There are lots of mesquite beans, but the sheep have grazed it hard. He may have to wait to put anything on it."

"Best go talk this over with Strickland," replied Maxwell.

"Does he know he'll have to wait to throw cattle on it?"

"Don't know that answer, but it sounds to me like he's pretty green when it comes to ranching. I don't know that we could get them off the ranch quick enough to suit Strickland, or Danner, but that seems to be the best solution to the problem. We'll talk it over with Pake or Strickland in the morning. Hope they'll be willing to work with us."

Maxwell sighed, shaking his head. "Let's go eat. That's one problem you'll have to solve your own self." He rose and walk-ed inside to join his wife. Silence reigned in the room as they moved to the table where Opal had finished setting out a light supper.

Maxwell took time to thank his Lord for the blessings of the day, the food they were about to eat, and the gift of his family. He threw in a request for guidance for Will and Matthew and the dealings with Sonny Danner. The meal was eaten without much conversation, which was unusual for that table. Usually there was talk of the horses, the ranch, the day's unraveling or mendings, but that night it was quiet. Only the rustle of utensils and cups being set down on the old wood with an occasional "Please pass me. . ."

After dinner Opal walked with Will to the porch, where they stood quietly for a long time. Simply being next to each other was often enough to satisfy them.

"You think this will turn to guns, Will?" she asked in a low, quivering voice. Her voice was soft, tainted with sadness. "If it does, there's no good can come of it, you know? You could be dead or in jail by the time this is over."

"Noooo," he drawled. "There's other things that can happen and we're trying to get movin' in that direction. Don't you fret none, cuz' that don't do me or you any good and it just makes your Mama worry more."

He'd felt a coolness in Lily's presence earlier. He was intuitive enough to know there were some hard feelings between them. It didn't take a lot of smarts to figure out why.

Impulsively, Will reached for Opal, drawing her close he stood holding her as though he would never see her after that night. Held her as though she were as precious as the stone she was named for, and something to be treasured and hidden from the world. She wrapped her arms around his waist and held him tightly, and he heard her quiet breathing. His shirt must have smelled of sweat and the dust, he should have dusted off better. But she held tight, and he knew she didn't want to let him go.

He kissed her quickly on top of her forehead, then pulled away and walked toward the corral, but stopped suddenly snapping his fingers in mid-air. "I dang near forgot." Turning back he reached into his pocket and pulled a small piece of paper folded neatly. "Found this for you yesterday, sorry it's a little wilted."

She wrapped her fingers around the paper and unfolded the layers to expose a pressed red Indian paintbrush, drying now but still holding what little fragrance was allowed by mother nature to enhance this wild, scattered color to their west.

Kissing her on the check again he turned on his heel, winked at her over his shoulder, and finished his walk to the corrals where he caught his horse and saddled quickly. The smell of her soap still lingered in the air around him as he opened the gate and led his mount through then replaced the latch.

He stood for a few minutes watching the other horses as they walked to the fence and nickered as if to say "Come back any time." He realized it was that sensation that he missed most of all these days . . . that "come back any time" response the townsfolk always had for him and Matt. Somewhere deep in his chest he felt a twinge as he realized he wanted that back more than anything right now. He felt ashamed at the tears that moistened his eyes, thought of the tears that filled her eyes, and led his horse to the house to say goodnight to Opal's folks.

***

For such a small woman, Lily had carried a large load in her life. She was born in the west to a mother who hated it, and she'd left Lily with her father and brothers for weeks at a time to return to her own father's house in West Virginia every year. As long as Lily could remember she had been the "chief cook and bottle washer" for her father and brothers. Her lonely, pampered mother had contracted pneumonia on one of those visits and died in the east where she was buried in her family plot.

Lily married Maxwell just before her sixteenth birthday and never went back to see her father or brothers again. She always said, "Maxwell got a wife and my father lost a housekeeper that day." Her brothers scattered throughout the west and her father had gone to some place in Texas where he sold dry goods until he died of influenza.

Opal was their only living child. Lily was such a small woman that childbirth had nearly ripped her apart, and the midwife who helped her through the ordeal said she'd probably never have another. She was right. No way of knowing for sure what had transpired within that tiny little body, but she never conceived again after Opal was born.

She named her Opal because she thought it was the most beautiful gem she had ever seen. Maxwell had sent through a mail order catalog for a "fiery opal" ring the first year he sold all his colts and she never took it off the third finger of her left hand.

She knew that Opal never thought of herself as beautiful. Her hair was the color of mud after a hard rain, her eyes were a common brown and her slight build had no redeeming features. As far as Lily was concerned, it was her loving heart and kindness toward others that made her such a treasure to those around her.

How many times had she heard the line "Pretty is as pretty does. Beauty washes off in time, but a good heart lives on." Between mother and daughter those words had passed frequently.

Lily had come to resent Will Martin deeply, but she kept that to herself and never spoke badly about the young man, much as she certainly wanted to at times. It was only from concern for her daughter and what Will could bring into their lives that made her bitterly disappointed in what seemed to be her daughter's choice for the future. He wasn't a bad kid, but she wanted more for her daughter than a slack-water ranch on the back side of nowhere. Hopes for her to marry a rancher with more to offer were slipping slowly away.

As Will rode away in the dusk, she stepped to the porch and stood near Opal. "You seem to be very attached to that young man, my dear."

"I know, Mama. I love him so much it hurts at times."

"Opal, there are times in our lives when love isn't enough. Now he's got himself in trouble. Stupid choices will do that to a person. I want you to stay away from him for a while, and sure and certain you stay away from the Danners."

"I can't, Mama. I won't leave him to face this without knowing he has the support of me and Dad. I would hope   you could find it in your heart to do the same."

"Well, daughter, as much as you can't leave him, I can't bear to think what he might bring into your life. So, we'll leave it there for now." She walked back into the house and began a fervent scrubbing of her kitchen and the dishes waiting for her.

Stickland and Sonny Danner met on the boardwalk in front of the café for an early breakfast on a particularly bright morning. Strickland moved to his left about a foot to avoid the stench from Danner's chapped, dried lips. It was obvious he'd been drinking heavily again the night before, but maybe a few cups of coffee would help. Tension had mounted in the midst of all parties concerned, in spite of efforts from all quarters to maintain at least a modicum of courtesy.

Seated together at a window table, they ordered coffee and Strickland ordered toast with his drink. The odor he would have to "breathe around" wasn't inviting eggs or oatmeal.

"So . . .beautiful day, eh?" Strickland tried to ease into a conversation.

Sonny's face winced as he spoke as though his brain was in pain and his ears overly sensitive. "Same ol' crap," he responded in a low growl.

Strickland was becoming weary of the tension, the sour attitude, and even the tales of the old west he sought earlier were now tiresome. Some seemed past believing. "I'm thinkin' I'll head back east in a day or two, Sonny. I don't know how much longer I can wait for things to change around here and   I have other business to tend to."

"You ain't goin' nowhere till we get this ranch deal settled." Sonny raised his face to glare across the table, and the low, menacing words were pushed through pinched lips.

For the first time since they met, Strickland bristled and felt his blood run a little cold. "So, let me understand clearly, Sonny . . . are you threatening me?" He waited, flustered, watching Danner's eyes for any sign of softening. None came, and a glassy stare raised the hair on his neck. When Danner spoke again the air wafted sour with swear words and personal accusations.

"You and I have a deal, Strickland. Those dam' kids are screwin' up the works, but you ain't off the hook. I may be an old drunk, but I remember things."

51

He leaned forward and reached across the table to firmly grasp Charles' arm. "You ain't backing outa this deal on account of them dam'dable sheep, you hear? I'll fix them boys if I have to run those crap-dealers off a cliff...every dam' one of em."

Strickland felt rather than heard the words enter his mind. *How am I going to get out of this café and to the sheriff's office without having an altercation with Danner?*

He rose from his chair and responded to the tirade, "Fine. I'll head for the hotel and you can pick me up there when you're ready. I will take one more look at the ranch and talk with

Pake to see what has transpired with young Will. Pick me up when you're finished." He turned to walk away, fully expecting a hand on his shoulder or another eruption of swear words to interrupt his departure. They didn't come, so he made his way out the door and up the sidewalk where he believed his movements would not be seen from the café window.

Dam' old fool . . .now I've got to find a way to get out of this mess without getting killed. His eyes . . . I've never seen such anger and hatred in my life. He slid around a corner then changed direction through an alley to find his way to the sheriff's office. He felt like a school-kid in some kind of trouble as he walked around the back of buildings trying to find a way to the sheriff's office without being seen by Danner. *This is getting absolutely ridiculous.*

He bolted through the door to find the sheriff pouring himself a cup of coffee. Startled, he met Strickland's gaze with, "What the hell's your hurry, Strickland?"

"That crazy Danner just threatened me, Sheriff. I don't know what he's got in mind, but he gave me the impression it wasn't going to be pleasant."

"What did you do to provoke him? Prob'ly didn't take much, I'm guessing."

"I told him I was leaving here in a couple of days without a deal if things didn't change."

The sheriff set his coffee on the desk, quietly looking at Strickland. "You know, from my opinion, you probably ought to do just that."

52

"Yeah, probably. Well, now I have to make another trip to the ranch with the old fool, and I told him I'd meet with Pake again, so I won't be leaving for a couple of days at least. I wanted you to know what happened in case I get dumped in some clump of bushes after this morning." Hearing the fear in his own voice seemed to intensify the possibilities housed within the threat from Danner. He was sure the buckboard journey would not be a pleasant one.

"Take it easy," the sheriff replied, seemingly with a little more sympathy. "Danner will grab a hair of the dog that bit him and level off a little bit in the next hour or so. Keep your head and don't say much, just let him do the talking. He won't do anything today because he wants the deal to go through, but don't let him know it might not." The young lawman tried to be encouraging, but Strickland knew he was upgrading the need for caution.

Strickland nodded, turned and quietly left the office headed for the rooming house, watching the street carefully for signs of Danner. He was overly cautious, not wanting to be seen leaving the lawman's office. Danner would put two and two together quickly should he notice.

He found his way to the back door of the rooming house and made preparations for a day in the buckboard with Danner. *I wonder if I can find Pake before we leave.* He went to the front room to inquire if the woman had any idea where he might find the younger Danner.

"He was over to the telegraph office a while ago," the heavy-set woman mumbled, waving her constant companion. "You boys need a secretary to keep tabs on each other." She returned to sweeping the floor.

Strickland walked a quick clip as he headed for the telegraph office, hoping to catch Pake. He saw the younger Danner step out of the door as he approached, and a smile crossed Pake's lips. This personable young man was so unlike his father.

"Mornin' Pake. Do you have a few moments?" Charles felt relief swell through his veins as he saw the smile, and heard the quick answer, "Sure."

They shook hands in the bright sunlight, so the squint he saw in Pake's eyes was for protection, not intimidation as would have been from the father. "Have you seen Sonny this morning?"

"Not yet. I had to send a wire, but am headed for the café. Would you care to join me?"

"No thanks, your father will be picking me up shortly for another visit to the ranch. You should know he's very irate this morning, and has threatened me. I told him I am leaving in a few days unless something shapes up with this ranch deal, Pake. I have business elsewhere, and I've been here several days with no sign of improvement where the ranch and the sheep are concerned. Sonny told me I wasn't going anywhere until it was finished and the ranch sold. I think you should have a talk with him later today."

"Let me guess . . . you saw him before breakfast."

"Well, during breakfast, yes." Strickland watched the young man's face for signs of concern, but he simply nodded.

"Give him an hour or so and he'll lighten up a bit. I under-stand your reasons for leaving, but I know he's banking on this deal going through so you should try not to talk about it unless you are pressed. I'll go talk to Will and meet you and Dad when you get back. I can't get out there and back much before late afternoon no matter what I do though. I'll do all I can to work something out today."

They stood together for a moment, watching a bird land on the sidewalk, then flit off as quickly as it came. When Pake spoke again, Strickland heard something in the young man's voice that made him leery of what the day would hold.

"It's just too bad you can't take that whole herd. Those boys will have to split and sort the sheep. They'll try to figure out what to do with the sheep they would be left with. That's going to take a while, and if you're in a hurry, that ain't gonna help much."

For the first time in a long while, Charles Strickland drew up to his full height and got enough gumption to reply, "That is not my problem, Pake. All I wanted to do was buy a ranch, and the situation here is not something I'm willing to deal with any longer. I said I'd buy two hundred head and that's all I'm interested in. The rest of the problem is not mine, and if it doesn't get solved I'll simply have to back out of my offer."

He finished his sentence, but when he saw the expression on Pake's face and the direction his eyes were pointed, he knew he'd been heard by ears that were not as receptive as the younger set. He turned sideways to see Sonny standing behind him not four feet away.

"You ready to go?" he heard Sonny's low voice ask. The hair on the back of his neck stood up again, and his inner flight or fight senses kicked into high gear. That same sense he had the first time he saw a rattlesnake coiled, quietly, with no signal he was there.

Pake spoke tersely to his father. "I'm headed to the ranch to find Will or Matt. Take it easy today, Sonny."

The trio split and two headed for the buckboard waiting outside the rooming house, while the third disappeared with the dust from a fresh shod horse moving at a trot.

Sonny didn't speak as he and Charles mounted the buck-board and he smacked the horses on the rump with heavy reins. His face was dark and sour, and he still smelled of booze and dirt, but not as bad as he had at breakfast. Charles could think of a million places he would rather be than seated here with this old range rider, and he couldn't think of a single thing to say that would have any sound other than that of a tinkling wind chime.

Dust boiled up around the wheels and the feet of the horses as they trotted at a brisk pace covering a lot of ground quickly.

Strickland watched the breathtaking scenery of the west unfold as they rode and he mentally tried to work out a solution to the ranch dealings.

Could he buy all the sheep? Why should he buy all the sheep? He was doing a favor buying any of them simply to aid the completion of the sale. Yet, it wasn't helping, it was making matters worse.

He was torn with a desire to own this piece of the west and the somewhat dubious "notoriety" of its current owner. But it was getting less appealing as the days went by, and he was losing interest in dealing with the issues that were attached to it.

Maybe I should just tell them I don't want any of the sheep.

Or maybe I should tell them I want all of them.

Or maybe I could just hire a rig and leave town in the middle of the night and catch a train in another town.

He quieted his thoughts with the simple pleasure of watching the horses as they worked and the land as it passed before him. He would figure something out with Pake later, and perhaps he would have news when he returned from visiting Will.

Up ahead someone was approaching horseback, he raised up in his seat to see if it was someone he recognized.

***

Pake rode hard to find Will, but his efforts were fruitless. Young Will had already left the ranch and the cook wasn't sure where he'd been assigned to work for the day. Matt hadn't been seen for a couple of days, he might be in the high country working. Pake felt his angst building as he rode for town, thinking of his father and what might happen if Strickland chose to walk away from the sale. It wasn't something he wanted to pursue mentally, that was certain.

What if he bought the sheep himself? With the proceeds of the ranch sale, he could buy the overflow of sheep and hire a Mexican to take them south and sell them. . . and right now he wasn't too concerned about a profit. Will and Matt would sell to him, no doubt. *There! A solution!* Why hadn't he thought of it sooner? He turned back toward the Mitchell ranch headquarters thinking to leave a note for Will or Matt. When he pulled his horse up outside the bunkhouse, he stepped down and hollered for the cook.

"Howdy the house!" he yelled, holding the reins in the crook of his arm and watching for signs of response from the window. He was taken off guard and surprised when the cook walked around the side of the house tucking his shirttail into his pants. He smiled a little as he thought of the little outhouse off about 100 yards into the trees. He stood nervously glancing at his dusty boots as he waited for the cook to stop in front of him.

"I'd like to leave a note for Will or Matt, if that would be okay with you."

"Sure . . . hold on and I'll fetch a paper and pencil." The cook coughed as he turned and walked through the open door. Pake could hear him continuing the old smoker's cough as he moved from place to place inside the darkened doorway. It was several minutes before he returned with a torn off piece of an old poster he pulled from the wall. "Sorry, we don't have much else here right now," he drawled as he handed the tools to Pake.

He scribbled across the piece of paper, "Will, need to see you as soon as you can get to me. Pake." Handing it back to the cook he said, "You'll see that he gets this, for sure? It's very important . . . *very important*." He accentuated the last line with a raised voice and looked the cook right in the eyes.

"Sure thing."

Pake rode away, hoping the cook wouldn't put the paper down somewhere and cover it up with a pot or bowl. Maybe he better try harder to find one of the cowboys. *No, just wait.*

At a slow trot, he moved toward town, and in a matter of minutes drew close to a fork in the road where he noticed a funnel of dust in the road ahead. He wondered if his father and Strickland were coming or going from the ranch. *Must be going, they haven't* had time to get out there and be on their way back. He touched his horse's ribs with a boot heel and moved into an easy lope to intercept the wagon before it turned up the fork in the road ahead.

He raised a hand and waved at his father and Charles, who was watching with his hand shading his eyes as they approached.

"Pull up, Dad." He spoke loudly to override the clanking and banging of the buckboard as it rumbled along. "I'll ride out with you. Had a thought I wanna run by you." He stepped off his horse as the wagon stopped and tied him to a ring on the side of the boarding, then mounted to slide into the seat with the other two men.

"Fine . . . but you ain't drivin," came the terse reply from the older version of a Danner.

He began to unfold the plan he was nurturing to his father as he chucked the horses on. Watching across Strickland's chest at his father's expression, he tried to talk loud enough to be heard over the noise caused by the lurching wagon and pulling horses. Sonny's expression never changed, not from the moment Pake began until he finished and sat waiting for a response. He found himself fussing with the seam of his Levis, which irritated him, as he felt a little like a child explaining away something he was sure he was going to get in trouble for.

Hells bells, he thought. *What now?*

The answer came eventually, and it wasn't what Pake wanted to hear. "If you wanna buy them dam' sheep from those two sorry little excuses for some kind of cowboy, you go right ahead. But you ain't usin' none of the ranch money to do it, you hear? I ain't payin' them to get the hell off my own ranch."

"It ain't like that, Pop! Some of the sale money is mine, isn't it? And I'll get it back when I sell the sheep, so they aren't making the profit off me." Words failed Pake, and he sat flushed and irritated. He knew there would be no further answer. "Stop the wagon . . .

I'm goin' back to town."

He stepped off before the wagon had completely come to a halt, and untied his horse hastily. His father had already smacked the team on the rump, so he had to walk along beside the wagon to fully release his horse, then stepped away from the wagon and watched as his father drove on. "Should have expected that one," he mumbled out loud.

He trotted back to town easy and slow, the sun was heating up the air, the earth, and his dark colored shirt. His horse broke into a

58

sweat within a mile or so. Slowing to a walk for bits and pieces of the journey he continued to figure ways to come up with whatever price Will put on the sheep.

His own financial supply was short, and he'd barely been able to sustain himself for quite some time. The mercantile belonged to his family, leased out to the current manager for a monthly income that had to be split between his drunken father and weakened mother. His own monthly "wages" would never stretch far enough to cover the cost of all those sheep.

The mercantile . . . maybe I could get an advance from Mr. Braden and pay it back a little at a time by deducting the lease amount monthly. His father need never know . . . yes . . . that would work if he could talk Braden out of the advance. He headed straight for the mercantile as soon as it came into sight, excitement building with each step. His hopes were higher than they had been for days.

He wasn't turning loose of the idea. Maybe he would find a way to come up with enough to pay for the sheep on his own. He would need to know if Manuel would be willing to take the sheep to Mexico for him, but first things first. Surely selling them a few head at a time would take a while, unless he could make some kind of contact with a rancher south of the border that would use them for food for his hired help. He chuckled to himself. *What a great thought . . . those dam' sheep becoming food!!*

***

Will had been at the campsite of his herder, Manuel, all morning. Matt had been there for two days, working with the old man to separate the sheep into three smaller groups. Push had come to shove and one way or another they were going to get sheep off the ranch. Who bought them, or how they got rid of them would have to be figured out, but the change had to be made.

Will and Matt were not sure which would be the easiest for them to sell, but they agreed with Manuel the mothers with younger lambs would sell better. These would be gathered and Manuel would take them to Mexico in the days that followed. One of them would travel south and catch up with Manuel and help get sheep sold and money collected, whatever that would come to. Then they'd pay Manuel and be rid of the yoke around their neck.

Later, if things worked out with Strickland, the rest would be taken to the shipping pens at the railroad. Will was nervous about all that, as he had never had a conversation with Strickland about the sheep, it was all based on Pake passing on the information. *This better work or we'll have a worse mess than we do now.*

Both cowboys were sick of the stench the herds of sheep created. They were used to the dust and grime of cattle, but these animals had a distinct odor, and neither of them had thought far enough ahead to foresee this part of the problem when they bought the animals. They were anxious to get this part of the process over and done with, and had given up many days work for their boss to get this far along. They were closing in on a solution, and were looking forward to meeting with Strickland and getting a date for shipping the rest of the sheep.

Will raised up to listen as Matt mounted his horse and hollered at him, "I'm headed up the canyon to take a good look through the brush. I think Manuel and the dog got everything, but I thought I heard some bleating up there earlier. See you in a while."

Their relationship had remained strained since the verbal confrontation over the sheep. Will felt an emptiness as Matt rode off. *I wonder if things will ever be the same again,* he thought as he watched his young friend working his way through the rocky creek bed. *Maybe when this is all over with.*

The rolling of rocks faded as Matt's horse put some distance between him and the holding pens. When the air cleared, Will heard distant sounds of a wagon coming up the narrow trail. *Who in the heck would bring a wagon up that trial?*

Aggravated, he opened the wire gate and stepped through, carefully closing it behind him, and stood with his hand on the rump of his horse tied nearby, waiting for the wagon to appear. The sounds of the wagon wheels bumping and the jingle of the harness stopped and he heard Sonny Danner's voice yelling at the team. Obviously, they'd run up against an obstacle they weren't going to get around. He stepped around the end of his horse and pulling the tie rope, gathered his reins and stepped aboard. He rode up the trail where he figured to find the wagon.

Will grimaced as it grew apparent that Sonny Danner had been driving carelessly up the trail. The wagon wheels mowed brush and cactus over as he pushed the horses to drag the buckboard along in spite of obstacles, until finally the team quit on him, exhausted. Their fetlocks were full of cactus burls and one horse sported a bloody knee.

"Mornin', Sonny . . . Mr. Strickland," Will spoke softly as his guts began to churn at what might be coming with the arrival of these two. Obviously, Danner was anxious to have this conversation or he wouldn't have pushed the buckboard as hard as he had to getting to this remote destination. "Can I tie on and pull you over that pile of brush?" he asked courteously.

"Don't bother." Danner smacked the horses on the rump again with heavy reins.

Will grimaced as he watched the horses strain and pull at the wagon, and the wheels moved slightly but then rolled back again. Danner gave up, and gave the horses enough slack they relaxed and stood breathing heavily as they waited for further instructtions.

Will sat quietly, watching Danner turn red in the face, then pale again into the gray complexion with the ruddy cheeks of a drunk. He nearly felt sorry for the man, but it faded fast as the old man began to stare at him with the expected and so familiar hatred.

Charles Strickland sat quiet, stiff and stoic. It was obvious there was tension between the two, which caused Will to lean forward in his saddle watching Danner's actions more carefully. His adrenalin pulsed as he heard Danner begin his usual tirade about the sheep and the ranch. His insults laced with profanity flowed freely as Will tried to maintain what little composure might have been present when he first rode up on the pair.

Finally, he flung at Will, "When you gettin' them filthy sheep off my ranch?" It wasn't really a question, he didn't want an answer, just a fight.

"We're workin' on it, Danner," replied Will in as controlled a voice as he could muster. What more could he say to this disgusting display in front of him?

Danner sat for a few moments chewing on a cold cigar before he suddenly announced, "I'm gonna' figure out what's under the wheels."

Reaching under the seat of the wagon he pulled out a shot-gun and set it across the fold of his left arm as he rose. But he didn't move to step down from what he apparently viewed as some kind of throne he was using.

Why the shotgun? Will was uneasy, his hand slid off the saddle horn and moved closer to the pistol near his right thigh.

Danner straightened, and stood staring at Will from his position near the seat of the buckboard. For well over a minute he stood, holding the gun, penetrating the atmosphere with venom. Will sat quietly watching, feeling the same adrenalin that would rise when a rattler would coil, sing out and move its tongue around feeling the air. His heart began to beat harder in his chest, and he tightened every muscle in his body as his mind began to assess the situation in slow motion.

Danner's demeanor, his movements, his expression, caused Will to tense. *Is he pulling that shooter up?*

Sonny's face grimaced, his right shoulder moved forward, and his body jerked as he pulled up the shotgun, aiming it in Will's direction. Before Will could clearly think through what was unfolding, by instinct alone, he jerked his pistol from its holster and pulled the trigger twice, not taking time to aim.

The first bullet took Danner head on, piercing his chest and knocking him backwards, the shotgun blasting off to release small pellets to Will's right. He heard the zing of the pellets more than felt them as he tried to control his spooked horse. Horses hooked to the buckboard reared and lunged. The air thick with the stench of gun powder and smoke. In seconds, the stench of fresh blood followed.

Danner fell backwards, lurched from the buckboard to fall on his back and lay on the ground. Blood spewed from two wounds, one in his chest, and one in his left shoulder.

Will's own blood ran cold. His breath left him as he tried to settle his mount who was jumping from side to side, tossing his head up and down like a nervous chicken. He glanced at Charles who grabbed at the reins of the team in an effort to settle them and keep them from bolting. Strickland turned white and his mouth twitched as his expression changed from fear to shock.

Will had his hands full with his own spooked horse, but managed to maneuver him in front of the team so they wouldn't run off. The horses settled down as the dust and smoke blew away on a gentle breeze that carried the stench of warm blood within its tendrils.

Strickland turned and asked weakly, "What just happened?"

"I've killed Sonny Danner." Will's voice cracked. Stepping off his horse, he dropped the reins to the ground and moved toward the fallen man.

Walking around the back of the buckboard, he steadied himself on the edge of the box as he drew into full sight of the old man on the ground. His thoughts were racing, his knees grew weak, and he stopped to stare as he tried to recall exactly what had unfolded. It all happened so fast he wasn't sure of anything, but he knew he better figure it out. He squatted down next to Danner for a moment to be certain he was dead. He stepped to the slicker tied to the back of his saddle, untied it and carefully laid it over Sonny's shoulders and face.

Should I ride to town and leave Strickland with Danner? No . . . the poor guy would probably never survive the afternoon. Better load Danner in the wagon and take him to town.

"Mr. Strickland, you better pull yourself together. You're going to have to get off that seat and help me load Danner into the back of the wagon."

Charles took a deep breath and blew it out slowly, but he couldn't speak when he tried to answer.

"Strickland! Get down and help me with Danner." He raised his voice and spoke sternly to the easterner as he tried tosnap him out of his stupor.

"Strickland!"

Charles finally pulled himself over the edge of the buckboard and stepped to the ground, standing for a few moments before he came around. He stood staring at the slicker, his face white and his mouth twitching.

"Drop the gate on the back of the wagon," Will instructed as he walked around the front of the team, gathered his horse, and tied him to the ring mount on the side of the buckboard. He wanted the man untracked and focused on something besides that gruesome vision. Approaching Strickland for the first time, he reached out to put his hand on the shoulder of the struggling gentleman.

"You gonna' be okay?" he asked softly.

Charles still couldn't speak, but nodded.

"Come on then. We have to get him in the wagon and take him back to town."

Will stepped to the shoulders, bent over to reach under the arms of the still warm, limp body and told Strickland to pick up his feet. When they lifted the body the slicker slid off into the dirt, and Will thought for a moment Charles would drop him, but they managed to slide him into the bed of the buckboard.

He went back to get the slicker and replace it over Danner's face and shoulders.

Matthew was breaking through the brush, riding as hard as the boulders would allow, headed their way. Will waited at the edge of the wagon, resting a hand on the sideboard to stem the shaking. *Dam' it all.* He struggled to draw a deep breath.

"What's goin' on?" Matt rode up to the off side of the wagon, dismounted and walked around the buckboard with a confused expression developing. His eyes fell on the body as Will pulled back the slicker again, then laid it back over the face of the old man.

"Hells' Bells!" yelled Matt. "What the hell happened here?"

"Help us get the wagon turned around, Matt. I'll explain later, we gotta' get him to town. Throw a rope on the side of the wagon so we can get it pulled off this brush pile." Silence ensued between the three as they worked together.

Strickland suddenly stepped around by the front side of the team. Will grimaced when he heard him upchuck everything and cough. He spoke to Strickland with as much authority as he could muster. "You'll have to drive the buckboard for a while, we have to hook on and pull it over the brush and get it turned around so we can get out of this canyon. You ever drive a team before?"

"Yeah." Stickland was finally able to get a word to pass his lips. He pulled himself back into the seat and found the reins where they fell. He could barely grip the lines, but managed to cooperate with Will and Matt as they tied on the wagon bed and with four-horse power they were able to get the wagon free and point it toward town.

Will rode at a fast walk as he made his way straight to the sheriff's office with a very shook up easterner and Matt following close behind at a steady clip. He took a deep breath as he reined in his horse and took his right foot out of the stirrup, shifting his weight. He stopped for a moment, dread rising up within him like ink spilled on a white blotter, spreading through his brain and his heart with a sensation like a bee sting would produce. He finished his dismount and hung the reins over the rail, knowing his horse would stand. He opened the heavy wooden door slowly, heard it creak and moan then release as he stepped into the room, stood in the light and waited for Sheriff Rankin to make eye contact.

"What the hell's the matter with you, Will?" The question came as Rankin stood.

"I've killed Sonny Danner," Will began to shake, feeling a cold chill down his back.

"You *what?*"

Will felt the words more than heard them, and he unbuckled his gun belt, pulled it away from his waist and handed it to the man walking toward him.

"You heard me," he replied tersely. "He pulled a shotgun up and leveled it at me, so I pulled on him and shot him twice. He's outside in the buckboard." Will tried to make his voice stop quivering by speaking louder, but it didn't work.

They walked outside together, and Will stood waiting on the boardwalk as Rankin pulled the slicker back and grimacing, set it back in place. "Can you drive this over to the Doctor's office, Strickland?" he asked of the still pale visitor.

Strickland didn't answer, but smacked the horses on the rump with the reins and moved the wagon in the direction of the town medicine man.

"You better get inside and tell me how this came about," he ordered Will.

Matt dismounted quietly as they moved back inside and joined them near the big wooden desk strewn with papers and books.

"You got any coffee?" Will pulled his hat off and sat in a hard-wood chair near the paper-strewn desk. He thought of Pake and Opal as he waited for the cup of java. Then he thought of her father, and for the first time he felt the sting of tears in his eyes.

He'd carefully thought through what unfolded all the way to town, knowing he would be called to give the sheriff a blow by blow of the incident. Shock was wearing off and his heart was growing heavy with the weight of what he'd done.

He felt justified, and knew in his mind that Danner had reached the place of being angry and loaded enough that he was quite capable of shooting him. Whether he meant to kill him or not wasn't clear, and it really didn't matter. It wouldn't change the outcome. His head swam with thoughts and fear hit him square between the eyes for the first time since he pulled his gun from its sheath and pulled the trigger.

***

It took less than five minutes for Will to relate what happened. Matt stood nearby listening intently. Will knew Rankin had all the facts, the threats and the animosity from previous days stored in his head. As he related the story the lawman's expression didn't change much. He nodded now and then as he scribbled notes on a wrinkled piece of paper in front of him.

The sheriff knew all parties involved quite well, and while his sympathies surely were with Will, they all knew that hell would break loose when word hit the streets.

"You know I have to lock you up, Will," Rankin stated.

Will stood and moved toward the cell. "Yeah, I know." he merely whispered as he moved toward the cage.

"You okay?" Matt asked as the door slammed shut and the key turned in the lock. A glint of tears passed through his eyes as he asked his friend of old, "What can I do?"

"My head's starting to hurt something fierce, I just need to lay down for a while." He looked up at the pale face of his friend and asked "I need you go tell Opal, then maybe in the morning you could ride up and tell my folks?"

"Sure, just exactly what would you have me tell Opal? Aw, Will . . . how the hell did this happen?" Matt watched as his friend nervously rose from his seat on the cot and stepped to the bars, resting his hands on the cross bar. His thoughts went to the slight little girl he'd known most of her life, and he noticed the sheriff turned away as his own face began to show signs of deep concern.

"It just did, Matthew. It's hell, that's all, just hell to pay. I been through it in my mind a hun'rd times and there's no way around it. I don't know how I could 'a kept it from happening short of gettin' shot myself, but I sure as hell didn't want this to happen."

"Aw . . . now, sure you didn't." Matt stood near the cell door watching the expressions on his partner's face, his own chest aching with what he feared would come to pass. "Hell, it would make better sense if it would have been me that done the deed. Surely folks will know you had to do it or you just couldn't have been the one."

Will stepped away from the cell door and eased back onto the cot. "Just go tell Opal and my folks . . . I'd like them and her to hear it from you before the word gets out. Rankin will send a telegram to the district judge, so I'll know pretty soon what's gonna happen. That's the best you can do for me."

Matt grinned at him, the impish tone of voice returned as he asked, "How about I just get rid of about three hundred sheep an' back up a day or two?" He stood and moved the chair back where he found it and looked at his friend again.

Will smiled enough to let Matt know he appreciated his attempt at keeping his sense of humor, stepped to the window of the cell to watch Matt and Rankin step outside to the boardwalk.

Matt skipped putting his foot in the stirrup and instead grabbed the saddle horn and swung up in one smooth motion. Rankin stepped back into the doorway and watched as Matt loped out of town, making tracks to the home of Opal and her family. In the morning he'd make the fourteen mile ride to Will's folks' house up the river.

They all noticed Pake loping into town, but Matt kept riding, simply nodded at Pake as he rode by.

Rankin stepped to the door to holler him over. "You need to go to the Doc's office, Pake. Brace yourself boy." He stood watching Pake, who spun his horse and loped toward the small building that held the office with a faded wooden sign.

Rankin stepped back inside and looked at Will. "There is sure gonna be hell to pay."

Pake stared at his father's face, still smeared with dark, dried blood, pale and gaunt. There'd been no love lost between them for many months, but the sight of his childhood hero lying there ripped his chest open. *I'll have to telegraph mother.* Tears filled his eyes, but he wiped them away quickly when the doctor walked up behind him.

"You okay, Pake?" he asked.

"Yeah. Anybody know how the hell this happened?"

"You better head up to Rankin's office. He'll tell you."

"In a minute," Pake responded with a weak, liquid voice. He sat down on a straight backed chair near the table where his father was laid out. He'd been cleaned up some, but still had dirt and blood all over him, and the stench began to nauseate Pake, so he rose again and walked to the door.

"I'll be back later, Doc." His eyes were lowered and his voice quivered slightly as he turned the door knob, he sucked a fresh breath of air and stepped through. The distance to Rankin's office disappeared quickly under dusty boots that had seen better days. The door to the lawman's office was open, so when he entered his gaze went straight to the face of the man who sat quietly waiting for him with a cup of coffee ready to hand over.

"Better sit down, Pake. Sip on that and breathe for a minute, then we'll talk."

"Buying time, Rankin?" He swallowed a sip of coffee before he realized there was someone in the cell to his left. He turned, knowing it would surely be the one who was responsible for his father lying in state up the street. When he saw   Will watching him quietly, he felt a hot ball of an old, familiar sensation from years ago rise up in his chest. His head buzzed inside like a nest of angry hornets. He set the cup on the edge of the desk, not looking where he set it. It fell to the floor, coffee spattered the room, but he didn't see or hear.

"YOU . . ." *Words failed him and he stood gasping for air.* His hands

69

grabbed the bars of the cell, and Will stepped back far enough to be out of reach.

Pake's rage erupted in a volcano of words and curses, his body shook visibly.

Rankin stood by the desk waiting for the "ash and smoke" to settle, allowing the flow to continue until it used itself up. "Pake! PAKE . . ." but the words fell on deaf ears. Rankin waited a moment then picked the cup off the floor and filled it with hot black coffee from the always full pot and moved closer to the young man in his tirade. Stopping just out of reach, he yelled again "PAKE! Knock it off."

Rankin moved in closer to put a hand on his shoulder. The touch of a hand jerked Pake around, and seeing Rankin he realized he was all used up for words . . . and hate . . . and anger.

He sat down hard in the chair, and Rankin handed him the cup of coffee.

"Here, slow down boy and let's talk this out."

"Talk . . . hell that's all I've heard for days."

Pake lifted the cup to his lips, not realizing how hot it was until his mouth was filled with a burning sensation. He winced, swallowing fast, but it jerked him to calmer senses.

It took a good half hour, but Pake was finally able to allow Will to describe the scene and what happened on the trail that morning. His emotional responses mixed with those of Will and Rankin caused plenty of disruptions as the tale unfolded. When it was finished, all three sat still and quiet.

A flock of birds on the limb of a nearby tree sang a light-hearted song. Pake smirked, *stupid birds.* They continued to fill the air with chirps and warbles as the men watched each other for a break in the tension.

Rising from his chair, Pake took his hat off and re-set it on his head, pulling it down hard. He stood looking at Will for a few seconds then turned on his heel and left the dusty little office. Stepping off the boardwalk, he froze and stood for several minutes as though he didn't know where to go, which way to turn or what his next step should be.

He made his way to the telegraph office where he carefully crafted a note to his sister and mother, paid the operator then made his way back to the doctor's office. Walking to the door, he stood for a few seconds with his hand on the knob, his head down before he entered the room to view his father's still, pale face. He'd been cleaned and combed and his clothing dusted off, and he lay on a wooden table with a pad and sheets under him.

"Dam' old fool." Pake spoke out loud, more to himself than to the doctor who stood near the entrance to a smaller room next door. There was no response from the doctor, so Pake looked up, his voice wavering as he simply repeated the words again. "If he'd have just held off a couple more days, I had things goin' fine."

"When you want to bury him, Pake?" The doctor seemed to be trying to pull his thoughts to the necessities at hand.

"Tomorrow ." Pake gathered his thoughts and settled his emotions. "My mother can't come, she's too frail, and my sister won't leave her. No fancy stuff, I'll just pick him up and take him to the buryin' yard if you'll find a couple of fella's to help me out. Is there someone who'll dig the place for him?"

The doctor stepped close to Pake, setting his hand on his shoulder. "I'll see to all of that . . . there's a couple of fellers who help me with this kind of thing and we'll have a place ready for you in the morning. If you want to drive the buckboard that'd be fine. You go on home now and I'll see you in the morning."

Pake made his way to the small saloon up the dusty road and stayed there until the bartender closed the place and made him leave by the back door. He didn't sleep. He faced the facts that he had to finish the ranch deal and bury his father. Then what? For the first time in his life he didn't have to drag his father out of a bar and follow him around to be sure he wasn't in trouble again. Should he go where his mother and sister were? Stay here and try to manage the few business dealings he'd held together?

Well, one thing's certain . . . I ain't goin' anywhere for a while. This ranch deal has to be closed and now there'll be a trial. Aw hell . . .

the trial. Pake's head spun with thoughts that bombarded him like a hail storm, stinging and cold, blowing through hard and fast. He wanted to hit something . . . someone. *That would be too much like him, and I'll be dam'd if I'll do it like he would.*

An empty room and the stench of old liquor and cigar smoke haunted him, called to his memories and drug them through the window of his soul. *I stayed mad at that ol' man most of my life, but I loved him.* Lying on a rumpled bed, he fell into a fitful sleep to return to childhood days and dreams filled with visions of Matt, Will, Opal and the years they'd played and romped through the school yard together.

Morning came and he hadn't changed his clothes, but he donned a clean shirt and wiped his boots then made his way to the café for a try at breakfast. Later he returned to the doctor's office where he was met by four men who helped with his father. They all made their way to the cemetery. The doctor was there, and a handful of townsfolk who came to pay their respects, including Opal and her folks.

The doctor said a few words and within a half hour the cemetery was empty save for two helpers who stayed to help Pake fill the grave.

Matt came to his side, gripping his hat in his hands. "Need some help with that, Pake?"

"No . . . Hell no! Get away from me."

Opal's father stepped between the two, settling the anger slightly. "I'll help you, Pake. You go on now, Matt. Thanks for the offer."

***

The service over, Opal and her parents made their way to the sheriff's office to check on Will. Rankin shook hands with Maxwell and doffed his hat to Lily. "I'll be outside. You folks stay as long as you like."

Opal stepped to the cell door, tears flowing freely. "I wanted to come last night but Dad said there would be plenty of time today. Oh, Will . . . *now what?*"

She stepped aside just enough to allow her father to shake Will's hand, watching Will's expression change as her father questioned him about the events of the day before. She listened carefully, imagining what it must have been like as Will related the story again. It must be getting more painful each time he had to relive what happened.

Her father had finally quenched his thirst for information, and her mother had stepped outside to talk to Rankin. Opal stepped closer to the bars on the cell, reaching through to place her hand over his, resting on the cross bar.

"Is there going to be a trial, Will? Or will the sheriff know it was self-defense?" She hoped for the later, feared the first, and was very confused about how this would stand up in court or how the judge would view the event. She wiped tears away again with a small stained hanky she'd tucked in her sleeve before they attended the funeral service.

"I'm sure there will be. I think Rankin telegraphed the circuit judge yesterday but he hasn't told me if he's heard anything back yet." Will didn't look into her eyes, but rather past her hair to the window behind her. Tears continued to make their way down her cheeks. They stood quietly, holding onto each other's hands, simply wanting to remain near each other.

Lily came back into the room and Maxwell stayed outside to stand quietly beside Rankin. Will looked into the eyes of the small woman who was so obviously struggling with her daughter being so entangled with what had unfolded.

Lily said nothing, but walked to Opal's side and put her arm around her waist. She looked square into Will's eyes, then pulled Opal away and said softly, "It's time to go." They walked to the door where Opal stopped, looked back over her shoulder and hesitated, but her mother kept pulling her to the boardwalk where the family gathered again and returned to their own wagon and tethered horses.

Will watched through the window across the room until they were out of sight, and then turned to settle onto the cot in the corner. He didn't want to think. Wanted to shut out the haunting memories that returned every time he closed his eyes. He dozed off and on through the afternoon and following night.

***

Rankin came into the office the morning after the burial and built a pot of coffee before he walked to the cell and addressed Will.

"I'll get you some breakfast here pretty quick, Will, and I stopped off at the telegraph office on my way home last night. The circuit judge will be here day after tomorrow. He's moving this case to the front of his docket . . . he and Danner were pretty good friends back in the day."

"Figures." Will ran his fingers through his hair to push it down after the night's rumpling effects. The smell of the coffee boiling over on the surface of the old wood heating stove was pungent and made his nostrils itch.

Rankin passed a cup of coffee through the bars and stood looking at Will for a moment. "You know, kid, I wish I could tell you which way I think this is gonna go, but the judge will be the one who decides that for you. I keep asking myself what I could have done different, and I'm sure you been doin' the same. But it's done, and you'll have to just see what happens. I guess I should tell you I don't think they'd hang you . . . but don't think they'll just let you go either."

Will felt sick inside. "Could they hang me?" He could barely push the words past his lips.

"They could, but I really don't think they will." Rankin left the room headed for the café and breakfast for him and Will. He was about half way across the street when he saw a dusty rider

74

coming up the road at a steady walk. Rankin waited in the road when he realized it was Matt, and watched as the young man rode up and stepped off his horse.

"Okay if I go in and visit with Will?"

"Sure. I'll be back in a few minutes. There's coffee on the stove." He didn't give a thought to the boys being alone in the office. It never crossed his mind that one might try to help the other get away. They just weren't that kind of kids.

Matthew took his hat off and wiped the sweat and dust from his face with a handkerchief pulled from his hip pocket, then stepped to the stove he used the rag for a pad and poured a cup of coffee as he spoke to Will. "I stayed with your folks last night. They're pretty upset, o'course. Your mama's takin it pretty hard and your Dad's mad as hell. He said they'll be here tomorrow as soon as he can get someone to feed and tend the livestock for him." He stepped close to the cell and sipped his coffee. Will nodded his head up and down, but no words came.

"Any word on a trial, or is the sheriff gonna' let you go?"

"Couple of days the judge will be here. He said they could hang me, but doesn't think they will."

Matt nearly dropped his cup, and swallowed hard. "Hell, Will. No way they'd do that. Danner threatened you and me both and why the hell did he take that shotgun when he got down off the buckboard if he wasn't thinkin' he'd use it. He sure as hell wasn't going quail huntin'."

Matt stood quiet until Rankin came back in with breakfast. "There's enough here for three of us, Matt." He handed out biscuits and pointed to a pot of oatmeal. "Dig in." Then he dished up a tin cup of oatmeal for Will and handed it through the bars. "I know you prob'ly ain't hungry but you better eat somethin'. Going hungry ain't gonna change nothin'."

It got pretty quiet except for the clink of spoons on tin and coffee bein' sipped up.

****

Will sat quiet, numb, through two full days of testimony and questions posed by the judge. Two long, emotionally charged days of working through what led up to the shooting. No jury had been drawn as the judge seemed to believe he could come to a conclusion on his own after hearing the testimony.

The morning of the third day, Will walked toward the school house beside the sheriff. Doubling as a courtroom, it was filling slowly with townspeople. Sleepless, restless nights had kept him awake, dulling his senses and his thoughts were muddled.

He remembered only vague bits and pieces of testimony. Several people had witnessed numerous threats by Danner against both Will and Matthew. While a few of Danner's friends had tried to justify his anger and reasons for his attacks on the boys, most of them remembered hard drinking and fits of anger.

Charles Strickland sat pale and calm as he gave his testimony regarding the scene on the road where Danner met his demise. He was also quick to add the threats to his own well-being where Danner was concerned.

The sheriff was called to the chair as well. "Strickland, Matt, Will, they've all been to my office on different occasions to discuss threats and fights with Danner. I warned all of them more than once to keep away from each other, but that doesn't happen in a town this size. I know my opinion isn't what's on trial here, but I have no doubt Danner was itchin' for a fight. I guess my personal testimony, with regard to the shooting when I wasn't there, would be to question why Danner felt it necessary to take the gun with him when he was getting down off that buckboard."

"I appreciate your opinion, Sheriff Rankin, but that's all it is, as you well know." The judge's tone of voice was nearly a reprimand.

Matthew's testimony was heated, and the judge had to rein him in more than once as he exploded under questioning. Will kept hoping Matt would calm down, fearing these outbursts would only lead the judge to believe the boys had possibly "egged on" some of the confrontations. In his own mind, Will found himself questioning what he could have done differently, said differently,

76

and he regretted most profoundly his decision to purchase that herd from the troubled old herder.

Will's sadness grew as he watched Pake listening hour after hour without saying a word, just doing a slow burn punctuated with dirty looks. When he had his hour on the witness stand he did more damage to his father than to Will, even though he tried to keep his testimony slanted toward his father's side of the case.

The doctor testified as to the position of the bullets as they entered and exited the body. His conclusion was that Danner had been facing Will when the first bullet entered the right side of his torso just under his right shoulder blade, near his armpit. He couldn't be sure of his position when the second bullet found its mark, but it had most certainly not entered fully from the back. The order in which they found their mark was uncertain.

Mr. Mitchell testified as to Will's character and how many years he'd been acquainted with both boys, standing up for them as young men with integrity. Will was acutely aware how grateful he was to this old man who had been like a second   father to him. Having him bear witness to his character meant more to him than he could find words to say.

Will himself testified that he was certain Danner intended to use the gun. "That old man had too many years under his belt to pull the shotgun out without intent to use it. There was no other reason for him to have pulled it out that I can think of. I never raised my voice at him that morning, nor did I threaten him in any way. Hell, I was just offerin' to help him get the buckboard back on the road."

The verdict was self-defense. The judge was quiet and deliberate as he spoke. "While I believe these young men brought a lot of their problems on themselves bringing sheep to this country, and while I had the utmost respect for Danner in his younger years, I cannot pass down any other verdict than self-defense."

Pake stormed out of the room and several in the room cried out in disbelief. One of the women in the back of the room who had been close friends with Pake's mother stood up and yelled out loud, "Murderer! You got away with murder." Several seated nearby voiced their agreement.

Maxwell Redding had been standing behind Will as the judge stated his verdict. His father also stood behind with his hands on the back of Will's chair waiting for the verdict. He heaved a resounding sigh of relief as the judge spoke the words from his desk. Will was thankful his mother had stayed home and hadn't had to endure these past few days.

Mr. Martin and Maxwell stood with him until the courtroom had quieted and was empty, waiting until the sheriff gave him leave and shook his hand.

Mr. Mitchell shook his hand and said quietly, "Job's waiting for you when you're ready, Will. Fall work starts before long."

Fall works. Will stood thinking to himself, a*t least that will be back to normal.* But he knew in his heart nothing would ever be the same again. Ever. Normal was now a vague word that held no real meaning.

Maxwell leaned into Will's ear; "Bring your father to supper, you can both sleep on cots in the bunkhouse tonight. It's too late for him to head home tonight and he can leave from our place in the morning. Pake will be around and could get riled up."

Will nodded. He looked forward to supper and time with Opal before he rode back to Mitchells' ranch and the familiarity of his own bunk.

It took several hours to finish paperwork and pick up his trappings at Rankin's office. Will and his father stayed close to each other the rest of the day as they ate lunch and gathered belongings before they headed for the Redding ranch. The air was thick with gossip and tension and both were anxious to get out of town. More than once he felt the angry eyes of townsfolk on his neck as he walked streets that for years had welcomed his boot tracks. The welcome mat was gone, and would maybe never be out for him again.

Throughout the day Will caught himself lifting his eyes to the openness of the sky, watching clouds mass and mill. Pines reached to the heavens all along the horizon. Across the way stood the old school house, now empty of everyone except the circuit riding preacher who stood quietly watching as the crowd dissipated after the verdict was read.

Will felt drawn to the old rider, and eventually made his way to the side of the leathered friend of his youth. Shaking hands, they stood for a few moments, then quite naturally settled on the three steps that led to the front door.

"Haven't seen you in a while, Will. Obviously the verdict was in your favor."

"Yes sir, the judge said it was self-defense . . . and I believe it to be so . . . but I'd like to speak with you for a bit if you could spare me the time."

"Don't need to spare it boy, it's God's time anyway."

Will poured his heart out to the kindly old gentleman, seeking some kind of absolution. "I'd give anything to be able to relive the moments before that gun came out of my holster. I keep thinkin' of ways I could get around doin' what was done."

"Have you seen in your mind a way that would lead you to another course of action?" asked the old gent slowly and softly. His eyes met Will's straight on as they spoke.

"No sir. Other than choosing to ignore the fact there was a wagon coming up the trail and leave them there to get themselves out of the pickle they were in, I don't guess there was any other way to run the course."

"Then be at peace with yourself, Will. There are things that happen in this west of ours that are contrary to the ways of peace and contentment."

They sat quietly for several minutes as Will played with the brim of his hat, rolling it in his fingers as he worked hard to control tears and a lip that would not quit twitching. Eventually he rose to his feet, reaching out to shake hands with the preacher. "Thanks. I reckon time will heal the ache."

"Most likely. If you let the peace of God soak through your heart and mind, Will."

After saying goodbye, Will found his father and shook off thoughts that carried him into the past and the disturbing events from the week before. They gathered their belongings and saddled horses to ride out of town slowly, carefully watching doorways and corners of buildings for possible retribution from townsfolk, or even from Pake.

Will imagined he felt a cool breeze being stirred by the rolling up of the welcome mat behind them as they rode away on dusty streets. Once again his heart ached for the days before the coming of the sheep.

****

Opal sat quietly staring at Will all through the evening meal as the men took up most of the conversation with cattle, horses, rain and the lack of it. She and her mother cleared the table and cleaned the kitchen while the men sat on the porch. After a short while, the conversation died down and they quietly watched the sun set in typical gold and crimson with bursts of what Opal had always called little stairways to heaven.

She took off her apron and hung it on the back of a chair before she stepped outside to wait her turn, wishing everyone in the world were gone except her and Will. She watched out of the corner of her eye as her mother moved to work on her darning rather than venture into the men's world. Mama had said absolutely nothing since they returned from the trial. Opal knew why, but that wouldn't change the way she felt about Will and her hopes for a future with him. Her thoughts were singular, focused on what could await them in days to come.

Relieved, she heard her father's words: "Why don't you and Will go feed the stock and tuck everything in for the night, Opal? Don't forget to put some smear on the sorrel's leg where he scraped it on the rocks yesterday."

Nodding she moved toward the steps, reached for Will's hand as he rose to join her. The touch of his rough, chapped hands was comforting, soothing to her soul that longed for something more than this friendship they'd nurtured since childhood.

They didn't return to the house right after chores, but sat on the top rail of the fence to watch the moon and stars find their temporary place in the sky. He would stay in the bunkhouse with his father that night and they would both leave before the sun was full up in the morning.

"I wish I could go with you, Will." She started a long awaited conversation. "You know I want to be with you and you know I don't care where we live or what it's like there, I just want to be with you always."

"Where would we go, now?" The sadness in his voice was painfully evident. "I gotta' get rid of those damnable sheep and try to figure out how to move forward from this awful mess I'm in." She heard him draw a deep breath, then heard it leave him as a heavy sigh. "At least I won't have to go to jail. I thought sure that judge was going to nail my hide to the wall. But that doesn't change the facts and there's no tellin' how long it will take for the hatred to die down enough where I can even go to town without folks glarin' at me."

Opal reached for his hand in the dark. "I know, but things will be okay in a while. You'll still be workin' for Mr. Mitchell and maybe somehow we could find a place and I could get a town job for a while."

Suddenly the reality of leaving her home and her horses caused her to bite her tongue. Over-whelmed with the reality of what would follow, she began to doubt her own ability to carry the load she saw rising before her like an undulating heat wave. Fear gripped her, she turned loose of Will's hand and slid off the fence.

"No way," said Will. "You'd go stir crazy workin' in town! You can't give up all this for me. Not until I can find a way to make things work for us. I can't think straight right now but soon as fall works are over I'll figure something out."

He slid off the fence next to her, pulling her to his side as he leaned down. He gently kissed her upheld face and eyes and then her lips. Her hunger for his love leaped as she pressed against him, they both felt the surge, a deep and longing desire. He stopped as she began to press against him tighter, knowing to continue would make it harder to let go. Pulling away he kissed the top of her hair as they turned to walk toward the house where he said goodnight to her family.

***

Opal folded herself inside the comfortable old quilts that covered her bed. Both were familiar to her shoulders and even after years they smelled of potions worn by her grandmother and her mother. Lying quietly, she knew he was awake thinking of her as she was of him. There was a nip in the air that evening, and she could smell the leaves beginning to turn yellow and curl their brown edges. In spite of her efforts to think of a solution to her dilemma she drifted off to sleep.

She slept through the sounds of Will and his father as they grabbed a biscuit and coffee and rode out as soon as they could see the roadway. Rising after the sun, she dressed in a split skirt and went to the kitchen to wash her face and wet her hair as she smoothed it around and braided it, twisting little strands of hair around the bottom to hold it in place.

"Must you persist in fixing your hair in the kitchen," asked her mother curtly. "I'm always finding your hair in everything."

Opal poured a cup of coffee and noticed there were four biscuits gone from the pan.

"Thanks for getting up early and making breakfast for Will." She pulled a crisp brown one from the pan, her favorite were the edges. "I know this has been hard for you to swallow, mother, and I appreciate you being there with me. And with him."

"I wasn't with him," came the terse reply. "I was with your father and with you. I could just bean that kid with a hammer sometimes. How could he get himself into such a rancid pot of spoils?" Her voice broke and she turned to walk out a back door with an apron full of scraps for the chickens.

Opal heard her talking to her little egg producers, but it wasn't the usual clucking and murmuring. She was tellin' them chickens her own little opinion in no uncertain terms.

I wonder what those chickens could tell if they could only talk. Opal headed for the corral and her father to find out what she needed to do for the day ahead. It would be good to be horseback again, and there were two young horses that could sure use some work.

"Just put some miles on the two youngsters," were her instructtions for the morning. She brushed them hard, and saddled them carefully, easy-like, and slow. They hadn't been ridden in a few days and they were feelin' the brisk morning air.

Thoughts of Will faded as she loaded her saddle on the first. She noticed he cocked his head to the left and laid his ears back when she pulled the cinch. Opal smiled to herself, she knew she'd better let him run in the round pen for a spell before she mounted. She tied the reins of the hackamore over the saddle horn and turned him loose in the pen, then stood with her hand on the gate to watch him for a few minutes. He was fresh, and drew her full attention as he threw his head in the air and snorted a long, rolling breath of air that sounded like a rumble of distant thunder. It gave her goose-bumps and she laughed out loud as he broke in to a trot, moving away from her. Crow-hopping a couple of jumps he settled in to lope around the outside of the pen.

Her second mount resisted arrest for quite a spell that morning. He was a bit of a juvenile delinquent and had been tougher to work with than the one she'd just left to loosen up a bit. She managed to corner him, waiting for him to turn and face her before she walked up and put her hand on his neck. Once she'd made contact he settled and reached his nose around to smell her arm and blow warm air onto her hair. She leaned forward and put her face close to his mane, breathing in deep, letting that singular, unique odor permeate her senses.

It was almost like she was taking in something of his personality, his qualities, his life, and feeding her own. She slipped the halter over his nose and tied it off, then turned to lead him to the front of the saddle house and repeated her grooming before she moved him into a separate part of the corral and let him run up and down the fence nickering to his buddy romping through the round corral.

She returned to the round corral with the younger of the two mounts who tried to accomplish a bluff and ducked to the side and ran around the corral. It wasn't long before he turned and walked up to Opal, reaching out his nose for her to touch. She laughed, saying in a soft voice "Silly bugger. Come on over here and pay attention."

She checked the cinch, pulled it up a notch, then unbuttoned one side of the front panel of her split skirt. She pulled his head around to the left just a bit, gathered the mane with her left hand and reached to the saddle horn, pulling herself slowly up on his back, watching for a change in expression or a flinch of his body. None came.

She worked him slowly at first, then at a trot, moving into a slow lope which she maintained until he began to break a sweat in the fold of his shoulder muscles. Reversing, she repeated her pattern. Cooling him out was the closing maneuver and then she stood him by the fence while she pulled her saddle and wiped the sweat from under the saddle blanket. She turned him out in a nearby pen, patting his rump as he moved past her.

Opal whistled as she worked, a habit she picked up from her father. She slipped the hackamore from the sweaty mount and walked easily up to the second pony where she wiped his nose, ears and then his face with her gloved hand. Talking to him constantly, she placed the hackamore carefully on his head, adjusting the fittings. She moved him into the round corral next door where she placed her own saddle on his brushed back and carefully cinched up once again.

She felt the fall breeze, sensed it held more signs of cooler weather, changing colors. It was certain there would be many days between Will's visits. The crew over at Mitchell's ranch would be starting the fall works. Gathering the herd, cutting out the culls, calves and shippers, riding the back canyons and high mountain range. Then for several days everything leaving the ranch would be moved to the railhead and loaded on cars to be shipped to buyers back east somewhere.

Buyers . . . her mind quickly turned to Charles Strickland and she began to wonder what he would do now that things had turned dark. Would he buy the ranch now? Would he give Matt and Will time to get rid of the sheep? They'd lost days during the trial and after all there was still blood on the ground where memories would surely swarm if he had to ride anywhere near the holding pens in the canyon. She shook her head and pushed thoughts away, focusing on the horse now responding to her knees and hands guiding him. *Too bad I can't move certain cowboys this easy.*

She opened the gate and rode this mount outside, finding herself on the trail toward the Mitchell ranch, wondering if she might catch sight of the crew in the distance. They'd be in the high country first, working cattle out of the mountain meadows before any early snow. She stopped frequently to scan the hills, riding out of the trees into clearings where she had hundreds of miles stretched out before her gaze. Each time, her senses swelled inside like a gigantic bubble, bursting, sending tiny drops of rainbows skittering through her brain.

By the time she rode through the corral gate back home, she wasn't so sure she really wanted to give up all of this and live in a cabin someplace with a man who probably wouldn't be able to give her the kind of freedom she had earned from her father as one of his "hired hands".

How many horses could I have to ride if I married Will?

Could I give all this up?

Would my father let me come home and ride for him?

Her hands tightened on the reins, as if to take a better grip on what was happening in her life, to regain some kind of control. *Who would ride for Dad? What rough handed cowboy would take over my horses?*

Too many questions without answers smothered her thoughts.

***

Pake Danner spent days following the trial breaking his time between the saloon and the café. He wanted desperately to pin down the sale of his father's ranch. Charles Strickland apparently wanted nothing more than to close the deal and return home. The younger Danner was beside himself trying to figure out how to make something happen.

Will and Matthew had left the care of the sheep to the old Mexican and gone back to riding for Mr. Mitchell, still waiting for Strickland or Pake to assure the purchase of the sheep and give them even a verbal commitment as to numbers and time.

Seated near the window one morning, Pake watched bacon and eggs grow cold before he stopped fussing about the situation and set his coffee down to attack his breakfast. He watched for Strickland to leave the boarding house and head for the small café. *This morning* he thought, *this morning I get some kind of answer.*

Strickland entered the room with some flair as he slung his coat over his shoulder and straightened to his full five foot six stature, pausing to look around the room as if to draw attention to himself. Standing, Pake stood and signaled to him to join him at his table. Shaking hands, they sat together as Strickland ordered and finished breakfast.

Pake addressed him abruptly. "I guess we better get this ranch deal settled or sacked."

Charles waited a moment, looked at Pake for a few moments, then finally began in a low voice. "I've been doing a lot of thinking and I have decided to buy the ranch, but not right now. I am leaving today, and when I get home I will begin making arrangements to buy and sell all those damnable sheep if Will and Matt are still of a mind to get rid of them, and I'm sure they are. I feel somewhat responsible for what happened here, Pake, and I would probably be able to broker a deal for them faster than any of you would. So, I'll leave a letter for Will, and once I'm able to accomplish the sale, I'll telegraph you, or Will, and we'll move forward then."

"Just telegraph Will," came the curt response. "I don't want to have to talk to him."

"I understand. But I will let you know once the arrangements have been made and we'll settle a sale then."

Pake sat quietly, digesting what had unfolded, flooded with relief to know the ranch would be sold. Relief mixed with disappointment that he wouldn't be able to make a quick sale, take the money and leave for a long-avoided visit with his mother and sister.

He struggled with overwhelming disgust as it sunk in that Strickland had just offered to broker the sheep. Did it really take his father's death to jog this man into helping broker the herd. *Why in the hell didn't he just do that to begin with?*

The pair finished, shook hands with stiff goodbyes and Pake walked back toward the saloon. Stopping outside the door, he shook himself and moved toward the mercantile instead. Life had taken on a sense of despondency with no direction, and no purpose. Slowly, gradually, as he wandered the streets he realized how much of his life had been consumed taking care of his father. From a safe distance, he had watched, guided, led his father without making him angry or causing him to feel like he was smothering him. Now, he had his life back, with no idea in the world what to do with it. Perhaps seeing his mother again would help bring him to his senses. He avoided the mercantile, making his way to the telegraph office instead.

"Ranch will sell later. Coming to you next week." Reading the telegraph he sat it on the counter, then watched the telegraphers hands move quickly over the key. The clicking stopped; he paid the fee and stepped out on the boardwalk. His eyes began to fog over as he felt tears welling up. Standing for a few moments, he looked slowly around the small town he'd grown up in. *Maybe I'll be back. . . someday.* But he couldn't think of a single reason he would ever want to return to this haven of sorrow and hardships.

The saloon door swung wide under his fist as he returned to a room with voices and the presence of fellow humans.   Familiar faces turned to watch him find a table and chair, order a drink, and turn his thoughts to his inward emotions. Even in this room full of people, with the clinking of glasses the presence of a woman serving drinks, the mumble of voices, the loneliness seeped into his bones like a slow-dripping jimson weed after a summer rain. Beautiful to watch, poison to the drinker.

***

Will and Matt finished the fall works with Mitchell before the first snowfall without a day off or a trip to town. Mitchell's wife brought the note from Charles Strickland and left it on the table in the bunkhouse, but it didn't find its way to Will for many days.

"Awww hell." Will's voice was low and terse as he read the note, and passed it to Matthew. Relief flooded his soul, but his next thoughts were, why now? In Strickland's offer to broker the sheep for the cowboys was something akin' to mockery for Will. Why didn't he just offer to do that before a life was squandered? But then . . . that life had been wasted and abused for years before Will came into the picture. Still and all, it tied his guts in a knot every time his memory flashed back to that ominous moment.

"Nice of the old boy to get us off the hook now," Matt's comment came with noticeable animosity and bitterness. "Well . . . I guess it's a gesture we should take kindly and be glad he's doing it at all. He didn't have to, he could have just gone on home."

"Well, for some ungodly reason he still wants that place. Looks like he's cut a deal with Pake and we'll just ride it out until we hear from him."

By the time the pair had the first note in hand, Strickland had found a buyer and a telegram was delivered to the Mitchell headquarters by a friendly local. The boys had twelve days to get the sheep gathered and to the railhead for shipment. Mitchell took pity on the pair and sent four cowboys with them to gather the sheep and get them shipped. It was time to put an end to this season of nonsense, and the putting an end to it was finished within the week.

Six worn out, sick-of-sheep-smell cowboys returned to the bunkhouse at the Mitchell headquarters after that long, hard, temper-testing week. The usual bantering that passed between Will and his peers had ceased by the second day, the usual "joking and jobbing" had become punctuated with swear words and some of what could certainly be considered animal abuse.

With their usual good humor returning, they finished the job, then wiped their hands clean of what both young men considered to be the biggest mistake of their lives.

As the last tail of the last "wooly" entered the railroad car and the gate slammed shut, Matt let out a war-whoop that split Will's ears to the core. Slapping him on the back Matt yelled, "Drinks are on me!" and ran as fast as his spur-clad boots would allow while three young cowboys followed suit.

Will chose to sit quietly on the fence until the train rolled out of sight, then shook his head and slid off the fence, mounted his horse and headed for the ranch and his job.

***

Opal hadn't been to a social gathering in weeks, and had no desire to mix with the prattling of women who had no idea what was behind all the problems they watched unfold. The townsfolk did not take kindly to the publicity Will's actions brought to their small town. Papers from back east had sent writers to cover the trial, dime-store novelists wanted to interview Will and Matt continually, and there was no end to the gossip that had the womenfolk stirred up.

Her father remained stoic and thoughtful, watching her work the horses day after day, her heavy heart betrayed through the wry, sad expression on her face. Where she once smiled constantly at her horses as she worked with them, now she was quieter than usual, and it was obvious the horses sensed her distraction. She found herself bucked off more than once due to her lack of focus.

The sun was leaving the freedom of sky to nest in the violet-gray mountain in the distance as Opal sat on the porch late one evening. Watching for dust from the trail she strained as the last bit of light faded, building shadows so deep and long they seemed to follow the setting sun into oblivion. Her father walked quietly up behind her, and she looked up to smile for the first time all day. Sitting quietly beside her, he reached out to touch her hand, an unfamiliar course of action between the pair. She knew her father loved her, but there was little-to-no show of affection other than an occasional pat on the back when he wasn't holding her feet to the fire for some stunt she'd pulled.

"Are you going to make yourself sick over young Will?" he asked quietly.

"Already am. Can't think, can't pay attention, can't get my head to go anywhere but to what must be going on with him right now." Her response was low and quiet, showing some embarrassment that revealed she thought it must be a weakness of some kind to lack the ability to forget and move on.

"I was thinkin' maybe I could find a place here on the ranch for him. Maybe let go one of the younger hands that hasn't been here long and put him to work with us."

Opal heard the words, but in the back of her mind she knew it was hard for her father to make this sacrifice. Once a man was hired on their ranch he was there until he chose to leave or showed he wouldn't ride for the brand. Which one would her dad let go to make a place for Will?

"Will wouldn't hear of it, Dad. He'd never take another man's job from him, you know that."

"Well, he wouldn't have to know about that part of it. I'll let someone go and wait a few weeks before we try to work it out."

"I don't know. I haven't seen much of Will and I fear he may be dealing with thoughts that just aren't giving him much room right now. I don't know if he's going to stay in this country or want to leave, and if he leaves I don't know if I could go with him. It's getting harder and harder to face what's goin' on in town with all the talk and hoorah. Will won't put up with that much longer." Stretching her sore legs out from under her riding skirt, she pointed the toes of her boots upward and noticed they were worn to a frazzle.

"Dam' that Danner," she mumbled. Her voice quivered like the quaking aspen on the far hill when the wind would whip through.

"Don't do that daughter. Danner was a good man in his younger years, he just let the bottle get to him and it cost him everything . . . including his life if you look at it that way." Letting go of her hand he leaned forward in his seat, poking at the toe of her boot. He grinned at her. "Think it's about time you had those fixed?"

"I guess," she replied, but the seething resentment still burned in her like a slow-boiling pot of brown gravy. Not wanting to spoil this rare time with her father, she bit her tongue, and they sat until the sky darkened completely and stars were all they could see.

Moving through the darkness without lamp light, she moved inside and slipped into her long-johns, then between the old flannel sheets and her quilts. The comfortable old collection of fragments had rested on her bed from the time she could toddle. It was more than a comfort; it was resting under a canopy of her roots. Fragments and memories of a grandmother she never knew but surely would have loved. Fragments of her mother's life and the years of worn out clothes and hard times.

***

Fall works were over, with only remnants to gather from the hills. Will and Matthew had experienced the first relief and peace in months as they were finally rid of the sheep, and the final papers had been signed for the sale of the Danner place. Will heard through the grape vine Pake had been staying with his mother for weeks. He'd left, saying he had no intention of returning to the town that left him filled with a rotten bitterness that would never leave him be.

The sun was beginning its trek across the purple hills, bringing with it a golden shroud filling the valley with vibrant explosions of effortless exposure. Will gathered a young horse from the corral, throwing a loose rope over his neck and leading him to the hitching post in front of the saddle shed. He whistled an old folk song from his mother's childhood as he brushed and saddled the colt, thinking of Opal and a good meal. His heart was lighter than it had been in a very long time, and his thoughts were clear. Memories from childhood years returned and brought a smile to his face . . . until he remembered his friends of school days and the face of Pake Danner filled his mind. The whistling stopped, and the colt turned his head as if to say "What happened?" his senses telling him Will was suddenly not the same.

Turning his horse around a couple of times, he pulled the colt's nose around slightly, set his left foot in the stirrup and gently lifted himself onto the back of the youngster. He felt the horse's muscles tighten and his back hump just a little, so he sat quietly until he felt the colt release. Moving easy he set him on the road to Opal's and began to whistle again. A ballad he'd heard an old cowboy sing one evening as they settled near the cook's wagon. The horse moved into an easy trot and ate up the distance quickly. Anxious to arrive, he spurred him into an easy lope as he drew near the last curve in the road before the Redding ranch would appear in his view.

Never thought they might not be home. He loped around a curve and pulled up to walk the last hundred yards to the corral gates, but pulled up as he realized Opal was working a young horse in the round corral on the far side of the barn. Walking slowly to the fence, he pulled his horse to a stop, and lifted his right leg to swing it over the neck of his mount. He laced it around the saddle horn and leaned forward on his knee to watch the love of his life working with the second love of his life.

Every muscle movement of the horse was matched by those of the lithe young woman with reins in her hands. The supple muscles of both horse and rider were obvious through a light shirt and a slick hide. She hadn't seen him, so he watched with keen gaze and appreciation for her execution of horsemanship, and the response to each request by the young horse. The pair looked like a couple on the dance floor working to figure out who was leading and which way to move. Realizing Opal had seen him, he rode close to the fence and smiled. She turned the youngster toward the edge of the corral responding to his, "Long time, no see."

"Hey, there stranger. I was hoping you'd make it down this week, I heard the works were finished out at the Mitchell place." Fussing with her reins a little, she continued with, "Can you stay for supper?"

"I was hopin' for an invite." He watched, amused when she tried to push her hair out of her eyes and smooth her shirt into the waist of her split skirt.

"When did you start wearin' skirts?" he asked surprised.

"I been wearin' these things for months! Can't believe you just now noticed. I wore out all my jeans and Mother had these things from back when she would ride with Dad sometimes. I gotta get to town and get some clothes bought up." She seemed nervous for some reason.

"Ride up to the house and let Mom know you're here. I'll unsaddle and be there in a few minutes."

She turned her horse toward the gate, then pulled him up and looked back over her shoulder. "Hey, it sure is good to see you." A perky smile parted the dust on her face.

"You too," he answered grinning from ear to ear. "You best hustle along with that horse you keep tormentin'." Turning his mount he leaned forward and urged him into a trot until he rode up to the hitching rail in front of the house, where he dismounted and loosened the cinch. He took the hackamore off the face of the colt and laying a loop from his rope around his neck, tied him to the rail. Lily Redding stepped to the open door wiping her hands on her apron, but no welcoming smile crossed her lips. Will stopped at the foot of the steps.

"Hello, Mrs. Redding." He spoke hesitantly. "I hope it's okay that Opal invited me for supper."

"Yep. But you better take that horse back down to the barn and put him in a pen. It's gonna be a while till we eat. Maxwell should be back soon, and you can sit a spell and visit."

He sensed her tone and felt unwelcomed, but he would stay. He'd pretty well braced himself for this wherever he went these days.

Turning slowly, he retraced his steps and untied his horse, leading him to the barn where he found Opal unsaddling her colt. Glancing over his shoulder to be sure Lily had returned inside, he stepped up behind Opal sliding his arms around her waist and pulled her close, breathing in the smell of her hair and the horse's sweat. It was a perfume that was unique to Opal . . . that homemade soap and her horses. The remains of that fragrance on his shirt sleeves had kept him awake many nights and caused his dreams to contain a pretty young woman who held his heart in the palm of her hand.

She turned suddenly and reached as high as her arms stretched to encompass his shoulders. His muscles tensed as he leaned down to steal a sweetness from her mouth like a hungry humming bird, hovering above a giving flower. They lingered, soaking in the long awaited presence of loved ones until they heard her mother calling from the porch. As they pulled away reluctantly, he reached in his pocket and pulled out one of those wonderfully familiar folded pieces of paper and she nearly tore it from his hands, unfolding each layer quickly.

"Easy there chickapea," he began. "That's a lot of work I put into wrappin' that little gift for ya."

She smiled as she unfolded a tiny bouquet of purple and white daisies that grew wild. They were limp, faded, and the petals had begun to fall from their gold center.

"Guess they ain't all that purty," he added.

"Yes they are . . . you picked them for me. Where on earth did you find them? It's been so cold I'm surprised there are any left." She folded the petals gently back inside the paper that was normally used to surround tobacco for smoking.

"There's a little clearing up the road where the brush grows close to the ground. I guess these are the last of 'em until spring."

"Where do you get these papers?" she asked as she noticed the shape. "You don't smoke."

"The cook over at headquarters does though." Winking at her, he turned to lead his horse to a small pen, pulled the saddle to fling it over the top rail of the corral, then hung the hackamore over the horn of his saddle.

Supper was laced with tension, Lily was terse and moved around a lot, but never reached a point of rudeness. Maxwell and Opal were full of questions and answers about the sheep roundup, shipping and the sale of the Danner ranch.

"I'm just glad all that's over and done with." Maxwell boomed across the table. "Let's just call it past and get on with what's coming."

"Tell us about roundup, Will," Opal begged. She loved his stories of the wild rides, the crazy things the cowboys did and most of all the pranks they played on each other. Leaning forward she waited, watched his face, and awaited what he knew was inevitable.

"Have you heard anything more about Pake?" Will changed the subject. "Has Strickland taken possession of the ranch yet and moved cattle on?"

Maxwell filled him in on both gossip and news, until Will's curiosity had been satisfied. Thus the hour flew by with lively conversation and even went so far as to bring laughter to the small group, something Will realized he had sorely missed.

Maxwell urged him to give them more stories about the fall works on a 'big outfit'. It was obvious he was hungry for what would come. The stories always renewed his own memories of a wilder, lively time in his youth.

Will leaned forward on the table, picked up a spoon and fiddled with it as he relayed a particularly amusing event from the weeks of gathering cattle with his peers.

"Ol' Rowdy rode off into the breaks of a little canyon after about eight or ten head we could see bunched up in an oak thicket just under the rim. I had four head in front of me I was takin' down the trail, but I kept an eye on him so's not to beat him to the creek below where we'd bring everything together. The fence line comes to a gate at the bottom."

He punctuated the story with a wave of his arm and the lilt in his voice said he was enjoying the sharing. "He was ridin' Salty, so I knew he was mounted right, but that ol' horse had already tested him a couple of times that morning an' I knew he could have a wreck if he wasn't careful. I pulled up and let my bunch spread a little and graze so I could watch him. He got to trottin' along the rim lookin' for a way down to those cows and calves an' Salty had his ears back an' nose tucked just enough for me to see he was gettin' kinda' cranky about the pressure.

"Pretty quick he found a trail off the rim and he an' Salty started rollin' rocks when they pulled off the trail, so the cattle took off like a herd of scared deer. Down through an oak thicket went Rowdy and Salty and next thing I know here comes Salty out the other side without a rider. He never slowed down, just kept after those cows and worked his own way above them and pushed them down into the creek bed."

He stopped long enough to take a sip from the lukewarm coffee in front of him to wet his throat, then began the story again. Both Maxwell and Opal were leaning forward with elbows on the table. Opal's expression caused him to grin. Wanting to keep that enthralled, wide-eyed look on her face, he continued.

"By that time I could tell I was gonna be behind the eight ball if I didn't hurry, so I pushed my little bunch off the trail at a high trot and we all come to in a little clearing near the bottom of the canyon . . . with no Rowdy in sight. Salty stood on one side of the bunch with his head dropped, breathin' heavy. That horse worked back and forth just enough to settle the bunch so I could leave them there and go see if that crazy Rowdy was hurt or okay. Well, here he come, walkin' down the creek bottom a'mumblin' to hisself like an old gramma. He walked up to Salty and climbin' aboard he looked over at me an' yells, 'Did you see this bugger brush me off in that oak thicket? Dam' ol hide!' I looked up at him and said "Well, from where I sat it looked to me like Salty was holdin' up his end of the bargain way better than you were."

Lively laughter rolled, then Maxwell began telling a story sprung from his own memories. Will lost track of time as the pair drank cold coffee and swapped tales. Every time the cups would be reaching empty, Opal would fill them up again, obviously hoping the stories would continue. She couldn't outlast the menfolk, but it was hours before Will noticed her dozing off now and then with her chin dropping off her folded hands.

Maxwell followed his gaze to smile gently at his young daughter. "You better stay the night in the bunkhouse, Will. We'll see you for breakfast." He nudged Opal and encouraged her to move to her bed.

The night birds called softly from the dead leaves of the dried lilac bushes in the yard as Will quietly found his way to the familiar bunkhouse and settled in. Thoughts of his time with Opal earlier that evening filled his senses, until he drifted into sleep and dreams that mixed horses, cattle and wild rides with a beloved face and precocious smile.

***

Opal sat quietly on the porch steps before the sun was fully up, waiting and watching for a Will to leave the bunkhouse and crew. Across the distance to the doorway of the quarters she could hear his laughter, and knew he was relating the same stories she'd heard the night before to old Tom and the young man her father hired to help for a few months. Patiently she waited for his face to appear as she watched a lone owl float across the meadow and find his way into the piñon trees at its edge.

Distracted, she didn't realize Will was nearly to the porch before she caught his form in the corner of her eye. Quickly rising, she stepped off the porch and hugged him briefly, then led him up the stairs into the kitchen and poured him a cup of hot coffee. They watched as Lily made her way into the small room to scoop her sourdough starter into a bowl and flop a hefty dose of flour into the mix. A pan of biscuits was quickly built as Opal sipped coffee and watched every glance, smile and wink from across the table. *Sometime, some way will he sit like this while I build the biscuits in our own kitchen?*

Her father found his way to a chair, holding his boots in his hands and rubbing his rumpled hair. "Mornin', all. Guess you youngsters beat us to the punch." He kissed his wife on the top of her per-fectly bound hair as he held a cup for her to fill with liquid mud. Sipping a taste before he moved away from her toward the table he smiled and joined them, setting his cup on the table and pulling his boots on before he began to converse with the group again.

She nearly jumped out of her chair as his voice rose quickly and she heard words she had only sensed were forthcoming.

"Will . . . I guess I best just get right to the point this mornin'. I'd like you to leave Mitchell and come to work for me. I need a good hand with the horses to help Opal, an' a man who can work into the position of a foreman as I get too old to push this crew around. It looks to me like you and my daughter are pretty well glued to each other an' I may as well get used to the idea. I know I can't pay you what you're makin' over there, but we'll feed you good an' as time goes by we'll up the pay." He stomped the second boot to secure the fit, then asked, "What say you?"

Opal watched Will's expression change as the older man nearly yelled the offer across the table. It was obvious her father was nervous, and in her mind he flubbed the offer substantially in the delivery, but she loved him even more for the trying. Her heart beat a little faster as she watched the face of her life-long friend change and his jaws tense.

"How does Mizz Lily feel about all this?"

She was amazed that his first thought was of her mother! Surely it must have been weighing heavily on his heart that she was still harboring bitter thoughts of past issues.

She glanced into the kitchen where her mother stood beating a dozen eggs for a scramble and winced as her mother's move-ments froze. Setting everything on the counter, Lily wiped her hands on her apron and walked directly up to Will looking down on his upturned face. She reached out, took his face in her hands and said, "I wanted to shake your teeth down your throat for a while, young man. I didn't want my daughter married to a man who could take another's life. I wanted her to marry some rich rancher and live a life high on the hog. But I do know you to have a truly good heart. I have loved you a lot and hated you a little since you first rode up here on that shaggy old bay and slid off to have a bite to eat. I've been feeding you at this table for a long, long time, and it won't hurt my heart none to do it some more. But the question I have for you is what will you give in exchange for her heart?" She stroked his hair, and pulled his face to her breast as she wiped the trail of tears that found its way down his cheek.

Opal wiped her own tears and her father "*hurumphed*" as he rose to fill his cup once again from the pot on the stove. Opal's tears continued, to her dismay, as Will replied, "I will love her, treasure her, and give her everything I can to make her life filled with happiness." She heard the words spoken softly from the heart of a young man to the woman he wanted to please.

Her mother kissed his forehead. "Then I bless you both with love and joy." She returned to the kitchen and finished her breakfast preparations. It was only a matter of minutes until she set steaming biscuits and scrambled eggs mixed with chopped left-over steak from the night before in front of her family.

The quartet was silent as they finished the meal set before them. Will helped Opal clear the table and returned to the table with the coffee pot, poured himself and Maxwell a fresh cup. "I guess you're waiting for an answer."

"You don't have to answer now, Will. Just give it some thought and let me know as soon as you know yourself."

She heard his response to her father, instead of her. "I'll have to talk to Mitchell . . . but I was wonderin' about a couple of things. Opal does a great job with the horses you have, and the crew finishes them off as they use them. Looks to me that you have a full crew hired on right now, so where would I fit into the mix?"

"I heard tell of a gal up North who has a string of horses that are well bred and good mounts. I was thinkin' maybe I'd stretch out my horse operation, turn that over to you and Opal and use you in the cattle end of things as well. Someone's going to have to go up there and check it out . . . decide if that's the direction we want to take the breeding program or if not figure out some other solution. You'd be that person, I reckon."

Opal held her breath as she listened to this news, surprised that her father had been thinking along these lines. Had this just come to him in the night or had he been chewing on this fodder for a while? Nobody spoke for what seemed a very long time.

They listened to sounds from the kitchen as her mother washed the dishes and started a roast for the oven. The space without words was awkward, and Opal began to fidget with the edge of a spoon left on the table for sugar, her eyes darting from her father to Will, waiting for a response from either. Finally, Will grinned that crooked little tilt that exposed only the white teeth on the right side of his mouth.

"I think I'd like that, Maxwell. I think I'd like that a lot. I'll ride home and give Mitchell my notice and tell Matthew goodbye.

Can I have a couple of weeks to tie up loose ends over there?"

"You can have what time you need. I have to figure out some things on this end anyway. I guess my next question is what to expect of you and Opal."

"Wait just a dang minute!" The spoon banged on the table and she knocked the chair over as she leapt to her feet. "I have something to say about all this, yes?"

Both men turned their faces toward her with eyes wide expressing surprise. They waited for her to finish, and Lily poked her head around the corner to watch with an amused smile.

Opal's short fuse had burned out so that her voice raised with a sizeable amount of irritation. "I haven't been asked about any of this . . . and just so you know, I can handle the horses I've got and a sizeable bunch more if I need to. If I'm going to spend the rest of my life in this mix, don't you two think I oughta' be *asked something*?" She stood glaring down at the two surprised men, and noticed the smile on her mother's face as she waited for an answer. It didn't come.

To her irritation, both men rose from the table, walked to the kitchen to dump their cups and headed for the door. Will stopped as he pulled his hat down, deliberately looked her right in the eyes and winked. She threw the spoon at him as he ducked and ran down the steps toward the corral. Her mother laughed, reminding her she had chores to do.

Will walked to the barn with Maxwell. Neither said much till he opened the gate to the horse pen. "She's right I guess. But before I ask, I need to square with you. Along with this offer for a job, I'm guessing it's okay with you that I ask her to marry me?."

"Well . . . that goes without saying, Will. Good luck with that one after this morning. She'll make you squirm for a while before she says yes."

They both chuckled, and Will caught up his mount, saddled and waved goodbye as he loped up the dusty road for what had been his home for more months than he had counted of late.

Don't know how Mr. Mitchell is going to feel about all this. Good thing we're done with the fall works. Then there's Matthew . . . wonder what he'll decide to do now that things are gonna be so different. His thoughts rampant . . . nothing came together in a clear picture until suddenly he realized fully what had unfolded. He spoke out loud, to his horse if no one else. "Well . . . I guess I better ask Opal about the marriage thing before I go quittin' a good job."

He laughed out loud, patted his horse on the neck. "I ain't wantin' to work for her an' her dad if I'd be answering' to a female that's been rubbed the wrong way." He pulled up and started to turn his horse around, stopped dead in his tracks, coming to the full realization of what lie ahead for him. His life was upside down and sideways, full of a hot-headed, full blown female potential bride. He chuckled, then burst into laughter again as he spun his horse and headed onward to the Mitchell place.

The sun seemed brighter, the world seemed a better place to be, and his mouth curled upward no matter how hard he tried to make it stop, until he finally just puckered up and began to whistle the old familiar folk tune his mother taught him as a child. Suddenly thoughts turned to his parents . . . how long had it been since he rode over to see them? *I better spend a couple of days and ride up to let them know what's going on. Well . . . as soon as I know for sure what's goin' on.*

He rode at a trot until his horse began to bead up sweat on his shoulder muscles. Slowing to a quick walk he rode to the saddle shed and unsaddled his mount, brushed him down and turned him into the horse pasture. Peripheral vision revealed Matthew watching him from the porch of the bunkhouse, obviously waiting. *This won't be easy, lots of years and water under that old bridge. How am I going to tell him I'm leavin'? And since I haven't even asked that little imp how do I know for sure if I'm even leaving.*

He wondered if he should have ridden back to the Redding ranch, but she was pretty hot under the collar, so he would wait a while. Not long, though. He needed to be sure of her answer. Would she say "yes"? Surely she would! But that little hot-head could not be taken for granted, of that he was very sure.

He walked up and leaned on the hitching rail in front of the bunkhouse. Matt stepped through the door and to the edge of the steps smiling. Those stairs seemed ten feet tall looking up at his friend.

"Mornin', Matt. How are ya?"

"Okay. I beat the socks of the boys playin' poker last night and have a pocket full of jingle . . . wanna head for town this afternoon?"

"Nah. I been gone two days already. I better check in with the boss. I need to visit with you for a bit right now though. You got a few minutes?"

"Sure," Matt answered as both settled on the steps. Will deliberately chose a lower step so he didn't have to watch his friend's expressions as he unfolded events of the day and evening before. Finishing he sat quietly waiting for a response, pulled his hat off and wiped his forehead.

"So . . . did Opal tell you she'd marry you?" came the quiet response from Matthew.

"Not yet."

"Well then . . . that little minx just might leave you danglin' in the wind till she gets good an' ready, pard. I wouldn't quit my good job before she gives you an honest answer."

103

"That's my plan." Will gazed toward the barn waiting for further response.

"Hell, pard. If that all works out you'll have a future bigger than anything we had planned."

"What'll you do?" Will realized this decision would change more lives than two.

"Well . . . I guess I'll stay on here and see what cracks." Matt stood, leaned against the pole nearby.

Will's heart was heavy for the first time in days as he thought of his life-long friend going through life without him. Things were sure shaping up to change a lot of lives in the valley. Standing, he reached out a hand and the pair shook long and slow . . . but eye contact was never made.

The next morning both were saddled and headed for high country to gather remnants. The day work crew had been paid and winter crew scattered to chores and duties.

This could be our last ride together, rang through Will's head hour ridge above him. Matt was reckless sometimes, but what a great cowboy he'd become. A little heavy handed with horses at times, but he sure knew how to read a cow herd. If he hung with Mitchell's ranch maybe he would make cow-boss one day.

He pulled up his horse and watched as Matt "whooped" at a pair of young cows brushed up and hid out in the oak thicket above. As rocks began to roll he pushed them across a shale slide and moved them toward the trail below. Holding his breath, Will watched as Matt's horse began to lose footing and slide with the rocks, then lunged to catch himself as the cows ahead seemed to be tearing off chunks of the hillside, pushing it toward Matt and his mount. He yelled, but knew Matt couldn't hear him.

He yelled again as Matt's horse went over backwards in the rock slide, then tumbled sideways throwing his rider beneath him and rolling at least 30 feet down the side of the hill.

Will pushed his horse toward the wreck, his heart beating so fast he could feel the blood hitting his brain pump after pump. Matt lay twisted and still in the midst of the rocks and dust while the horse made his way to his feet and moved to the edge of the rock slide, then stood shaking himself in a bunch of algerita brush.

Will nearly fell to his knees as his feet hit the ground. Leaving the horse ground tied near the edge of the rock slide he made his way toward Matt. *Lord, please don't let him die!* He crawled over the rocks the last twenty feet to Matt's side. Reaching out to touch his chest he realized he was screaming his name over and over. Blood streamed from cuts along the side of Matt's head and face and as Will pulled him out of the rocks he noticed blood coming from his nose and mouth and out of his ear.

"Matthew . . . *Matthew*! Come on man, come to. *Come to!*" No response.

How the hell am I gonna get him out'a here? Then his mind turned off and his body began to move in perfect response to fear and necessity. He pulled Matt completely out of the rocks and worked him over to the edge of the slide, moving carefully so as not to start the slide again. He whistled loud and hollered at his horse. Both lifted their heads to look his way, but neither moved toward him . . . *hell.*

He kicked rocks out of the way with his boot heel and laid Matt in what spot he could without a bed of malapai beneath him then leaving his still silent friend gathered both horses and brought them to the spot where he lay, still unconscious. *I don't dare move him until he comes around. No tellin' what's busted up inside him.* Kneeling near the body, again trying to bring him around, he pulled his bandana from his back pocket, spit on it and wiped the blood from Matt's face. He spoke firmly, fear gripping his tongue making it hard to speak.

"Hey, pard. Hey . . . Matt, come on buddy, come to me." Adrenalin coursed through his veins like hot oil then seemed to freeze solid as Matt's eyes fluttered. He groaned hard then opened his eyes and said, "Stop beatin' on me . . . what the hell's the matter with you."

Falling back on his butt Will breathed deep. "I ain't beatin' on you ya dam' fool – yer all busted up from a horse wreck. Just lay there for a minute till we know if you can move."

"I can move just fine . . . what's the matter with you?" Turning his head Will watched as Matthew gathered himself and sat up, holding his head and looking at the blood that had dripped all over his shirt and hands. "What the hell. . . ."

"You took a bad fall, pard. I don't know how bad you're hurt, but it ain't good. Let me take a look at you . . ." Will eased to his side, careful not to set his knees on a cactus. Pulling Matt's scarf from his throat he began to wipe the blood away and look at the cuts and scrapes. The blood in the ear was from the cut above, not coming from inside, but two of the cuts were deep and still bleeding. "Sit still. I'll be right back."

Untying saddle strings he pulled his saddle pouch from its place, yanked a couple of long strands from his horse's tail and made his way back to Matt. Digging through the small pouch he pulled a thick leather stitching needle from the depths and began to thread the horse hair through the eye.

"Don't look at me that way. You'll bleed to death by the time we ride home if we don't stop it. I've sewed up horses an' leather, but never skin. This is probably going to hurt like hell." He pulled the edges of the first wound together and began pushing the needle through the edges as Matt winced and tears washed the blood from his face. Second wound wasn't as deep, but by the time he finished Will was sick to his stomach and he kept hearing buzzing in his head as he pressed through to get the job done.

Pulling Matt's canteen from his scraped up saddle he gave Matthew a long drink and washed blood from his face and hands, then washed his own hands. *Dam' . . . that very nearly was the last ride we ever took together.* Looking up at Matt he asked "Think you can climb aboard and ride for home?"

"Where'd those cattle get to?"

"They're prob'ly off down the canyon somewhere, but you ain't goin' after them today, and neither am I. We're goin' back to the house."

"Let's just gather 'em up an' take 'em with us." Matt began as he rose to his feet for the first time. "No sense in wastin' a full day."

Will chuckled as Matt staggered and sat back down, holding his head. "You're going home, and then I'm takin' you to town and have the doc look you over. I hope nothin's busted up inside but we better be sure."

He helped Matt rise again, setting his boot in the stirrup for him, he pushed him into the saddle as Matt grabbed the horn and tried to help himself, and they rode carefully and slowly back to headquarters. It took several hours after they reached the home place to convince Matt to go on into town and find the old man known simply as Doc. It was dark before they tied up at the rail near the little building that served as home and hearth, as well as receiving room for the old man who tended the needs of the town.

Banging on the door Will stood with his friend who kept insisting he didn't need to see the doctor. When the door opened wide, a young woman stood before them asking, "Can I help you?"

Completely taken aback by the unexpected face before them, Will finally responded, "Isn't this where Doc lives?"

"Yes . . . he's busy right now. Can I help you?"

"W-e-l-l-y-e-e-s-s, ma'am, you surely can." Will heard the familiar voice coming from behind him as Matt moved around in to the light of the lamp she held in her hand.

Good gravy, for a sick compadré that idiot sure came around in a hurry. Will felt Matt's hand on his arm, moving him out of the way so he would be in full view of the pretty young woman in the doorway.

"I got smashed up in a horse wreck this afternoon and my pard here thinks I need to see the doc."

Will stepped back and the corner of his mouth ticked up in a slight grin as the young woman responded, "You can come in and wait, but he could be a while. Seems horse wrecks were running rampant today, he has another patient in the back who came in all banged up as well." She moved aside and the trio filled the small entry. Will and Matt took a seat on hard backed chairs against the wall and watched the young lady disappear through a curtain that led to another room.

"Who's the other fella'?" Will asked as she swished through a curtain across the doorway. She didn't respond, but he heard her exclaim as she moved down the hall, "Cowboys . . . they all think they're ten feet tall and bullet proof."

"Who you reckon that gorgeous piece of humanity belongs to?" asked Matt in a whisper.

Will turned his head, reached up to uncork his hat and tipped it to the side as he grinned at Matthew. "Well now, I don't know the answer to that little question . . . but I reckon I know who'd like be on the top of the list." He nearly laughed out loud as Matt stood up to look at his reflection in the glass of a picture hanging nearby. . . fussing about his hair and looking close at his swollen, battered face that didn't really look much like the youngster that left the ranch earlier that morning.

"Sit down you fool, you look like a plate full of hamburger. She ain't gonna look at you twice till you heal up some. She's prob'ly visitin' the doc." His mischievous nature took over and he impishly began to hoorah his friend. "Or . . . well . . . maybe he took a wife and just apparently robbed the cradle."

Matt groaned and shook his head no. Will patted him on the back. "Cheer up pard, maybe you can wait around until the doc kicks the bucket and you'll be healed up enough she'll take a look at you." Suddenly he felt rather than saw that the young woman had re-entered the room, and his neck began to flush. Moving up through his entire face was a blush of embarrassment that silenced him completely.

"Doctor Anscom will be with you in a few moments. And just for your information, I am his niece, not his wife, and if I were you I wouldn't be speaking so lightly of him 'kicking the bucket' since there isn't another doctor within a hundred miles of here to take care of you idiot cowboys who are forever coming in here banged up." She flipped her hair over her shoulder and swished back through the curtain.

"Now you done it, you dam' fool." Matthew groaned and punched his shoulder.

"Aw cheer up, Matt. Maybe she'll be around until she could stand to look at you and you can take her for a peekneek sometime." He left him alone to stew and wait for the doctor, went out to keep an eye on the horses and the night.

The two young friends did not heed for long the warning that Matt was to avoid hard riding for a few days and get plenty of rest. They saddled the next day to find the cattle they'd lost the day before.

**

Opal stomped and fumed for several days after Will rode away . . . with a wink and a nod he simply left her stewing in her juice. Pestering her father for information, she tried to find input while she waited for Will to ride back into her days. She heard from folks in town that he and Matthew had been in town, but didn't make their ride pass by her window. Her fuming increased, the fussing accelerated, and her frame of mind was such that had Will made his way to her company she quite probably would have dismissed him with a similar wink and nod, then a slammed door.

Thinking of a dozen ways to answer the question she was sure would come soon she fluctuated from revenge to full on submission:

I'll make him squirm . . . I won't answer for a long time.

I'll fly into his arms and make him ask me before he can think straight.

109

Maybe I'll just sit and rock and won't even look at him . . . no . . .

I never could pull that one off.

What if he decides to stay with Mitchell?

What if he doesn't want to work for my dad?

What if things just don't work out for us to be married?

Standing in the barn door watching the horses flip their hay around searching for tastier morsels, she sensed rather than heard someone behind her. Fully expecting to see her father, she was quite surprised to find that Will had ridden quietly up behind her. He stood watching her with his reins draped over his right arm. Startled, she jerked around and stood silent as he drank in every expression on her face, watching for a sign of welcome and relief. It came quickly . . . she moved into his arms and hugged him hard, holding on to his neck with both arms and resting her head on the soft curve of his shoulder. No words formed, no space developed, just a warmth of presence that fed the longing in hearts long ago forged in tandem.

"Will you?" His voice was low, soft and haunting.

"Will I WHAT?" she demanded, still holding fast to his frame.

"You know what . . . you *know* what!" he whispered. She held on tighter, wanting to stay close to him longer.

"And you know I will." Looking up into the edge of his jaw she saw his chin quivering slightly and her heart grew warm with liquid longing. She felt his breath on her forehead, then his lips on her cheek, and finally they found each other in that deep exchange of love and caring that only lovers in the depth of submission experience.

She watched Will's every move as he unsaddled his horse and led him into the corral where he charged two of the horses and nosed them out of his way while he raided their pile of hay. Moving to meet him as he closed the gate she held his arm close to her shoulder as they made their way to the porch where her mother waited.

Reaching again into that familiar shirt pocket he pulled out the little folded paper and held it in front of her as they walked. She looked up at him, smiled that quirky little tilted familiar grin, stopped and unfolded the papers. "Oh . . . a sago lily!" One of the rarest of wild flowers in their area, she lifted it gently to examine the little cup that had been carefully pressed to dry. In life it was shaped so very delicately to catch and hold perhaps one or two drops of rain. "Will . . . it's so beautiful. So tiny, and delicate. When did you find it?"

He didn't have time to answer before they heard, "I guess I can tell what just happened." Lily quipped.

"How'd you know that?" responded Opal, wondering how much her mother had heard.

"Well child . . . if you could see your face and the silly grin plastered all over his, you'd see just how easy it is to read that lingo." She laughed and turned to walk back into the house.

Pouring each a cup of coffee, Opal sat beside Will and sipped coffee, unable to take her eyes off him until she heard the clink of her father's spurs on the steps. Will rose from his seat and waiting for her father he reached to shake hands and greet the old cowboy friend.

Maxwell looked from Will to Opal and smiled. "Looks like we have your answer . . . yes?"

"Yes, sir."

"When will you start?"

"I quit this morning."

Opal raised up straight in her chair. "You must have been pretty sure of yourself."

"No . . . just sure of what we've had for a long, long time."

His eyes met hers and all sense of self defense faded quickly from her thoughts.

Maxwell sat and abruptly continued, "Good. I'm lookin' to send you North to bring back a new stud and some mares from that female rancher I told you about. Sooner we get that settled the better." Maxwell stated firmly as he lifted the coffee pot from the back of the stove and kissed his wife on the very top of her carefully contained hair.

"I'm goin' with him." Opal inserted her own concerns to the conversation.

"Hold on . . ." came from the lips of both men nearly simultaneously.

"No, you hold on . . . I'm goin' with him," she responded firmly, then braced herself as she watched her mother moving to stand near her husband. Dwarfed beside him she looked just as intimidating as her counterpart, and Opal knew whatever happened next would be the final word on the subject.

"Only if you're married, young lady!"

She felt Will's hand covering hers and his fingers gripping tightly. "Yes, ma'am . . . that's going to happen as soon as possible."

"You two ride into town in the morning and talk to the preacher." Then she returned to the kitchen to stir potatoes just starting to burn on the bottom.

Will drew Opal to the porch when Maxwell turned to walk to the bedroom. They sat quietly waiting for the sun to completely disappear over the pines along the ridge. Words were flying through the mind of each, but there would be time for them later.

***

Finding the preacher was easier said than done . . . he was making his "rounds" and the note on the door said he'd be "Back by Sunday." Sunday came and went, the congregation met without him, sang hymns twice as long as usual, had a special prayer for his safe return and dismissed.

Word came by special rider that the pastor had succumbed to some kind of fever and passed on before he could get home.

He would be buried in the cemetery of the town where he'd died, and since there were no family members or wife to mourn him, the service was short and the headstone was small. The congergation took up a collection the following Sunday to have a larger stone placed on his grave with the name of their town to be displayed clearly in site. After all, he had been their shepherd for nearly ten years, visitors should know that.

A few days later, Lily and Maxwell sat quietly at the table waiting for Will and Opal to return from a long ride. There was a very acceptable solution available to the quandary regarding their marriage. Maxwell would perform the ceremony before witnesses and the congregation, then when the judge came through again, or a traveling minister visited, they would re-new their vows and have the papers signed. It was perfectly legal in the law of the land, and had been done many times in western states where both judges and ministers were limited and quite often circuit riders.

The date was set, the congregation, friends and families were invited, and Maxwell prepared what he intended to say at this very auspicious time in his life. The words didn't come easy for him and he continually asked Lily to write down what she thought he should say.

"You'll figure it out," she responded.

The morning came too soon, and he stood in his best Sunday-go-to-meetin' clothes with his tiny wife seated before him and his mouth as dry as a cotton ball. His only child stood tall and proud waiting for his words of blessing. The small gathering made him nervous, but he read clearly in spite of his hand shaking the page so hard he could barely keep his place. Will's parents sat on a wooden bench provided for the congregation in the little clapboard sided building that doubled as a school and a church.

"Folks, it wasn't all that long ago these two young'uns here in front of me were just kids playin' in this school yard and sitting on benches right where you find yourselves seated today. It ain't no surprise that they have ended up here in this place to do what they're about to do. Since there ain't no preacher, nor circuit ridin' judge, I'm about to perform the ceremony and you all are witnesses here that this marriage is takin' place and put your blessin's on it."

It was hard for him to keep his voice from cracking as he watched his daughter and her soon to be husband beaming like a pair of fresh cleaned lantern glasses. He continued, reading the words he'd heard a preacher say when he and Lily were married. Standing steadfast, he finally did let one tearful trickle escape as Lily prayed and blessed the pair.

He took off the jacket as soon as the deed was done, and invited everyone to step outside where they'd find a table filled with offerings from all the ladies present. He shook more hands than he'd seen in a coon's age.

Watching the sun across the sky, he waited for the time to pass and hopefully all would head home. Which was where he'd take his own little wife and let his new son-in-law and daughter spend the night in the boarding house in town. "Where the hell am I gonna' put those two now?" he asked Lily quietly.

"I'm workin' on that little problem, don't you fret yerself. Is this really the first time that thought has crossed your mind?" She shook her head in amusement.

"What have *you* got in mind, woman?" He smiled down at her and deliberately ignored her question.

"You'll see when we get home. Me and Opal got it all figured out." Lily closed the conversation and moved off to help clear the tables and shake the tablecloths out. She hugged women and said goodbye, and putting her portion in the back of the buckboard waved goodbye to the last wagon.

Glancing around one last time to be sure doors were closed and nothing left waving in the breeze, Maxwell helped her into the seat, then climbed up next to her. He sat holding the reins for a few moments, his head down. Lily reached over and put her hand on his, smiled that wonderful little crooked smile of hers and once again all was right with his world. He smacked the horses on their butts with the reins and rocked a little as the wagon lurched down the road. Lily leaning against him and the evening was quiet until he voiced what was on his mind.

"I gotta get that boy headed north after those horses within the week . . . else wise it's gonna start snowing and we won't get them back here till spring."

Lily patted his hand gently, smiling as she leaned her head on his massive shoulder.

***

Opal stretched on the bed, suddenly feeling the masculine leg next to her. Jumping a little she turned her head to view the face next to her on the pillow. Watching her quietly, Will reached out to smooth her rumpled hair and kissed her on the cheek gently, slowly, and then on to her eyelid, her nose, and finally her lips as he pulled her closer. The night before had certainly been a surprise, and since neither of them had much practice at this thing called love-making it hadn't been exactly a breeze . . . but it was certainly exciting. She touched his face and looked into his eyes smiling like a child about to open a Christmas gift.

"Wow. . . what a night," he whispered softly.

"Mmmmm . . . yes it was." She giggled and wrapped her leg around his, enjoying the sensation of skin on skin. They kissed again, longing and enraptured with all this new pleasure, only this time with new-found and slowly learned responses. Seemingly hours passed before they rose from the covers, washed and dressed.

"Let me brush your hair," Will stood behind her watching their

reflection in the mirror. Passing him the brush she tilted her head and watched as the brush passed time after time through her hair.

I've watched him brush a horse like this so many times, so much care, so much love. Turning she reached up to embrace his face with her hands and she kissed him again and again; laughing between each touch she felt like her heart would explode within her chest.

"So this is love," she said quietly.

"Yes ma'am . . . ain't it somethin'?"

Grabbing his hand she ran for the door, down the stairs and out onto the boardwalk. "Let's get something to eat . . . I'm starved."

They made their way to the little café and ordered breakfast. The waitress mockingly answered, "Little late for breakfast, ain't it?"

Opal felt her face heat and knew it was turning red. Will's was too.

She looked up and said crisply, "What the hell do you care when we eat breakfast?" Will kicked her under the table as the waitress shook her head and walked toward the kitchen. "You little firecracker . . . she was just makin' conversation. I can tell we have an interesting life ahead of us."

"Don't you forget it, either." She reached for his hand across the table.

Finishing quickly they returned to their room and stuffed clothes and shoes and hairpins into old beat up suitcases and satchels then headed for the livery where they threw every-thing in the back of a ranch buckboard, hitched up the horses and quickly moved onto the roadway headed home. Life had taken on a new brightness, a new excitement and she couldn't wipe the smile off her face to save her life.

Resting on the seat of the buckboard behind the horses, she watched old visions come and go wondering why it looked so much more beautiful this morning. She held fast to Will's arm and watched the horses putting miles beneath their feet at a quick trot. When they pulled into the yard her mother came to the porch, wiping her hands on the apron she wore and waiting for them to step off the buckboard into her arms. Opal felt her mother's tears on her shoulder as she hugged her hard, then released her to grab Will and hug him around his middle, just as lovingly and welcoming as she could muster.

"You two bring your stuff inside . . . Opal, take Will to your room and settle in. Your dad wants to talk to both of you when you get done there. He's out to the barn."

Opal threw their belongings on the bed and pulled him outside by the hand toward the barn and her father's hugs and handshakes. They all stood looking at a pen full of horses as her dad set his boot on the bottom rung of the fence and began what must have been a well-practiced speech.

"Will, I need you to leave within a couple of weeks or so, and head north after some brood mares I'm of a mind to bring into our herd. I know it's short notice and cuts into your honeymoon time, but if we don't get it done quick there'll be too much snow up north and you'll have hell gettin 'em home." He moved restlessly around the perimeter of the pen.

"I know Opal wants to go along, so you two work that out. Maybe take the train up and ride a couple of the horses back leading the rest. We'll map out the trip back and figure some things this afternoon. If things go well for us this winter and we sell some good colts in the spring I'll build a cabin for you two over the meadow there next summer. Till then you're stuck in the house with me an' 'yer maw but we'll get around that as best we can. We'll try to give you some alone time as we can, and you'll have to do the same for us, but I think we'll all figure this out and be ok."

"How about I check the freight office and see if we can bring the horses back on the train?" Will asked. He wasn't overly comfortable discussing the sleeping arrangements with his father-in-law.

"Too costly for me, Will. I don't have the extra right now to handle that kind of expense."

"I have some money saved up and it would be my way of buyin' into the business." He squeezed Opal's hand as they stood leaning on the pole fence in front of them.

"I'd rather you save that to put into the cabin come spring."

Will stood quietly, turned his head to look into her eyes and waited. Opal smiled. "Let's talk it over this evening over supper. Right now I want to spend some time with the horses." She walked to the gate and slipped through as her father turned and walked to the house. Will leaned on the fence watching her walk through the pen, touching each horse's nose, neck and scratch their ears. She spoke softly to each one, calling them by name and asking how their day had been. They were her friends . . . they were her playmates. They were her life's blood and he knew that would never change.

"Whatcha' gonna' do when you get babies to tend?" he called through the fence.

"Maybe we just won't have no babies." She laughed and threw back at him.

"Yeah . . . right . . . whatever you think." He chuckled.

They spent hours at the corrals and barns, walked through the meadow looking for a perfect spot for the promised cabin, stopping over and over to share a kiss or an embrace. They watched young colts that were being weaned ducking and nipping at each other, then stopping to take in their every move as the made their way through the tall grass.

Happier than she'd ever been in her life she was frequently overcome with emotions that brought happy tears to her eyes and smiles to her face at every turn of their steps.

"You as happy as I am?" she asked him.

"Oh . . . I don't know . . . I reckon it's growin' on me."

She punched his arm hard. He winced and smiled, then pulled her to his chest and wouldn't let her go until she finally pulled away with a tug and a grin. The hours passed as they simply enjoyed the presence of love and simple belonging, then she drew him toward home and hearth.

***

It was nearly a month before Maxwell convinced himself and Will it was time for him to make the trip to purchase the horses. Will agreed to leave within the week by train, then would trail the horses home rather than ship them. Opal insisted she would go along but the jury was still out on the common sense of that kind of trip for her. The whole thing was settled quickly with the switch of a horse's tail.

The sun was barely up, they'd gone to the corral to morral the horses and feed. She was slipping the burlap over a young horse's ears when the shadow of an owl floating toward the open hay loft and the swish of its wings caused her horse to spook and jump backwards. He leaped forward and to his left, knocking her aside, then he jumped ahead and kicked at her as he broke loose. His hoof caught her right leg just below the knee.

Will threw his hands in the air as the other horses spooked and jumped around, moving them away from Opal. She was rolled up in a ball on the ground, hands over her head to protect her from more flying hooves. He reached her side within moments and knelt to feel her leg and check to see if the colt had done any other damage.

"I don't think it's broken," he said with relief. "But it's gonna swell up and be sore as hell." Blood ran from a long gash in open flesh.

"Help me up." She reached for his shoulder.

He lifted her to her feet and supported her with his arm around her waist, giving her time to settle the sickness and dizziness that followed. "Let's get you to the house."

"Easy m'lad. I can't put any weight on it." Her voice cracked with pain and she grabbed hold of him to steady herself.

"Be still a minute, let me carry you up to the bed. We need your mom to take a look at this. I'm thinkin' we might need to get you to the doctor."

He saw Lily drop her spoon in the wash pan as they stepped

through the door, and felt her behind him as they reached the bed in their little room. He moved aside at her prompting and stepped to the far side of the room to watch as she deftly lifted the edge of the riding skirt covering Opal's leg. Finally looking up toward Will she said, "This ain't good. But it ain't broke, just bruised and scraped up pretty bad. Help her get out of this rig and I'll go get the water hot and some clean cloths."

Will stepped around the bed to replace his mother-in-law near Opal, helping her remove her clothing without moving her unnecessarily. He was pulling the covers over her when Lily returned to move him aside again and pulled her daughter's leg over to the bedside.

Will watched as she cleaned and bound the wound carefully. "Looks like you may have done this a time or two."

"Yep. More than that you can bet. And more than just a time or two for this little scoundrel."

Relieved, Will's chuckled as Opal joked about the rough handed ways of her mother. She laid her head back on the pillows. Some of her color returned and the wincing ceased so he moved into the kitchen to wait for Lily. Pouring coffee he stood at the window watching for Maxwell to return with the boys he rode out with before sunrise.

The old man's gonna be mad as hell.

Lily's voice startled him. "Funny how fast a life can be changed with a simple switch of a horse's tail or crack of a hoof. I never cease watching for Maxwell, waiting for Opal, wondering what simple incident will change our lives. It's never whether they'll get hurt, just how bad and when."

Will nodded as the little woman return to washing dishes, fussing through the preparations for a noon meal. Suddenly she stopped, lowered her head and tears began to flow and her shoulders jerked with her sobs. Completely at a loss as to how to respond he stepped closer and put his hand on her shoulder. He waited, consumed with an uncomfortable desire to help, and fear of making things worse. She stiffened, then leaned into his strength, seeming to draw from his simple presence.

"I'm okay, Will."

"I know."

"That little wife of yours won't be goin' north with you, that's certain. You can't postpone the trip any longer so she'll be staying home. Can't say I'm not happy about that."

"Same here. Never was thrilled about her goin' along but tryin' to stop that girl from doin' what she's set her head to sure had me stumped. I was hopin' her dad had more clout."

Chuckling with Lily, Will returned to sit by his wife's bed.

The swelling and discoloration had set in, making him aware just how serious the injury was. Relief settled, his hands shook, and he realized how scared he'd been through the ordeal. What if that kick would have been to her head? What if he'd lost her? His stomach turned over, he reached to hold her hand.

"Love you girl." he whispered as she fell asleep.

***

Opal sat quietly, seething as her father passed a leather folder tied with braided horsehair into Will's care with instructions, a bank draft and contact information. He unfolded telegraphed information as she listened to the two discuss the journey ahead. More importantly the return trip with ten mares and a new stud horse.

"Why don't you take Matt with you?" she asked suddenly, playing with the sugar spoon in a small glass container with blue flowers around the rim.

"He's got work to do, m'dear. I can't ask him to take weeks off. I got it handled."

"Stubborn . . . that's what you are!" was her retort.

121

"Takes one to know one," came back as she poked the spoon in the sugar and left it standing straight in the air. Limping to the kitchen, she stood at the window, holding tightly to the curtains that lay softly in her hands. She fought back tears as she watched young horses nipping at each other as they trotted around the pen. With Will gone they'd be unridden for several days, and she'd have to find a way to get past her mother back to the corrals to at the very least continue daily contact with them.

She sensed more than heard Will quietly slip up behind her, felt his arms around her waist as he pulled her against him and held her gently.

"I know," he whispered in her ear. Leaning against him she let the tears overflow and wiped them away with the corner of the curtain.

"Dam'dable colt." They stood saying goodbye without words. She stayed by the window, watching him step from the porch and walk to the waiting buckboard. Her father waved goodbye to his wife on the porch, then to his daughter's face in the window. Will's wave followed, she wanted to run screaming after the disappearing buckboard.

"Come on girl," her mother called.

She stood at the window, anger and disappointment flooding her soul as she fought back being angry at her mother. Why was she so angry at her, anyway? She had done nothing, but someone was going to get the brunt of it. Opal gathered herself, preparing to unleash hours of a boiling pot of emotions, then caught herself and began to take deep breaths to calm herself. "Lord help me get through this," she prayed softly.

As Lily returned inside, Opal reached out to hug her, something that rarely occurred between the pair. In a rare display of emotion her mother held her daughter close and began to reassure her with words of experience. "You'll be okay. We'll find things to do and time will pass quickly, you'll see."

On the contrary, Opal found the days passed very slowly. She was able to limp to the corrals and in obedience to her father only reached through the slats of the corral fence to make contact with her colts.

A younger hired hand was assigned to ride them daily and keep the training process moving forward, which irritated her even more. *That's not the right way . . .* ran through her mind more often than not.

Her father built a crutch for her but it stayed by the doorway more than under her arm. She used pages of paper and smeared ink all over her record book. She preferred that name over "diary". Diaries were for girls, not riders of the horse such as herself. Yet she found herself acting very girlish over the absence of her husband, missing him and writing lines that held traces of loneliness and sorrow.

Days passed, as the one before, until she could finally put her full weight on the leg and set her left foot in the stirrup to pull herself onto the back of a mount. Her father and the crew rode out daily and she began to ride and work with the youngsters as she watched the meadow below for signs of a man on horseback with a string of horses tied behind.

Time stretched into weeks and weeks into a month before she began to quiz her father as to when they could expect Will's return. She tried hard to ignore her father's obvious concern over the young man's term of absence. She found little relief as he came up with numerous reasons why it was taking so long for Will to find his way home. Night after night they sat at the table while her father named reason after reason, none of which fully extinguished her fears and apprehension. By the end of the month the family had begun to sit quietly without sharing reasons and excuses. They simply went about daily duties with internalized worry and concern.

"I want to go with you." Opal responded as her father   announced at breakfast he was riding into town to send telegrams. "I won't stay home."

"No need to, Opal. Just get yourself ready and we'll ride in as soon as I get old Tom lined out." He pulled his hat on and walked outside to stretch and continue to the bunkhouse where the old hired man was having his own brand of breakfast.

Through the years, each of the hired men took their turn at building biscuits or pouring pancakes and scrambling eggs. Lily kept their cupboard supplied, and for special occasions invited them to the kitchen to take meals with the family. Only two remained after Will was hired on . . . the youngest left after the bulk of fall works were finished.

Opal was very fond of the older of the remaining cowboys who seemed to pull more kitchen duty as the years moved through his life. Tom had been with Maxwell for a little more than twelve years, more than half of her life. She loved the old gent and she'd learned a great deal of her horse-sense from him as they worked together through the years.

She walked to the corrals, favoring her leg slightly, watching her father as he stood talking with Tom, both heads down and shoulders slumped. Her heart leapt as she watched Tom shake his head back and forth then return inside the bunk-house. Her father walked toward her, "Who do you want to ride this morning, daughter?"

"Red. But I can saddle him myself."

"Just let me catch him up for you, pull your saddle out'a the shed and I'll bring him to you." He walked quietly into the little bunch of horses against the fence, two of them turning toward him and reaching their nose out to sniff and nibble at his coat sleeve. Her father was a horseman, had been all his life. "Cattle are just a good excuse to get horseback," had been his mantra as long as she could remember.

She remembered watching him from a perch on the fence and waiting for him to ride by and pull her onto the back of a horse to ride in front of him on a saddle. She couldn't remember anything before those moments. She could barely climb up on the fence when they started that little game, and never in her life could she remember being afraid of horses.

Several accidents had not changed her love for the animal God spoke of in the Bible as being his choice of transportation when

124

he would return for the second time.

As she saddled her horse, her mind turned to one of her favorite scriptures in her Bible. From Job, it spoke so clearly of horses, of their power, of their usefulness. "Have you given the horse strength? Have you clothed his neck with thunder? Can you frighten him like a locust? His majestic snorting strikes terror. He paws in the valley, and rejoices in his strength; he gallops into the clash of arms. He mocks at fear, and is not frightened; nor does he turn back from the sword. The quiver rattles against him, the glittering spear and javelin. He devours the distance with fierceness and rage; nor does he come to a halt because the trumpet has sounded. At the blast of the trumpet he says, 'Aha!' He smells the battle from afar, the thunder of captains and shouting."

She couldn't remember the rest, and she felt warm tears welling as she silently prayed that the horses Will was bringing home would be filled with power and ability to bring him back to her.

The pair were pulling their cinches tight when a rider came loping up the road, stirring dust behind him in little puffs as hooves left the ground. Opal's heart began to beat hard and her mouth went dry when she saw the badge peeking out from under the jacket around the shoulders. She felt her father's hand on her arm as he moved away from the horses toward the rider. She couldn't move her feet, and reached up to steady herself with the saddle horn as she watched what unfolded before her in a profound slow motion.

The sheriff reached into his coat, pulling a familiar leather folder from inside. It was tied with a braided horse hair string. She tried to move toward her father, but her legs were weak and she felt sickened and dizzy. Pulling herself together she was   finally able to step slowly to join her father. He put his arm around her shoulders and they listened quietly as the lawman delivered a message that had been dry-rehearsed over and over as he had ridden from town.

"A package came by stage last evening. . . addressed to me. There is a letter here for you, and there was one for me in the wrapper. A rancher and his son found loose horses on a water tank not far from their headquarters and gathered them up. A horse that was

125

saddled was in the mix, so they began to backtrack and about seven miles up the trail they found Will. He was mashed up pretty bad and there was nothing they could do for him . . . he was already gone."

Reaching out to take the leather pouch from his hand, she began to shake uncontrollably. Instead, her father took the package and asked the sheriff if he wanted coffee. "Not this morning, thanks. I best head back to town." She knew he was avoiding any further contact with the family. His own voice broke as he spoke. She reached for her father's arm as her knees buckled beneath her, and he grabbed her, calling for Tom to come quick. They lifted her between them carrying her into the house. She felt helpless and empty, groaning inwardly as they entered their home.

Her mother ran to them from the back of the house where she'd been feeding chickens, stopping cold as she saw the leather pouch and her daughter's face. "Oh no – dear God," was all she could mutter.

Opal sat sobbing as her father read the letter. "We found this pouch with the young man who met his death as he was moving horses through open range near our ranch. We want you to know we have buried him near our own family plot and you are welcome to come and visit the grave any time you can. We are holding the rest of his belongings, and the horses here at the ranch. Come when you can to restore them to rightful owners." He turned the envelope over to read the return address. "Well, he made it to within sixty miles of home."

She wondered what possible difference that made, rose from the chair, and made her way to the bedroom where she closed the door and threw herself on the bed where she stayed hour upon hour.

Opal walked into the cool night air, her feet finding loose boards as she carelessly missed the bottom step and lost her balance. Staggering, she moved toward the stone fence she had been trying to build near the porch to occupy her time in weeks past. Her heart beat hard and she found it painful to breathe. She stood under the moon for a few moments, and then lifted her face toward its light, and from the depths of her soul she felt a ball of noise begin to find its way to her lips. When it erupted in what should have been a scream, it left her mouth sounding more like the howl of a lone wolf as it cried for a mate.

She dropped to her knees, filling her fists with rocks and dirt, squeezing until it hurt so bad the pain in her heart began to be less noticeable. As the sobs began to wane, she turned to sit quietly, losing herself in thoughts and memories. She wondered how many other women had heard a similar cry from the depths of their souls, one that tried to shock them into some small bit of comfort.

The pain began to wane, and tears stopped for brief periods of time. She sat quietly reflecting on the years that, like the stars, seemed to hover just above her tousled hair. So many days, so much had happened. Her heart slowly returned to beating normally, and her thoughts were simply filled with the wonder of life near Will.

Eventually, she stood and returned inside to climb into a warm bed and pull her mother's quilt over her shoulders. As the patchwork folded over her, she realized even the quilt held memories of him, for within the pieces were remnants of old shirts he'd passed on to her mother when the elbows were worn through for the second time. Tears began again, so rather than lay sobbing she rose and moved back to the wooden table in the kitchen of her parents' home.

She found the memories overwhelming, and as one facing death her life began to flash before her eyes in brilliant colors and images. She gave in to the flood, and began to drift with the current of visions and thoughts.

Her mother joined her quietly, sitting nearby without words, simply being close seemed to be enough for the time being. They watched and waited for the sun to rise over the horizon. Joined by her father as the room began to brighten with the natural light of the morning. Lily moved to the kitchen where she started the coffee pot.

When Tom knocked gently on the door, Maxwell opened it and stepped aside as Tom pulled his hat from his tousled hair. Holding it in his hands he asked softly, "Is there anything I can do for you, Miss Opal?"

She shook her head slowly . . . tried to smile at her old friend but found that only tears began to flow again.

"I heard you in the night, Miss Opal . . . and I want you to know I been where you are. That pain in your heart will take a while to ease, but it will in time and you'll be able to bear it one day." He pulled his hat back down over his leaking eyes, turning on a heel to leave the house quickly.

She watched him walk toward the corrals and barn, taking notice he was bent more than usual and his stride was shorter than she remembered.

Time was taking a toll on everything and everyone she loved. She felt the wad of pain in her gut begin to rise and call out to be released again, but she swallowed hard and stood to follow her old friend to the barn and corrals. Solace would be found there, time would slow down and when she touched the hide of the horses, surely then she could stop this pain from overtaking her. But the opposite was true. When she touched the mane of one of the horses Will was riding before he left it was like he leaned from the saddle to touch her hair. When she closed her eyes she felt his hand on her face, his thumb on her chin, saw his curling lips and clear eyes and so went the journey back into the depths of her despair.

Old Tom came to her and lifting her from her knees led her to the gate away from the horses who, one by one, were hovering over her as though they would help if they knew what to do. "You go back up to the house now, Miss Opal."

"No . . . I need to walk. I'm goin' up to the meadow, you tell Mama I'll be back."

The place they were to call home now called to her soul as though a haunting voice was beckoning, beckoning her to save it from loneliness and sorrow. Those two compadrés were the haunting ones, the overwhelming presence of them would not leave her be no matter where she moved her thoughts.

Will seemed to be everywhere. Yet . . . he was not here, he was in the ground somewhere miles away in the family plot that was nothing of his family, nothing of his own.

"I cannot bear it. I will die of this, I hurt so bad. Where now will I turn? Where now will I ever find his hand in the night, his laugh in the morning, his heart through the day? Oh God . . . *oh my God* . . . she screamed into the pines that whispered gently back to her, "Why?"

Her anger toward God overwhelmed her. "I asked you to protect him, I spoke with you of this. Where were you that day? Where are you now?"

Sobs began to wrack her small frame again . . . and yet again. Suddenly the face of his mother came to her.

"Oh no, Father will have to ride and tell his family." Trying to lift herself from the earth that held her, she moved her eyes to the house of her childhood, watching as her father saddled a horse and kissed his wife goodbye.

"He's going. God go with him. Oh God . . . please go with this one this time! Don't let harm come to my father." Tears began again. "Please don't let harm come to my father."

Doubt and fear filled her brain with tormenting visions and thoughts of her father lying somewhere as Will had. Shaking it off, she forced herself to rise and return to the kitchen table where she found her mother seated, crying softly and wiping her eyes with a wadded up apron. Walking up behind her, she bent over Mama's body with her own, lovingly placed her arms around her shoulders and they spilled each other's pain out onto a very old, very worn table.

When they had emptied themselves of enough tears to sufficiently soak the apron, the question surfaced again. "Why, mother? Why did God take this from me, from us? I asked him to keep Will safe and bring him home to me. Did he not hear my plea?"

"God always hears us when we cry out to him, daughter. Always. But he is not the only force on the earth . . . there is another it says comes to kill and destroy. He is the one we should be angry with, not God. I don't know why . . . I don't know why . . . I asked God the same thing when your older brother who you never met was taken from us. I have decided not to torment myself with the asking, but rest in God's comforting arms until I leave this earth."

"My older brother?" Shocked and amazed, Opal was snatched from thoughts of her own pain and looked into her mother's face that had twisted ever so slightly and her chin quivered unexpectedly.

"We never told you. There was never any reason to speak of it, but you must know others have suffered that kind of loss and pain. You will survive, you will grow through it, and on the other side you will find a love for the Lord you have not had before. He will comfort you if you only allow him to do that for you. If you do not, Opal, if you remain angry at God it will only hurt worse and it will surely hurt longer." She stopped to gaze into her daughters eyes. " You must let him fill the empty place in your heart and rest in the knowing that Will is experiencing things today that all of us look forward to when we finish what we have to do in this place." She rose and moved to the kitchen where she hung the wet apron to dry, and taking a bowl and a drying cloth went out the back door to visit her chickens.

Opal sat for what seemed hours, thinking only of her mother's words and keeping her mind on what would come next. "When Father returns I will ask him to take me to the place they have laid him. I must say goodbye . . . I must know where he is." She felt the tears begin to well up, shook her head and returned to the corrals and the horses she would draw strength from once again. Her focus became their needs, their attention, their breathing and the moving of their muscles and thus she left the grieving of the day and began to breath normally again. This . . . this then would be her saving grace.

***

Her father returned safely mid-morning of the following day with word from Will's ailing and elderly parents. He handed Opal a note; "Our son was loved. One cannot ask for anything more precious in life. Be well, dear Opal, live your life and love again."

"Will's mother is very ill," Maxwell said softly. "She may not last long. Her lungs fill up with some kind of fluid and she can barely breathe. Will's sister is there with her, the boys are helping with the orchard and the fields, but the outlook is dismal over there. I hated to be the bearer of that news."

"I would have gone with you, father," Opal reminded him.

"No – you needed your time. Now we must think ahead. I have to ride over and get the horses, I was thinking I'd ask Matt to come with. I know you will go as well, you must go see where the boy is buried. We'll talk about it tomorrow. Do you want to take ol' Tom with you in the morning, ride over to see if Matthew can come along?"

"Can't I go without a caretaker?"

"He's not a caretaker, girl," came the sharp retort. "I don't want to think of you out there alone, you little fool."

"We'd best get past that, Dad. I have to get back to work and Tom can't be my side-kick forever."

"Well . . . for a while he will be. Till I can be at ease with you riding out of sight."

Nodding, she watched him shaking his head as he turned on his heel and stormed to the house. They would talk in the morning.

131

Tonight the meal would be quiet. *Maybe I'll ask ol' Tom up for supper.* She turned quickly and walked to the bunkhouse.

After supper she said a fond good evening to the old friend of her family as they agreed to rise before sunrise and leave for the Mitchell ranch and Matthew. *I wonder if Matt has heard yet. That won't be an easy thing to do.* She folded herself into their bed and the familiar old quilts she grew up beneath. Reaching for Will's pillow she drew it near and lay quietly then cried herself to sleep again.

She was out of bed long before sunrise, filling herself with hot coffee. She poured a bowl of sourdough from the crock and folded a pan of biscuits. They would need a few for lunch if there was no one home at the Mitchell place. Finding Matt could take more time than just a ride over and back.

Watching past the curtains in the window she saw Tom's shadow moving among the horses and knew he was feeding so they would be ready for the ride. She was anxious to have the task done and past, wondering if she would be the one to have to break the news to Matthew. *Maybe Tom will do it. No. it should be me. It should be me.*

Her mother came into the kitchen to inspect what was in the oven, and began frying bacon and scrambling eggs. "You will need more than a handful of biscuits young lady. Go holler at Tom and we'll feed him up here this morning before you go."

Gladly she left the house and ran toward the corrals, free of the household duties she so disliked. They waited together until the horses finished their grain, then threw out piles of hay and made their way through the light filtering through the trees and rising dust. She found herself wanting to walk as close as possible to Tom without touching him. Strange . . . she wanted companionship this morning.

Breakfast was finished more quickly than usual and the pair saddled in short order to mount and ride. She was anxious to be horseback, but not so much for the duty that lay before her. She tried to enjoy the sunrise and the changing colors of the sky and hills beyond as she rode quietly beside her old friend. Time seemed to drag as they made their way to the Mitchell ranch and yet before the shadows had shortened they rode up to the hitching rail near the long building that served as a bunkhouse. Opal wondered how many nights Will had slept under that shingle roof in a hard bunk with smelly blankets and hard pillows.

She started slightly when Tom reached out to touch her arm. "You wait here, Miss Opal. I will tell Matthew if he don't already know it."

"I should be the one to tell him."

"No, ma'am. You've had your fill." He stepped gingerly off his horse, stood a moment to let the stiffness pass, and handed her the reins. He moved to the old wooden door and reached to knock, but it opened before he could, and Matthew stood filling the doorway with all six feet of his frame.

"I know." He spoke to Tom, then moved toward Opal to catch her as she slid off her horse with renewed tears flowing past her cheeks and down her neck. It felt good to be held and allowed to cry, but suddenly she realized they might both fall to the ground if she didn't get hold of herself.

Pulling back, she patted his shoulder and blurted out, "We gotta go get those horses and I have to see where they've laid him. Can you go along?"

"I will . . . I'll talk to Mitchell. When do we leave?"

"Dad wants to leave day after tomorrow. We'll ride over and lead the horses back. The folks who found Will and kept the horses for us seem kind. I think we can stay over with them, but better bring along your bed roll. Can you be there early?"

"I'll ride over as soon as there's enough daylight to see with. Well, come to think of it the moon will be fallin' down and I can ride to its light so I might get there earlier."

Mounting, she reached for her saddle horn and Matt gave her a boost as she set her boot in the stirrup. "I'll see you then." They both nodded, faces twisted and lips quivering as they held back the tears.

"Opal..." Matt took a deep breath, "You'll be okay. Will knew you were strong. Sometimes too strong, ya know? But he was proud of you, girl. He was dam' sure proud of you."

"Thanks Matt . . . that don't help much right now." Pulling her horse away from him, she trotted toward home, forgetting Tom was along. He caught up in short order and rode silently beside her homeward. She wanted to relax and enjoy the ride, feeling comfortable and safe with her old friend riding beside.

"Tom . . . you ever lost someone you love?"

"Yes, ma'am, a long, long time ago."

She waited for more, but it never came, and the longing silence lasted until they finished unsaddling horses in the home corral.

"Thanks for comin' along . . . it felt good to have someone nearby."

"Sure . . . . sure 'nuff." Tom wiped the moisture from the crow's feet that lined his weary, old smoky eyes and headed for the bunkhouse.

"You'll be fine, miss Opal," drifted back over his shoulder, then in softer whisper, "You gotta be just fine."

***

Maxwell Redding was an impressive man for his age, holding his health and well being in spite of the hard life he chose to spend with his wife and daughter. As they readied themselves for the journey to collect his horses and help his daughter say farewell to her husband, he was forced to "buck up" and remain even stronger than usual. His eyes and the pinching around his nose and mouth would give him away when he found himself watching his daughter for signs of breaking.

Proud of her, he watched a strength arise. She was stubborn, determined, even belligerent when things didn't go her way, but this was something deeper, something he had never seen in her.

A gentle, calm, quiet kind of strength that came from something or someone bigger than any of them.

He knew his words hadn't been the birthing of this strength, nor had her mother's. While they constantly tried to en-courage and build her up, any efforts on their part seemed to fall on deaf ears. As the days passed he watched this girl become a woman, become more like her stalwart ancestors.

"Better take extra canteens of water, Opal." He spoke firmly to her as they packed food and water. "It's a long haul, and I'm not sure where to find water once we've passed over the divide. It's nearly forty miles that far, and another ten or so to the Johnson ranch and our horses." He paused to watch for her to move in obed-ience. "Go down and tell Tom to fill two extras if he can."

He had mapped out the roads and trails where they were to ride, and he and Tom had talked it over carefully, but this trip just might be a little harder than he anticipated. "Throw your sleepin' bag over the back of your saddle, and I'll have Tom put the rest of this on the pack mule."

She obediently and quietly turned and walked to the bunk-house. They finished packing the mule and horses, then she and Tom sat on a top rail awaiting Matt's arrival.

Maxwell walked to the house, and into the kitchen. He and Lily stood arm in arm near the window watching and waiting for Matt. Lily leaned against him for just a moment as he confided, "I'm a little worried about her. She seems pale and she ain't eatin' much lately. Maybe this grievin' will come to a stop after we get this trip under our belt."

His wife hugged him. "She'll be fine, Max. Just keep an   eye on her, especially when you get to the Johnsons'. I'm glad Matthew is going along, it will be soothing for her, I think."

He kissed her goodbye, and returned to the barn, anxious to be on the way. It was a hard two day journey but that might not be possible with winter pressing and the cold dropping down from the high country closer every day. Traveling too early or too late would be difficult if it turned hard cold. It could turn into a three-day journey each way very easily.

Standing with his arm over the pack he watched as Matt rode up at a trot with his own pack mule in tow. "Little late aren't you?" he snapped at the young man.

"Sorry . . . this dam'dable mule is more trouble than he's worth and it took some doin' to get him loaded. Can I help with anything?"

"I ain't wantin' to get caught in a snowstorm before we get gathered up and head home." Maxwell repeated and pressed the trio to get loaded and on the road.

He moved to a stump that had been placed beside the old hitching rail, stepped up on it and pulled himself into his saddle. It was harder to reach places he'd taken for granted all his life, and he didn't spring into that saddle as he had even a few years ago. It took a little settling to get his butt where he felt comfortable.

Turning in his saddle he hollered at Lily, "See you in a few days, darlin'." She stood on the porch with a corner of her apron in hand, waved, and he turned quickly and hit a high trot. He felt Opal and Matthew slide in behind him. Tom brought up the rear with the pack mule dallied around his horn and a chew of Red Man in his cheek.

Maxwell watched Opal carefully as they trotted, walked, loped, then trotted in spurts to make time as quickly as they could. She seemed tired, and smiles were hidden somewhere in a box inside her that wasn't going to open any time soon. "You doin' okay, daughter?"

"I'm okay." No joke or comment followed. Nearly twenty miles behind them, Maxwell settled them in for the night near a small stream that flowed from a spring above the trail. They re-filled canteens and let the horses drink their fill.

When they rose with first light of day steam burst from their lips like smoke from the wood stove at home. "Good grief it's cold!" He laughed as he beat his arms and pulled his coat tighter. "You okay Opal? I know you hate the cold almost as much as your mama does."

"Give me another jolt of that coffee an' I'll be ready to ride." They stood drinking what was left while Tom poured out the dregs and tied the pot to the pack horse. He handed out jerky and day-old sourdough pancakes, then threw their sleeping bags over the back of the saddles and tied everything down tight. Maxwell moved to her side, reached to draw Opal into his long arms, wanting to encourage her and bring some kind of smile to her face.

She stiffened obviously, and said tersely, "We better get going." He felt her pull away as she threw the rest of her drink in the fire and moved to replace the halter with a bridle and tighten her cinch.

"Thanks for saddlin' my horse, Tom." She pulled herself into the saddle. She was stiff, didn't move like the nimble horse-woman he knew her to be. *The cold probably.* Maxwell tucked their cups into his saddlebags.

They weren't but about half an hour up the trail and he heard a strange sound from behind. Turning he saw Opal on the ground, bent over and heaving up everything she ate for breakfast. Tom was holding her horse, head turned away as though it hurt him to watch her.

"Hell, Opal, what'sa matter?"

"Just didn't set well with breakfast. I'm all right." She pulled herself back on her horse and motioned him to move on.

It was nearly dark the next day when they found themselves on the outskirts of a small town with not much more than a post office, sheriff's office and a little rooming house with a sign out front reading "meals". *Could be our own home town,* thought Maxwell.

"I'm puttin' up here for the night. Opal, you go see about a room and I'll visit with someone to find out about the Johnson ranch and we'll pull out for there in the morning. Tom, see if you can find a place to bed down the horses."

"Me and Matt'll sleep with the horses tonight, boss. You get a room for you and Opal."

They split up and within a few minutes Opal reported, "There's a room available, so we'll share that one tonight, Dad. Matt and Tom can throw bedrolls out in a back porch at the rooming house. It's too dam' cold to stay at the stable." "Let's find something to eat. Bound to be some place round here. How about that roomin' house, Opal? Any place to put on a feed bag over there?"

"Yes, sir. She'd finished feeding her boarders, but I think we can talk her into feeding us somethin'."

 Maxwell barked instructions again. "It's about three hours to the Johnson ranch from here, so we'll head out at daylight."

***

The four found themselves pulling cinches as the sun filtered through pines on the horizon. They made their way onto a narrow two-track-road with no breakfast in their stomachs. Maxwell was anxious to get to the Johnson ranch and settle things as quickly as possible. Home seemed a thousand miles away that morning, and with Opal upchucking frequently, he was even more anxious to get her home to her mother. She'd been sick all the day before and wouldn't eat dinner. She'd even turned down coffee that morning.

He shook his head. *Dam' it all, this trip ain't helpin' her much. By the time she gets done sayin' farewell to Will and the stress of the ride I just hope she doesn't have some kind of breakdown before we get her home. She's got a lot to tend to with this new bunch of horses, and with Will gone she's on her own.*

Silence reigned as they watched the sun rise over fields of winter wheat and calves pastured for shipping. "Pretty country." Maxwell tried to break into conversation with Tom. They rode side by side and Matt brought up the rear. Opal seemed to be dropping back and slowing down. Maxwell pulled up and let Tom ride on as he waited for his daughter.

"You sick again?" he asked softy.

"Just tired. Didn't sleep much with all the snorts and snores last night." She smiled at him and with a side glance added, "Had to pull that pillow over my head, I have no idea in the world how mother gets a minute's sleep with you for a bed-mate."

"Well now, I reckon she does just fine there, missy." He grinned back and rode beside her for a while, taking note of the pinched lips and furrowed eyebrows. "Seriously, Opal, are you all right?"

"No . . . I'm dreading what lies ahead. It's over, Dad . . . it's dam' near over and I'm scared."

The sleepless nights and stomach troubles had taken a hard toll on his girl. Reaching for her hand he tried to make a connection that might help her with what was coming. She grasped his hand like she had when she was such a tiny little child. Heart hurting in his chest, his eyes teared up and memories overwhelmed him. *Seems like that was only a few weeks ago.* They rode hand in hand for a spell, then he rode on ahead to lead out when he saw a gate and corrals looming in the road ahead.

As he stepped down to open the gate, a man about seventy-something came from the house to meet them. Slightly behind him walked a thirty-year younger version. "Yawl get down and come in the house. We'll talk some and have somethin' to eat and drink. We've been expecting you to show."

Glancing at Opal, Maxwell thought she turned a little darker shade of green at the mention of food. Two very young cowboys came for their horses and moved them to the corrals. Matt helped as they unsaddled and lifted the pack saddle down. Maxwell wondered if they were family or hired day help. *Were they possibly the ones who found Will lying out there, alone, so still?* He felt comfortable enough to settle in to getting acquainted with the kindly folks who seemed to view them simply as friends they had never met.

"I wanted to say thanks for taking time to send the letter and hold the horses for us," he blurted out.

"No need. It could have been us on the hard side of the fence, ya' know?" came the response from the older man as they entered the front door of the comfortable warm home.

"This is my wife Junie and my daughter-in-law, Amy. That young man who followed us in is my son, James."

"There's tea and coffee on the stove, whichever you prefer," came the offer from Junie. "And I baked a pie and some short bread this morning so if you're ready for a snack it's no trouble."

"I think Opal would like some tea and short bread." Maxwell replied. Settling into a hard back chair at the edge of the table he added, "As for us fellers, I think we'll take pie an' coffee." He motioned Opal into the seat next to him. "I really can't thank you folks enough for helpin' us out this way. It's enough to keep the horses and all, but I guess what we really owe you a debt of gratitude for is takin' care of our Will." Under the table his hand covered Opal's cold shaking fingers, and felt her grasp his hand, again like the little child he remembered toddling along with him. His heart hurt for her and he struggled to find words that were not coming easy for him.

"I guess we best get right to it," he blurted out. "I think my daughter would like to see where Will is laid to rest." He heard her breath leave her body and her fingers went limp in his hand. "If . . . if that's okay with you, Opal?"

"Sure." The word was clear but it was very obvious she was most unsure of what her father had opened before her. *What have I done*? He knew that before her was a deep chasm of black water that she would have to ford alone, no matter how much he wanted to help her swim through. He tightened his lips.

Sometimes I'm a dam'dable old fool.

Their host stood slowly to his feet, moving pie and coffee aside, watching Maxwell from across the table. His eyes shifted past Maxwell to watch Opal quietly. "You ready for this?"

Standing, Maxwell pulled Opal to her feet. "She's ready."

Mrs. Johnson was beside Opal in three quick steps. "Men are such idiots, dearie. I'll go along with you if you like, but if you're not ready we'll just wait a while and they can just set themselves back down at that table."

140

"There's something more I should tell you before we do anything." Johnson's voice dropped, and his stance softened. "I haven't said anything because I didn't want to add to the pain of your loss, but there's more to what happened than what you've been told."

Maxwell stood quietly for a moment, waiting for the forthcoming piece of information. Johnson watched Opal carefully, and Mrs. Johnson put a hand on Opal's arm.

"Well," asked Maxwell, "What is it?"

"Will had a bullet in him when we found him." The words came like a bucket of cold water in the face, and stunned silence filled the room. "Nothing was gone from his pockets, everything we gave you was left where he fell. We didn't notice the bullet hole right off, but when we buried him it was obvious he'd been back-shot."

Opal's gasp was audible. Maxwell couldn't bring himself to look at her face, he knew what he would find there.

"Who could have done it? You got any other hired men working for you?" Matthew asked.

"Nope, it's just my family. We got no reason to shoot that boy." Johnson replied. He looked Matt straight in the eye.

"Did you call the sheriff?" asked Maxwell. "What did he have to say?"

"We've got no sheriff here. That's why I sent all that stuff over to yours, but I didn't say nothin' about him bein' shot. We figgered if anyone showed up we'd tell 'em how we found him and give 'em the facts, which there ain't many to tell. There were no tracks anywhere to read, those horses had walked all over anything fresh. We never saw another person around here all week, and we watched. Someone could have come earlier and waited, but since they never took anything off his body we couldn't figger how it happened or why." He stopped to look at Maxwell with sincerity.

"We asked around town if anyone knew the boy, or had talked to him. Nobody there even saw him ride through, except the old man n the stable. He fed his horse, corralled the little bunch overnight and was gone before daylight in the morning. He may have seen someone in the bar, but nobody there would say so."

He went on with finality. "It could have been somebody shot him by mistake, and when they saw it they got scared and run off. They sure didn't need or want what we found in his pockets, cuz we sent all of that over to your sheriff."

Matthew walked to the door, jerked his hat low and walked out into the dust, stopped to grip the pole holding the porch roof up, and stood there.

Maxwell watched Opal from the corner of his eye, waiting for a response. None came. Maxwell realized he truly was on strange ground, in so many more ways than he was comfortable with.

I don't think pickin' at this is going to make it any better. We better just get this over and head for home. She'll have to figure this out later. He was getting antsy as his eyes moved from face to face. *Maybe I'm looking the fool to them, but I know my daughter better than they do, and she won't be any more ready than right now.* "Well, let's get on with it."

***

Opal reached for the arm of a woman she did not know, turning loose of her father's hand. Suddenly it felt cold to him, so he carelessly stuck it in his pocket. For some reason the face of his little wife loomed before him, and he knew he should back up about three feet and take a deep breath. *This woman will have to be to Opal what I cannot, nor can her mother right now.* He felt sick, his face flushed with humility, and his heart began to know a deeper gratitude toward these kindly people.

Opal left him standing in his own puddle of concerns and fears. Reaching for friends instead of him, she asked, "Matt, will you and Tom please come too?"

They all moved to the narrow porch and stepped onto strange ground. Opal stopped, stood for a few seconds then reached for Matt's hand to help her. Maxwell felt that haunting sense of helplessness again, knowing she would have to find her own way.

The grave was simple, a mound of dirt still showed above the ground and an unobtrusive wooden cross stood tilted on the west end of the mound. Will had been laid facing the rising sun in the east, even though his eyes would never again greet that spectacle.

Matt squeezed Opal's hand just enough to remind her he was there for her. She held fast, both feeling stronger for the presence, yet even with her father and the small group of people nearby she realized a loneliness she had never experienced in all her days.

She wanted to scream . . . wanted to throw herself on the chest of this boy she knew was beneath the brownish gray sod. Wanted to pitch a tent under the branches of this ancient oak and live there until her life was finished. *It is finished,* she thought carelessly. At that moment she felt Matt squeeze her hand harder, comforting and strengthening her. She swallowed hard several times, feeling the twinge in her gut that wanted to bring back the tea and shortbread she had just eaten.

Taking a well-used bandana from her pocket, she walked to the cross and tied it carefully around the cross beam. Still damp and wadded up from her tears, it hung limp. *Looks like I feel.* Then all thoughts, all concerns left and she sobbed softly into the sleeve of her jacket. Mrs. Johnson moved to her side and held her waist gently.

"That's enough of that!" her father barked.

Jerking upward at his command, Opal's chin jutted out and through clenched teeth she responded tersely, "Yes, sir." She naturally responded to her father's commands, but there was an anger rising up inside her that made her want to scream, tell him to go away, run as far away from him as she could. She felt Mrs. Johnson tighten her grip and heard her muttering something about a sad old man with a blind side.

Moving back toward Matthew she reached again for his hand saying quietly, "Let's go. I need to be somewhere else." She drew

143

him back toward the corrals and house, knowing her father would be looking to gather horses and begin the journey home while they still had daylight.

"You okay?" Matt pulled at her hand.

"Hell, no. But I will be. I have to be. Thanks, Matt. I don't know what I would have done if you hadn't been here to help me. Prob'ly would have kicked my dad in the shin, that's for dam' sure and certain." Hearing him chuckle brought a hint of a smile to her tight lips.

Within two hours they found themselves on the road home with horses and pack mules tailed together, dallied to saddle horns. Moving at a trot was strangely difficult for Opal, but she began to post to ease the pounding that seemed to take a more vengeful toll on her body than usual. Silence had folded around the group, fully overwhelming her. She had not spoken since they thanked the Johnsons as they were leaving the yard.

"You come back any time you want to, my dear," Mrs. Johnson had whispered in her ear as she hugged her, longer than Opal was comfortable with.

"Thank you . . . for everything. I will never forget you," she whispered in return. "Put a flower on Will's grave for me when they bloom in the spring . . . will you?"

"Oh my goodness," blurted Mrs. Johnson. "That's why . . . wait right here!" She returned to the house briefly, then rushing to Opal's side she slid a packet into her open hand. "This was in his shirt pocket."

Afraid to look down, she steeled herself, then realized she was holding on of his familiar "smoke rollers" folded carefully around a faded dark blue flower. Where he found it or when, she would never know.

Choking back tears she turned quickly, mounted and gathered the lead rope on her share of the new horses. She rode in behind Matt and once again Tom brought up the rear in his capable, stoic manner.

She stiffened, breathed slowly, tried hard to think of home and the work that lay ahead . . . but there was an invisible string tied to something deep inside that screamed at her, "You're leaving him behind. Don't do this! Go back and bring him home."

"Opal . . ." she heard a voice from somewhere. "Opal . . . you will be okay, just give it some time." She was unsure of the source of the words. Had they been whispered from Matt or Tom? Was Will speaking to her from the grave? She knew it wasn't her father's voice. . . or her mother's. *Maybe it's my own heart speaking.* She straightened in the saddle, checked her lead ropes and reins again then settled herself for the journey home.

***

Opal moved comfortably into her daily routine of riding, working and training her father's horse herd. Days turned into weeks. The new horses were working well, the stallion had been turned out for a few months, waiting for a decision to be made as to which mares her father wanted to breed when the time came.

Maxwell and Matt had been to visit Sheriff Rankin when they rode back from the Johnsons. He took all the information they gave, listened to the story, and they all agreed they may never know who shot Will or why. Rankin would keep an ear out and sent information to other law enforcement so if anyone said something or a tip came to the surface they would know about it. Opal had settled with herself that it would remain an unsolved mystery all of her days. It was time to accept he was gone and her life would be forever changed.

"Dam' it all, I wish this nausea would quit." She stood leaning against the shoulder of a quiet little mare. Suddenly she remembered something her mother spoke of years ago, her own morning sickness when she was carrying Opal. Numbness set into her knees and elbows, head spinning with this possibility. Could it be?

Ground tying the horse she went the house and found her mother in the kitchen. "We need to talk." She grabbed her mother's sleeve, dragging her to the table. "Sit."

"What in the world is the matter with you, Opal?" Her mother brushed the hair away from Opal's face with a tender hand.

"I think I may be with child. I've been sick in the morning, and most food won't stay in my stomach. I remember you said something about that a long time ago when you told me about the early time of carrying me. Could that be?"

Lily leaned forward, smiling just a tad, wide eyed "Good grief, child, why didn't you tell me?"

"I thought it was just bein' upset over Will and all the changes and trying to settle into the horses and what Dad needed me to do. Just tell me, could it be?"

"Of course it could be, silly. What a miracle that would be, yes? You would have a part of Will with you forever."

"How am I going to carry a child and do what Dad wants done around here? Will I have to stop riding?" Her voice took on a hint of panic, she jumped to her feet, paced a few steps then threw herself back into the chair.

"No. Not right away. Lots of women ride through most of their pregnancy, especially when you've been horseback as much as you have. You'll have to be careful about getting thrown, and the last month or so you'll not want to be packin' what will become a big ol' tummy in front of you on the saddle. We better tell your dad."

"Not yet. Let me finish these new horses and get them doin' what he wants. It won't be long until snow flies and it's gonna be too wet for me to ride much anyway, so we'll tell him after a while. Maybe I'll drop the news on him as a Christmas present." Rising slowly she looked at her mother's face carefully. Was that joy or fear in her eyes? *Maybe both. I don't really want to know.*

*S*he picked her gloves up off the table, pulling them back on her shaking hands. Leaving the room, moving toward the porch, she was amazed to hear her mother begin to sing as she returned to her kitchen chores. *Already . . . really?* She hoped her mother wouldn't let the cat out of the bag to her father before she was ready to spill the news. *Oh, I bet she'll slip* up . . . she won't be able to keep it to herself. She's already singing!

She bounded down the stairs and moved back to the corral and work. Stopping at the gate to meditate a few moments, her thoughts swayed like a waterfall slipping over a rock pile, white, dark, deep and bouncing all at once. Wiping tears away with her worn leather gloves, she wasn't sure if she was happy or sad. She struggled to bring her thoughts back to a single focus. *I will have his child, God willing. But what will that mean for my future now?*

A child to care for, to provide for, to raise up in a way that would please Will . . . his family . . . her family. She shook her head, and moved toward the gate and back to work. *Focus . . . focus . . . focus . . . or you'll end up kicked again.*

She slowed down, moved cautiously, watched more carefully as the horses flinched, switched tails and laid their ears back. It was strange to be more concerned about each move than before. She realized she was thinking about a child that even now needed protection. Realizing she was keyed up and causing the horses to be nervous, she removed ropes and halters, hung them on the gate and moved to the house to sit at the table, to be near her mother, to ponder this reality that was causing her confusion and a pinched ability to think clearly.

She wondered if her father had any inclination that he was about to become a grandfather. She didn't think so, not yet. Would he be happy for her, or would his first reaction be to question how she was going to do her work and tend to her horses? Nothing mattered, it was going to happen and he'd have to deal with it. She felt more closely tied to her family than ever, knowing her life was going to remain intimately wrapped into her parents, and her father's ranch. Beyond that, she dared not wander in thoughts, or hopes, or even dreams.

Early morning sunshine was breaking over tree tops along the ridge, working its way through the window, making the light curtains shine around the edges as she came awake. The breeze was cold, a fire crackled in the wood stove, heating the house nicely as her mother prepared breakfast. Opal watched her father make his way from the barn where he'd helped feed the horses . . . a job the hired help could easily perform, but he'd always done it so he always would. His shadow moved over the rocks and weeds growing along the trail and for the first time she noticed he was bent over more than usual, his hair was grayer than she remembered, and his feet moved slower and more carefully.

"Mom . . . how old is Dad?"

"He'll be 80 next year."

"How old are you?"

"Why do you ask?"

"Seems Dad's stove-up more than usual, and you're not. Is it hard livin' or are you just a healthier specimen?"

"Your father was nearly thirty when we married, girl. I was very young, and life was hard at home. When I saw that tall, strong, good lookin' cowboy ride past our house, I wanted nothing more than to be in his life. And, nothing could be any harder than the life I was living back then. It took some doin', but I got his attention and I was bound to hold it."

"Guess you did. He loves you somethin' fierce."

Her mother walked over, put her hand on Opal's shoulder, and together they watched Maxwell approach their home. Life stopped being about her and her child as she watched him make his way to the house, up the stairs of the porch until the door burst open. Her eyes met his and a smile cracked the surface of his leathery face, tracked all over with wrinkles and little sores that would become skin cancers. She wanted to gather him up and put him in a safe place, never to let him be hurt by life and her sad little mistakes. It was time.

"I have something to tell you, Dad." Her mouth went dry and she stumbled through the words in her mind trying to find the right ones to break the news to this old man of the mountains. "I am carrying Will's child, Daddy." It didn't sound right as it left her lips . . . it was too short, too abrupt, too matter of fact. She never called him Daddy. Watching his face for tell-tale signs, she waited while he stirred a spoonful of sugar into the coffee cup her mother had set before him.

Her mother froze as the words left Opal's mouth, and she moved to stand beside her husband, gently laying her hand on his shoulder.

"Hell . . . I knew that, daughter. I should'a figured it out on the trip. You've never been one to carry any weight on you, that skinny little girl I used to train up in the ways of a horse just ain't all that skinny anymore."

Nervous laughter filled the silence after a few seconds, but Opal wasn't sure if she liked the response her father was expressing. Was he happy? Sad? Scared? How did he feel about having another mouth to feed . . . would he be . . .?

"That had better be a boy, my young girl. You'll need some help runnin' this outfit after I'm gone. And I ain't all that good with girls. Look at you! Tomboy. Tomboy to the core."

She waited, he stopped talking and finished his coffee. The stack of pancakes on his plate disappeared as though being devoured by some kind of vacuum.

As he finished his meal, she spoke honestly. "I'd like for it to be a boy. You can pour into him what you tried to pour into me all those years, and I know Will would like for his own legacy to remain."

"What will you name the little feller?"

"That's a long way off, Dad. Somehow I'd like for it to carry Will's name."

Maxwell's eyes sparkled with mischief. "Willhemena if it's a girl."

149

"*No.* Absolutely NOT Willhemena." She snorted, stood to her feet. "I gotta get to work. I was gonna ride with the boys today and get those colts out in the rocks for a while. They're getting soft footed and every one of em's purt near ready for the boys to take em and go."

"I was wonderin' if you've ever let that long-legged little sorrel mare run." True to form, her father's thoughts turned to the horses.

"Not full out. Why?" She couldn't help but entertain the vision that filled her mind of the wind in her hair and a horse running full out beneath her. It gave her chills, made her smile.

Her dad continued, "She looks like she could fly low if you gave her a chance. I was thinkin' about getting her shaped up and run her in the July 4th matched horse race over in Springerville next year. There's a pretty healthy purse goes with that win. What do you think?"

"Don't know. Guess I'll find out." She gathered her gloves and pulled a coat over her flannel shirt, but barely got it over her shoulders when she heard her mother literally yelling at her from her post in the kitchen.

"*NO, you won't, young lady!* You let one of the boys do that . . . take no chances with a fall or falter horseback."

Smiling at her Dad, Opal winked and grabbed the last hotcake on the platter then slid through the door listening to her mother at the window, "You hear me Opal? I mean it girl."

***

Christmas came and went with little celebration and simple gifts exchanged. Lily's special meal included one of her chickens baked to perfection, a bowl of cooked cranberries and a pile of boiled potatoes dressed with some dried parsley she hid in a drawer for special occasions. She peeled a few treasured oranges and diced them in a bowl with a little salt and sugar, and set them out with a pound cake. Everything was served with a flourish and a smile. All hands were "on deck" for the meal and good wishes.

The family agreed no gifts would be exchanged. Oranges laced with cloves, unshelled walnuts and hard candies filled special glass dishes. The family invited Tom to dinner and gifted him with a new handkerchief and five silver dollars. Maxwell took advantage of the gathering to read from his "good book" and urge all present to remember with due diligence the birth of a child that was so wonderful, so powerful, so filled with love that he had a whole book written about him.

Lily had quietly listened to his yearly dissertation, wondering if there would ever come a time he would touch on the real reason for the birth of that wonderful child and leave off the part about the "whole book written about him." She loved that man, truly she did, but he was a little thick between the ears when it came to tenderness. Probably a sign of the years he'd spent alone before they married, working as a cowboy and being with animals more often than people.

Snow fell twice after Christmas, with its fresh beauty, sparkling in the sun with all the brilliance of pure unmarred white. Just after the second falling, Lily stood in the window with steaming coffee in hand, waiting for Maxwell to return from his morning chores.

"Why do you suppose he won't just let the hands take care of everything out there?" asked Opal as she walked into the room.

"Guess he just loves the horses so much he has to be in the midst of them to start his day off right."

Turning, Lily watched her daughter move heavily about the room, pouring coffee and reaching over her batter bowl to wrap puffy fingers around yesterday's biscuits and pull one to her.

"You should wait for breakfast, girl. Too much of that kind of food isn't good for the baby."

"Well, since we don't have an abundance of spring vegetables around I guess I'll just eat what I can."

151

"I've got pancakes and eggs nearly ready . . . can't you wait a few minutes for your father?"

"Y-e-e-p-p. While I'm fillin' the gap with a few bites of your *m-a-g-n-i-f-i-c-e-n-t* biscuit." Opal wrapped her arms around her mother's shoulders and hugged her tightly.

"You silly thing. It won't be long now and you'll be rockin' that little bundle and feeding her or him every few hours. I want you to go into town and see the doctor. I'm sure what he'll say, but I'll take comfort in knowin' he'll be ready to help when the time comes. He needs to know about when you'll be ready so he won't be goin' off to some warmer place just when you need him."

"Aww . . . Indian women been havin' babies in the bushes for years, Mom. I think you and me can handle this."

"You think so, but just you wait," she responded as Maxwell blew through the door with a flurry of powder-like snow. "You wipe your feet on that blanket before you track mud in on my floor. That horse pucky smells everything up when it gets warm."

Moving to the stove she wiped the waiting pan with a swab from the bacon grease bucket kept on the edge of the stove, and poured a cup of batter on the warm surface of the black skillet. It sizzled around the edges and within moments bubbles surfaced, broke, and stayed open. She flipped each plate-sized flat cake and stacked them on a serving plate. She listened to her family discussing what should unfold for the day.

"I want you to stay inside today," Maxwell instructed Opal. "It's colder than a witches titty out there and the boys and I will tend to what needs be done."

"I was hopin' you'd say that."

Lily made fresh syrup in a small pitcher and flipped more pancakes. Sugar, boiling water just until dissolved, and a tablespoon of Mapeline. She watched her family devoured the fresh cakes. She listened to Maxwell's strong, loud voice over the sizzle of more pancakes and smiled as she heard Opal's responses to his comments about the horses and the cattle. *He should have had a son. Maybe this grandchild will fill that need before he gets too old to enjoy it.*

She refreshed the pancake pile on the table, then sat down herself to enjoy breakfast as the second and third cups of coffee were enjoyed and the conversation waned. "You and I need to do a little sewing this morning, Opal."

"Sewing? What for?" The mention of housework or women's handiwork always ruffled her daughter's feathers.

"I have some material saved up in the hall shelves that needs to be built into a quilt for that baby. You haven't done one thing to get ready to receive her and take care of her."

"Him."

"Well, that remains to be seen . . . nevertheless there are some preparations you have been ignoring and I am not going to do all of it. You're going to be a mother and you need to start leaning that direction. You do the dishes this morning and I'll gather what we need."

"Dishes! Ahhhh yes . . . my least favorite chore in the whole wide of all creation."

"Just do it. I'll start with the material." She moved to a shelf in the hall and began riffling through stacks of items she had stored away, searching through a ranch woman's treasures. A paper of pins, package of needles, thread in three colors, and way in the back a stack of material. Old shirts that had been cut into pieces stacked separate from the heavier pant material from worn out clothing. A treasure of yard goods purchased months earlier during a trip to the mercantile to be hidden for just this very moment. Light colors of gingham folded carefully with the cotton from flour sacks washed carefully and kept. Stacking all of it carefully on the big table she used the surface as Opal and her father removed all signs of food and eating utensils.

"What's all this, wife?"

"Just you go read a book," she responded. "I been savin' up for this day."

153

Stopping for a moment she rested her head against his chest as he patted her shoulders and kissed her soft, clean hair. Then she pulled away and began to spread the material and sort it into piles of similar colors and weight. She deftly decided which would be used for a backing and which would make up the colorful surface that would be wrapped next to the sweet baby's face and hands. Softer material and brighter colors found their way to one pile, most of them cut from faded shirts Maxwell had worn through the years. Heavier material from his worn out pants she set aside for another project.

Sorting through the material she found two shirts that hadn't been cut into useable pieces, but rolled together and tied with a string then shoved to the back of the shelves many months before. Sliding them off the surface of the table she tried to hide them in a chair that had been pushed under the edge.

"It's okay Mom," came a voice from behind her. "Those are from Will and Matthew, aren't they?"

"I forgot they were there."

She watched as Opal reached to untie the shirts, opened them and set one aside, then pulled one to her face where she breathed in deeply. "It still smells like Will," she whispered with tears in her eyes. "How does that happen, Mother?" Turning away she began to sway just slightly as she held the shirt close.

Lily moved to stand beside Maxwell's chair with her hand on his shoulder and they watched together as Opal drifted into another world. A place where she found memories of her childhood sweetheart flooding her mind and emotions. The smell of his sweat, soap and horse hair filled her nostrils. No amount of washing had completely done away with days of work and wear from the shoulders of the wearer.

Watching her daughter brought tears to her eyes, and they began to leak severely as she watched. Opal stretched the arms of the shirt out, holding the sleeves, and then with all the grace of an overweight hippopotamus, she danced around in a circle with her eyes closed.

She felt Maxwell rise and heard his voice over-ride the moment with, "Opal . . . that ain't gonna help none, girl."

"I know. I just wanted the moment, Dad. I'm done." She laid the shirt next to the one she set aside earlier, lifted both to stroke the material gently. "It just brings back so many memories of those two crazy boys I grew up with."

"You ain't even grown up yet, Opal. You need to get over actin' like the carefree girl who did what she wanted and rode with the drift of the wind every day. You're gonna be a mother and things are gonna change around here." Maxwell's voice was gruff.

Lily reached for his arm, sensing he was about to unload an opinion on his daughter she didn't need to hear, and especially not right now. "Another time, Maxwell. Another time," came softly with a stern note.

Surely this was a response to his own carefully hidden sorrow at the loss of the young man he thought would become the son she was never able to give him. Maxwell stopped, returned to his chair and book, mumbling to himself.

"Let's get back to work." She drew Opal away from the past into the present need for scissors, needles and yards of thread. Searching, she found six small cardboard pieces cut into specific and carefully measure shapes. Choosing two she handed one to Opal and instructed her how many pieces of each color of material to cut. They used scissors like small weapons and attacked the pile of material with fervor. Gradually a bright stack of four inch diamonds grew into what looked to be a mish-mush of pieces of rag, but within a matter of hours had been laid out into a pattern formed much earlier in Lily's creative mind.

Taking a quick break to spread butter and sugar on left over pancakes, they ate a light lunch washed down with cold water and returned to the project at hand. By evening, the top of a small quilt was taking shape as each woman stitched the diamonds and triangles together in stars and squares of brightly colored memories.

"Remember when your father came home with this one shredded

155

to pieces?" Softly she brought other memories to light to turn Opal's mind from the painful ones. She wanted to remind her there were others to smile about. "He got bucked off in the buckbrush and ripped it to pieces. He was so mad at that horse."

"Here's grandma Jared's apron . . . be careful when you place these pieces as there are only a few. Look, this was your baby blanket; you drug it to the corral so many times it only had about twelve inches of clean savable material, but these pieces have to have a place in your baby's blanket for sure. " Her mind raced with facts and dates and times that came back with the lifting of each fresh stack of clean, faded cloth remnants.

Watching carefully for the upturn of Opal's mouth, Lily smiled to herself as they began to relive moments that so many of the pieces of material brought back. They merged pieces together in blocks and stars, working deftly with a woman's tools. It was cold and dark when they moved the material to a corner and found meat and potatoes to make the evening meal.

Later, as they spread the pieced treasure on the table, they both beamed at their day's work. "We'll see if some of the church ladies can help us quilt it later. If not, I'll work on it a little each evening and quilt it for you. I know you won't keep the stitches tiny and even."

Opal laughed out loud. "Why mother . . . how wise you are." She had never been one to take to the finer duties of housewifery.

Lily folded the quilt top carefully and put left-over pieces of material back on the shelf. Suddenly her mind returned to the day Maxwell had married the pair, and she gasped softly to herself. There would now be no way to go before a judge, or a preacher to have her daughter legally married by the laws of the land! With Will gone, would the proper paperwork be done so her granddaughter could legally bear her father's name?

She waited until Opal had gone to bed, then she approached Maxwell with her questions. He sat looking at her and realization hit both of them squarely. He had no answer.

Late winter held snow and rain beyond what had come for many years. Mud was deeper than Maxwell remembered, and work was limited to what could be done without riding or driving wagons through gummy masses of rich black sod heaving with moisture. Becoming more and more frustrated with being indoors he spent long hours with Tom at the barn, "holed up" with plans for spring gather and branding.

"If this don't let up soon, we'll be branding yearlin' calves before we're done," he concluded.

He'd grown uncomfortable in the house watching Lily fuss over Opal who had grown a huge belly full of baby as the weeks grew longer waiting for a delivery. He kept a horse close to the barn so he could ride for the doctor when the time came. Putting Opal in a buckboard and slogging through this gumbo was not going to work.

"Wish things would dry up and that baby would pop out," revived the stalled-out conversation. "Seems like it's way past time."

"Babies always come when they're ready, Maxwell," commented the old puncher.

"Well . . . that baby could have been ready a long time ago and I'd have been happier. I think Opal would too. Dam' she got big as a barn, and barely fits behind the table at dinner. Yu'd think she would'a left off some of the biscuits and pancakes in the last few months."

"She'll lose it later on," Tom remarked with that droll tone of voice he used frequently with Maxwell these days.

"Awww . . . how the hell did we get on this women's gab, Tom?" Maxwell snorted with disgust. "Let's go chop some wood and fill up the wood boxes. Where's Jimmy gone off to? I ain't seen him all day."

"Went to town yesterday. I told him he mas'well take advantage of the down time."

Lifting his head and tilting an ear toward the house Maxwell asked, "Did you hear someone call me?" Pouring out the dregs in his cup Maxwell moved toward the house and waited. The call came again, and the urgency in the tone pushed him forward in earnest. He opened the front door and stopped in his tracks as he watched Lily helping Opal rise from the table and moved to help get her through the bedroom door.

"You go for the doctor . . . an' don't you slow down for nothin'. This could happen fast."

He set his cup on the edge of the table and grabbed a heavier coat from the hooks near the door behind him. The cup teetered, then fell to the floor with a crash, splintering into a thousand pieces. He stopped to look at the pile, thinking he might clean it up, but as he heard deep groans wafting from the bedroom he quickly dismissed it all and made for the barn as fast as he could slog through the black sucking earth.

As things go, the trip went well, short of being slow. The mud sucked his horse's feet as they slogged through puddles and mud-bogs, like the thoughts that pulled him into worriment.

The doctor was home, which eased Maxwell's mind substan-tially. As the sun had been up without cloud cover the road dried out just enough here and there and allowed them to make pretty good time on the return trip. There was still plenty of daylight when they stopped horses in front of the Redding ranch house. Never-the-less, both men were shocked to be greeted by the crying of a healthy, very upset newborn baby.

"Wha'du you s'pose happened?" asked Maxwell.

Doc Anscom laughed. "Well . . . I reckon that baby came when it was ready, Maxwell." He pulled his bag off the saddle horn and moved into the house while Maxwell gathered the horses and retreated to the barn. Horses unsaddled and settled with hay, he stood in the barn door reluctant to return to the house.

Tom walked up and stood beside him, reaching out to settle a thorny hand on his shoulder. "Guess you better go on up to the house."

"I'll just wait a bit." Maxwell fidgeted with a button on the frazzled corner of his coat.

"Guess you better go on up to the house. Lily will be needin' your help, Maxwell."

"How come you to know so much about what the hell a woman might need, Tom?" Irritation tainted his voice.

"I had a wife once, and almost had a baby." Tom's voice dropped to nearly a whisper as he pulled his dirty hat from a graying head of hair. Maxwell turned to look full into his face with an unspoken question on his lips.

"They both died during childbirth." Tom pulled his hat down tight and turned to walk back to the bunkhouse he called home.

Watching him move away, Maxwell wondered why it had taken so many years for this old friend to reveal the secret he'd held in his mind and heart, hidden from the world, hidden from friends, maybe even somewhat successfully hidden from each day's pressing thoughts. It had taken a new baby to bring all that to the surface again. *Hell . . . what if Opal didn't make it through this ordeal?* Maxwell's heart leaped in fear as he finally made a move toward the house.

Lily was in the kitchen when he stepped through the door, carefully peeking around the edge of the heavy wood. She looked tired and strained, so he walked slowly toward her and asked, "Are you okay?"

"Yeah."

"Is Opal okay?"

"Yeah." She tensed as she rinsed out the cloth in her hands, wringing it harder than necessary.

"Is the doctor with her?"

"Yeah." The wringing intensified.

"How about the baby – is it okay?"

"Yeah."

"Oh . . . good. . . you think we'll be eating dinner soon?" He watched the strained face of his wife twist into the form of anger

159

with a trace of insanity. Her chin jutted out a little more than usual and she looked up toward the ceiling as if to say some kind of reverent prayer, but instead of peace there seem-ed to be a veil of what he slowly, ever so slowly, began to perceive as anger.

"What's wrong?" he asked, puzzled.

"Well, Maxwell . . . *what do you think is wrong*? I'm at the end of my rope, that's all. You fix your own damdable dinner tonight, and make extra for Doc."

He ducked the wet towel she threw at his face. *"And clean up that broken coffee cup!"*

"Well, you don' have to get mad . . . I was just asking."

"Now you know," was the terse response as Lily moved toward the door to the bedroom. Glancing over her shoulder she said, "By the way, it's a girl."

Maxwell flopped into a chair nearby with a gasp. *Well . . . there go my plans for the future.*

***

Weeks passed as Opal nursed her newborn, fussed around the house helping her mother and yearned for her horses and the fresh air she could only breathe from the window. She paced the porch like a caged lioness, watching as a young cowboy rode her horses, working them his way, not hers. Then seethe with envy as he rode out for spring works and the scent of wild cliff roses. *Just a few more weeks and I'll be able to join them.*

She found herself yearning for the manzanita bells Will would bring her during his scattered visits. She only allowed her mind to wander through the past few months on rare occasions. Only a little more than a year had passed, and she had experienced love, loss, marriage, death and birth. A whirlwind of memories wafted through her internal vision, but only a handful of faces came and left quickly as the winds of change took their toll.

She stopped, watching the horizon as a familiar figure appeared through the morning sunrise. Her heart leapt into her throat . . . *Will? How could that be?*

It was one who sat his saddle much like Will. One who sat like he'd been there before he could walk in the high heeled boots his father gave him early in life. Leaning forward he urged his horse into a long trot, then a slow lope. *Matthew.*

Stepping from the porch she waited by the hitching rail nearby and waved as he lifted the reins and slid to a stop. In one swift, easy motion he found earth beneath his wings.

"Mornin', Matt . . . what brings you along?" Her voice lifted with her heart as this friend of many years smiled and stepped away from his horse. It was good to see a face besides her family and the hired hands.

His face lit up with a wide smile. "On my way to town for the boss . . . wanted to stop by and see how you and the baby are comin' along. Sorry it took me so long to come by, but weather, mud, and bein' a little overworked kept me. We've been in the midst of works for months. This weather has us hamstrung half the time."

"Mmmm . . . come on in and grab a cup o' coffee. I'll gather up the baby." She moved gracefully up the stairs. "What did you name her?"

"Willene Jewel. We just call her Willy."

He followed close behind and found his way to the kitchen and a coffee cup. Laughing, he commented, "Well at least it ain't Willhermeana."

"Look who's here, mother," Opal called to the little figure coming through the back door with a basket of eggs. Reaching the corner where the baby lay sleeping she lifted her to her breast and held her close for a moment, then carried her to the waiting, rough, clumsy hands of a surprised Matthew.

Matt gasped. "I don't wanna hold her." His eyes were wide with surprise and even a hint of fear. Something she was not used to seeing on the face of these hardened cowboys.

"Sure you do . . . just keep one hand under her butt and the other behind her head and you'll be fine." Passing the baby over without hesitation, she watched his hands rather than the expression on his face.

The contrast enveloping the pair did not go unnoticed by the women. His twisted fingers on tiny soft; his jagged brown skin against milky white; his dirty, sweaty hair drooping slightly over her soft brown, freshly washed.

That could have been Will, she thought sadly. *It should have been Will.* Opal felt hot tears in her eyes and a catch in her throat.

"Oh, Opal . . . she's really pretty," Matt offered.

"I know, she really is isn't she? And she's a great baby girl. She only cries when she's hungry. She's already watching us and trying to turn her head toward voices. Can't wait to set her on her first horse."

"Hold on with that," came a voice from the direction of the kitchen, and they both broke into laughter.

"What's that in your hatband?" asked Opal.

"Oh, take it out'a there. I know you love those things." He tipped his head to the side so she could easily reach the little flowers tucked so carefully into the sweaty, dusty hatband. Opal pulled a stem of the familiar manzanita bells . . . milky white and soft rose bells that hung in small clusters from a red stem with olive green leaves playing a supportive role. Tears filled her eyes and her lip quivered.

"I'm sorry . . . I didn't mean to make you cry. I thought it would make you smile," Matt offered softly.

"No . . . it's okay. You know how I love them."

"Yeah . . . never have been able to figure that one out! You women love 'em and us cowboys hate 'em. They just overtake the land and build hidey-holes for cattle."

Lily was refreshing the coffee near Matt's elbow, so Opal bent to relieve him of his package.

"She really is pretty, Opal," he commented as the little bundle left his arms.

Chit-chat continued for nearly an hour as the family caught up on the happenings of neighboring ranches and families. "Have Will's family been to see her yet?" broke into the conversation around wild cattle and bronc rides.

"Yep. His dad came over when she was a few days old but they haven't been back since. It's a hard ride in a rough ol' buckboard and his mom is gettin' up in years, ya know. She really isn't well, and couldn't make the trip, and I couldn't take the baby over there yet. I need to soon, though. I want her to see her grandchild before something happens."

Her father stomped up the stairs and burst into the room, shook hands with Matt and pulled up a chair. Setting it down hard with the back facing forward he straddled the seat and began quizzing Matt about all the cowboy wrecks and wrongs. Hanging on every word, Opal listened intently to the conversation that had turned back to bronc rides and the men who had come and gone as the works started and were coming to a close. Within the hour Matthew rose to his feet several times as if to leave, then pulled the chair back under him to remain and continue conversation.

"This time, I really gotta go." He stood to his feet, pushed the chair under the table, and reached for his hat and coat hanging near the door. "Walk me out?" he asked of Opal.

She handed the baby to her father, who had learned to hold her without scrunching up his face and twisting his mouth around into a wad. Walking out to say goodbye to her old friend felt good. She missed the language of the cowboys, and it made her feel warm to hear him laugh and talk about the men and the livestock and the life she yearned to return to.

"Thanks for comin' by, Matt," She leaned against the hitching rail near the porch.

The reins draped loosely over his arm as he stood holding his hat in his hands, flipping it front to back and rolling it over carefully. "Could I come again?"

"Of course you can . . . any time you like."

"No . . . I mean . . . could I come again to see *you*, Opal?" He set his hat back on his head, tipped back just a little so she could see his eyes clearly. His dark curly hair poked out from under the edges of the dusty ol' thing.

She stopped thinking for a broken moment, looking into those eyes for a signal that she understood what he was asking. His boyish face covered with freckles and scars eagerly watched her so that she became nervous, unlike herself.

"What, exactly, are you asking me, Matt?" She noticed he had begun to perspire slightly just below his hair line.

It took a long breath for him to look up and answer her question. "Well, this ain't exactly how I had this planned . . . but here goes." Reaching up, he nervously pulled his hat from his damp, dark locks and moved two steps closer to her shoulder as she leaned against the rail.

"I loved Will, Opal . . . you know that. But I've loved you all this time right along with the love he had for you. I ain't trying to be disrespectful of his memory 'cuz you know I will hold him dear to my heart for all of my livin' life. But with him gone, you got a baby to raise and a heart full of love that sure don't need to be held inside 'cuz he ain't here to get it. I ain't thinkin' he'd be objectin' to me giving you what we both know you deserve and he would want you to have."

 She straightened up, holding her hand out to touch his forearm and keep him a step away. "Oh gosh," she gulped. "I had no idea you felt this way."

"Sure you did." He smiled slightly and held his ground.

"Just you figured it was more like a brother instead of the way I'm sayin' it right now. And . . . for all these years I was okay with bein' like a brother and happy to share that with you. Now I'm askin' for a chance to be somethin' more to you and that little lady up there in her blankets. I don't mean right now." He ran his hand through his hair, and searched for the right words. "But after a while if you and I could work it out, maybe you'd begin to feel about me a little like you felt about Will, ya know?"

Standing quietly her heart began to beat faster and her mouth felt suddenly dry and parched. "I don't know Matt . . . I ain't been thinkin' about nothin' like that. I figure I'd just be here on the ranch with the folks and raise Willy up same as I was."

"You think on it." He spoke low and soft, stepping back to pull the right rein over the horse's mane and reach for his saddle horn. "You think on it and I'll come back in a few days." He didn't bother to put his foot in the stirrup as he returned to his lofty perch, but rather swung up with a hand on the horn. "I'll be right here," she mumbled without looking up at him, fidgeting with a piece of horse hair stuck in the cracks of the hitching rail.

"That's good enough for me." He spun his horse to the left and trotted slowly on his way. She lifted her head to watch as he looked back over his shoulder, pulled his hat off, and dipped it her direction briefly. She moved away from the rail when Willy let her know she was hungry.

***

"Willy" was weaned early. She was happy with cow's milk by the time she was a few weeks old, and Opal was ready to return to her horses. Her mother was happy to keep tabs on the good-natured baby girl, who grew fat and sassy on the rich white liquid.

Old Tom had received a letter from his sister in Nebraska one sad evening. Her husband had died, and she desperately needed help raising her sons and keeping their farm and ranch operation held together. Through broken hearts and tear-filled eyes they lost another family member. She could barely stand to look at the bunkhouse those days.

165

Spring flowers were in full bloom as she rode out each morning, working the horses, building a quality performance in each as their turn rolled around. Her father began selling them as they reached what he considered to be a solid salability. She found a little cash on her side table as each was sold. A special hug was reserved for her dad as each sale trotted down the lane to a new home.

She stood near the corral gate frequently, watching one of the new colts learning to romp on his spindly little legs and his mother nuzzle him each time he returned to her side. "You're next to the halter, little guy," she advised him quietly.

Matthew rode over once in a while. She wasn't sure about her feelings where he was concerned, but willing to let things unfold quietly and slowly. He was a great guy, but he was far from being her Will. . . *nobody will ever be like Will. So strong, so tender, so right minded.* Her chest still hurt, her eyes still filled with tears when she thought about him. *I wonder if I'll ever stop missing him. No . . . he'll always be with us. Willy will be so like him that it will be like he's living on forever in her, and in our love.*

It was sunrise on a Sunday morning as she stood with her arm

over the mane of an old mare in the corral, talking to her as though she could understand every word. She heard a voice, like a still strong echo, calling her name in the distance. She waited, listened, but it stopped.

Then she heard it again, only this time it was inside her head, maybe in her heart, she wasn't sure. The familiar voice beckoned her . . . "Be Happy . . . live life . . . love again."

Smiling to herself she whispered, "Yes sir. You never quit tryin' to boss me around, do you?"

***

At first glance he seemed to sit pretty tall in his saddle. He rode up to the corral fence and sat quietly watching her, waiting for her to finish schooling on the colt she was working with. She pulled his nose around and started up the fence toward the man waiting.

"Howdy!" She didn't yell, but raised her voice above her usual quiet drawl.

"Back atcha." He pulled a sack of Durham from his left pocket.

Opal watched silently as he rolled a cigarette, placed it between his lips and lit it with a flourish of snapping the top off the match and watching it burn for a second before he put it to the pinched end of the home-made "twig".

"Can I help you?" she asked as he shook the flame off the end of the match. Up close she could tell he wasn't as tall as she thought. Just thin and wiry, and his horse was short and stocky which gave her that first impression.

"Lookin' for some work." He looked straight at her. "Heard you'd had a fella killed out here a while back, and another left not long ago, so I thought you might have a spot."

Hearing him use those particular words felt like a bucket of cold water in her face. It was a harsh way to refer to the loss of her husband. She sat staring at the strange man as smoke curled around his nostrils making him squint a little.

"I don't think so." Her reply was curt and direct. She decided she didn't like him much.

"Is the boss around?" he snapped back.

"I AM THE BOSS, if you're looking for horseback work." Her voice was prickly. "Maxwell Redding is my father."

"Well now, ain't that the chiggers." The corners of his mouth curled. "I didn't mean to offend you, ma'am. Just that there's usually a mister around somewhere and I figured you bein' as young as you are that just stood to reason."

"My dad's out riding right now. He'll be back shortly and if you wanna talk to him you can." She watched his face for change of expression but none came. "I don't think you'll be needed around here. Now if you don't mind I've got work to do." She reined her horse to the inside, which she rarely did, but she wanted her back to him as soon as she could arrange it.

"That horse will respond better if you rein him to the outside and use the fence."

She felt her face burning, her throat tightened and her butt muscles tensed as she pulled her horse up and turned in the saddle. "You go to hell."

He pulled the cigarette from his lip as he chuckled.

Her anger erupted like a mouthful of hot coffee being spewed past quivering lips. "You . . . you . . ." words escaped her mind like water down the drain hole. "Just who are you, anyway, besides a jackass?"

"Just a drifter lookin' for work."

"You can water your horse over by the barn and wait for my dad by the corral. But I'm thinkin' you ain't gonna be needed anywhere around here." She kicked her horse's ribs hard and he jumped into a lope which she continued until she saw the rider leave his spot on the fence.

Dad better not hire that idiot. She was still hot under the collar, and her horse must have been sensing it because he began to pull at the bit and stretch his nose out a little farther than usual. *I better catch Dad first, when he comes back.*

***

Opal was intent on her horse's progress so missed her father's arrival when he rode around the corner of the barn on a dinked horse and stepped off to slip his saddle. By the time she realized he was home, the drifter was shaking hands and he'd put out the cigarette he'd been nursing.

It was too late to interfere with her father's decision, but she was pretty sure he wasn't hiring new help. The young colts were doing fine and work was light for now. Old Tom had been gone for weeks, and a younger want-to-be cowboy had hired on. She missed Tom fiercely! He was part of the family, and losing him was hard after Will. It had been hard to see him ride away, and she wasn't yet over missing him, but Johnny was working out well and she had her hands full trying to help run the ranch according to her father's specifications and instructions.

I'm just glad he didn't come in a couple of weeks from now. Dad would sure hire him on for the spring works. She was hopeful he would at least talk to her before he made that decision!

She pulled up her horse and sat, letting him blow for a few minutes while her father shook hands with the drifter again. To her surprise he pointed to a small pen on the side of the barn and the stranger walked his horse over and began to unsaddle and set his tack on the fence rail. She whistled hard to get her dad's attention, and her horse spooked a little as she motioned for her dad to move her way.

"You didn't hire that fella' did you?" she asked abruptly.

"No. But I did invite him in for some dinner. Do I need to ask your permission to do that these days, young lady?"

"No, sir. But I had a run in with him earlier and I ain't particularly anxious to sit down to eat with him."

"Well, then I guess you'll have to take your meal to yourself, girl." Her father turned on his heel and headed for the corral where he met the drifter again and pointed him toward the bunk house. She knew he was cleaning up and like it or not, she could eat on the fly or sit down to a meal with the man.

She was sure Lily would have a meal on the table that would be hard to pack outside. Besides, Willy would be up and playful and she wanted to spend time with her daughter in spite of the unpleasant company that would be found at the table.

She unsaddled her horse and brushed him carefully before turning him out in the small holding pasture behind the round corral. Standing quietly for a few stolen, delicious moments, she watched him lope toward the other horses, crow-hopping along nickering softly. When he reached the group of young horses he nipped and romped for a few minutes before lowering his head to graze.

She never tired of watching horseflesh of any kind, doing anything. They fascinated her, mesmerized her at times with their grace and beauty. Her love of these animals was almost unhealthy at times according to her mother, but her father's pride in her horseback accomplishments simply fed her inner being with strength and love for the species.

They gave her nearly everything she needed to make her feel useful and productive. Even sometimes gave her a sense of prowess and accomplishments beyond what other women could produce, and that gave her a jolt of intense pride. So much so that if any part of this arrangement in her life was unhealthy it was that intense pride.

Little Willa was walking now, and it wouldn't be long before she'd be wanting to be in the corrals or horseback with Opal. She'd already had her first ride, and many more. She would stand at the window and yell for Opal when forced to remain at the house with her grandmother. She was barely talking, but her first words were the names of horses as Opal took her with her to feed morning and night. Letting her pat them and rub their soft noses as they smelled her hair made her happy, never afraid. How she giggled out loud when their warm breath would blow her hair out of her face. She was indeed Will's daughter, but she was her mother's child as well.

Leaving the gate Opal headed for the house and a meal with her family . . . and that stranger who had already ticked her off. She set her jaw and gritted her teeth as she entered the house to find her father pouring coffee for two. She moved straightway into the kitchen, picking a happy Willa from the floor as she entered her mother's sanctuary. Seated in a small chair near the window she played with her daughter, laughing as they made faces at each other. Nothing brought joy to her heart faster than this laughing, playful, happy extension of her late husband.

So like her father, this child of her heart was gentle, quiet of spirit and strong willed as a willow groping to find its way through a rocky creek bank. Once her mind was settled it took intense effort to get her to change direction or by-pass her willful desires. Having a grip on something required balancing determination to pry her little fingers from possession.

"She's just like you," her mother often reminded her.

"Mmmmm . . . more like Will I hope."

With supper set on the table, seating required that she sit next to this stranger and directly across from her mother. Willa had taken her own special place at the head of the table. That simple arrangement made it easier for both Opal and her mother to share the feeding and care of the little girl who wanted nothing more than to feed herself. An act that created more mess than management. She was uncomfortable sitting next to this man who set her teeth on edge.

As they began the meal, Opal found herself increasingly

uncomfortable. Who did he think he was to tell her how to handle a horse without having even bothered to ask her name. She fidgeted with her flatware and spent more time feeding Willa than entering into the conversation.

"So, where you hail from, Jacob?" Her father tried to draw him into conversation.

"Originally, from Kentucky. Blue Grass country."

"What brought you West?" Maxwell pressed for information.

Talking with his mouth full, this man now known as Jacob offended her again. Her mother wouldn't tolerate bad manners at her table under normal circumstances, but she ignored this rudeness.

"I just got tired of bein' my father's flunky and decided to see if there was somewhere I could be my own person for a change, so I took my two horses and sold out."

"So what happened to the other horse?" her father asked. "I see you rode in single."

"I sold him some time back for travelin' money. I've been able to find some work here and there and stayed on steady for a couple of years up country a ways. I'm good with horses and fair with cattle. I work hard when I work and play hard when I play."

Opal decided it was time for her to enter the conversation. "So, why did you leave the place you were steady workin' for a couple of years? Did they get tired of your rude behavior and run you off?"

He father slammed a spoon down on the table. "Opal Anne."

She and Willa both jumped and stared at Maxwell. "Sorry," she said softly as she patted her daughter's chubby little hand holding her own little spoon.

"I apologize for my daughter's rude behavior." He spoke directly to Jacob. "You carry a last name around with you?"

"Yes sir. It's McCallister. Scottish along the line, but there's some Irish and English in there somewhere I'm told." He paused, helped himself to another biscuit and some butter.

"I guess I made her pretty mad when I popped off at the corral earlier. Seems she holds a grudge for a while."

"She does." Maxwell glared at Opal, his face red.

"I'm sorry, sir." She responded, feeling her own face flush.

"Don't tell me . . . *tell him!*"

"But I'm not sorry I said it to him," she began. "I don't like him and I don't like his attitude and there ain't much sense in covering it up, ya' know?"

Jacob laughed. A jolly, rolling, belly laugh that surprised everyone. "Well now, I reckon she's got a right to her opinion, and a right to say what she thinks. Let's just call it good and maybe I'm the one who should apologize first."

"That's not necessary," responded Lily. "There's no excuse for her rude behavior."

"Sure now . . . I guess there is," Jacob replied. "I had no right to correct the way she was handling her horse out there, and even though I didn't agree with what she was doin' I should'a kept my voice hushed and let her do what she thought was right."

"WHAT?" Opal heard her voice before she thought what she might remark. "*What I thought I was doing right?* There you go again . . . who do you think you are? What makes you think I don't know what's right?" She stared at Jacob with venom seething out of her muddy brown eyes, and her voice quivered with anger. Willa began to whimper and her eyes widened with apprehension.

"I think it's time for me to be riding on." Jacob spoke to Maxwell. "I don't think this is gonna get any better pickin' at it an' since you don't have work I better get on and see if I can make town or another ranch before evening." He rose and pushed his chair under the edge of the table, leaning on the back slightly. "Thanks for the meal, ma'am. It was right kind of you to include me." He stepped to the door lifting a filthy black hat from the hook, but held it in his hand rather than put it on his head inside the home.

Maxwell rose. "I'll walk you out to the corral, Jacob." As he shut the door behind them he paused to give Opal one of his "I'll beat the tar outa you girl" looks. She'd never had the tar whupped out of her yet, so she wasn't worried about more than a tongue lashing when he returned.

***

The tongue lashing was short-lived, and directly to the point. Opal listened, pinched her lips together, and built an argument in her mind. But her father was right, she had been very rude to this drifter.

She held her argument, but responded curtly, "You're right, but there's something about him that just rubs me the wrong way. I hope he keeps on riding and stays outa this part of the country. Sorry."

Lifting Willa from her messy supper plate she carried her to the kitchen and carefully wiped her hands and face. The squirming, grimacing little girl made her laugh. "Time for bed, missy."

"No, no! No beddie." The writhing bundle fussed, as she always did when it was time to give up for the day and sleep.

She whimpered, and then burst into outright tears and wailing, which brought her grandmother to the rescue.

"How about a story?"

"Tory. Tory." The wailing stopped, and Willa shot her mother a frown.

Opal resented her mother's ability to soothe the child when she herself seemed to bring tears and fussing. "Spoiled. That's what she is, you know," she commented to her mother as she moved to clear the table and wash the dishes. All she received in return was a patronizing smile. Her mother's quiet voice reading softly to her child made her own soul quiet again.

174

She washed the dishes quickly, stacking them on the counter to dry. She still hated housework with great disdain. Thoughts of the drifter returned, much to her consternation, and she re-lived his early comments. *The man's a know-it-all, to say the very least. Wonder how old he is.* She remembered how easy he sat in his saddle, how comfortable he seemed compared to her own frustration and unsettled responses.

He's not young, that's for sure, but he's not all that old either. Looks could be deceiving, he must have had a hard life and it's always hard to tell a cowboy's age. Too much sun and leather. I just hope he moves on.

Yet there was something about him that drew her, something so strong she couldn't seem to quit thinking about his apology at supper, and wondering where he would ride next.

Later, she climbed into bed next to Willa, who rolled over and snuggled into her arms without waking completely. Her hair smelled dusty and her little feet were cold, but it was nice to have her so close. She fell asleep to dream of the smirking face of a man she barely knew.

When she woke with the crowing of an early rooster, she pulled herself away from Willa and dressed quickly. She was irritated, agitated, and looking for an argument before she even left her room. She beat her father to the barn and fed the livestock, leaving morrals on the horses as she threw hay into feed bins. Then she stood quietly, settling her soul to the sound of horses crunching oats and blowing, listening to them contentedly filling their bellies. She scratched each horse's ears as she removed the morrals and hung them over her arm to return to hang inside the barn door.

When her father walked to the gate and opened it for her, she smiled as he said, "Up early this morning, eh?"

"Yeah. Willa was restless, so I didn't sleep much." She lied to avoid the issue of her dreams and agitation.

She didn't dare say anything to her father over breakfast, afraid she would start an argument and that would make everyone's day harder. She was glad Willa slept on into the morning.

After breakfast she stopped to peek in on her sleeping child. This soft-haired baby made her heart swell with pride and love. Her little feet twitched as she dozed. *She must be dreaming.* So like her to be in motion, even as she lay quiet on the pillow with her thumb near her mouth.

Leaving the house, she walked to the barn with her father, listening half-heartedly as he gave instructions for the course of the day. She knew the drill . . . she'd lived it nearly every day of her life since she was old enough to walk. Yet, every day he had to give her instructions as though she was still a child, needing to be told every move to make. He told her which horses to ride this morning, and why. She already knew. *Is he ever going to just shut up and let me do my job?*

About mid-morning she sensed more than noticed someone riding up the road toward the corral. As she pulled up her mount and turned toward the rider, she was relieved to see Matt Baker trotting toward her. She let out a quick breath she'd been holding, irritated at the realization she was expecting it to be the drifter again.

"Hey . . . what are you up to?" she hollered at Matthew.

He'd apparently taken it upon himself to keep an eye on her and little Willa since Will's death. Still not sure how deeply involved she wanted to get with Matt, she was guarded with the proximity of their visits. She didn't dismount, but rode to the edge of the fence to visit.

"Just headed for town and thought I'd ride by," Matt commented with that crooked little smile. He reached up and set his hat on "tilt" which had been his habit as long as she could remember him owning a hat. Slinging one leg over the saddle horn he reached in his pocket and pulled out a sack of Bull Durham, then rolled a cigarette and lit it carelessly.

"When did you take up smokin'?" she asked curtly.

"Awww, I been smokin' a long time, Opal. I just didn't do it around you much. Keeps me busy and I don't crave goin' to town so much."

"Well, you look silly." She sniffed the air and snorted. "Stinks, too."

"Huh! Ain't you the little stuffy miss mouth this mornin'." He chuckled.

"Say . . . you boys over at the Mitchell place haven't seen a drifter by the name of Jacob, have you?" She turned the conversation to her liking quickly by doing a little snooping into the whereabouts of the man from Kentucky.

"Yeah . . . he came by day before yesterday lookin' for work. Mitchell told him maybe in a few weeks, but there wasn't anything now. I didn't catch his name, but it must be the same one. Is Jacob his first or last name?"

"First." She grimaced.

"Hmmm. He come by here too?"

"Yeah. Dad sent him on. Struck me as bein' a pompous jackass."

"Say . . . what's eatin' you this morning?" Matt leaned forward on his knee with a smirk and a wink.

"Nothin'," she responded too quickly. "Just a comment. I better get to work. If you're headed home around supper time, stop back by." She dismissed him with a wave and spun her horse too quickly which nearly unseated her, but she regained her composure and moved into a slow lope around the outside of the corral.

She noticed Matt didn't move for a while, but sat quietly watching her. It was making her nervous, but she refused to recognize that flush as being embarrassed.

He finally slung his leg back to the stirrup and giving her a little salute turned and loped on toward town. She stopped her horse, stepped off and ground tied him, headed for the house. She needed a drink of water and maybe a biscuit from breakfast.

Men! They think a woman is just waitin' around to be impressed by their simply bein' there.

***

It was only a few days later till her father began making decisions about starting spring works. "I need you to get horseback and help with the cattle end of this outfit today." Opal's father pulled his hat down hard. "We need you all day and probably for the next few days too. Pull your best colts out and let's see what they can give us." *Breakfast was over!* Her dad was on his way out the door.

Relieved to be looking forward to a day out of the corral and away from the house she hugged her mom and grabbed a handful of leftover pancakes. "You okay with Willa all day?" she asked quickly. She already knew the answer. Her mother was raising Willa while she moved into a place of managing the ranch with her father. She was completely comfortable becoming the son he never had. That would have fallen to Will, had he lived. Matthew made plain he was up for the job, but life with Mathew wasn't all that appealing at this point. He was a great friend, but a lover? She shivered.

Stopping to peek through the door at her growing daughter, she smiled at the sweet face and curly hair that folded around a soft cheek. Her thumb had found its way to her mouth again, in spite of her mother's efforts to break the habit. Hot sauce hadn't worked, nor had vinegar. Willa quickly found the dogs would lick it away and then her thumb would find its way back into her little mouth.

Life in the mountains held excitement and change. She was tired of the confinement of a round corral and long trot through a horse pasture day after day. The mountains held testing and pushing the horses too. Rocky trails, steep cliffs and narrow places through long canyons would provide the testing time.

A wet fall had quickly been absorbed by years of drought, and early spring rains were brief and fast moving. Pulling the cows with calves off the ranch was becoming a necessity, not the choice her father would have made some other year. They'd already moved them out of the worst of the mountain range to the lower end of the ranch where a few springs were still producing water. Fresh grass kept the cows producing milk, and calves were filling out and putting on weight.

Rushing to catch up with her father she stuffed two pancakes in her jacket pocket, glad she had eaten some breakfast. Two of her colts walked up to her sniffing for their share, but she pushed the soft nostrils away and threw a lead rope over the neck of the older of the two. "You'll earn your keep today, young fella."

She saddled quickly, merely dusting him off with a gloved hand rather than brushing him as she would have with more time. Pulling the cinch snug she led him through the gate and turned him around a couple of times, then led him to the saddle house where her father and a young cowboy were waiting.

"Sorry to hold you up," she handed the lead to her father, then returned to the other horses to choose one for their young hired hand to ride. Maxwell had let all the men go during the winter months, finally. This new young man had only been hired on a few weeks.

For herself she chose one that had several weeks of training and riding time.

"Cinch up and let's get outa here." her dad groused. He stepped up on an old stump that had been moved near the   saddle house to help him mount, and Opal noticed it was harder on him in the early morning cool than after the sun warmed things up.

She pulled the cinch hard, set it up a notch and pulled her stirrup around. Her left foot hit the stirrup, and swinging her right leg into its perch she settled easy into a saddle seat that was as familiar to her as a kitchen chair.

Turning her horse she rode in behind her father and in front of the young cowboy who had just recently turned fourteen. They moved at a quick trot, needing as much time as they could squeeze out of the daylight. She glanced back at the young man who followed her respectfully. Some months back he'd left his own home where a mother and father were trying to raise nine siblings. Her kind-hearted father hired him straightway. He was going to make a hand, and he was hard after learning everything her father had to offer a young cowboy heart.

Within the hour, they began finding traces of cattle moving from the small spring fed pools into the breaks of three canyons that merged about seven miles above the home pastures. They left a gate open here and there as they made their way to a point above the feeding grounds. Later they would bring what cows and calves they found back through those open gates.

Her father pointed out parts of country to her and to Johnny, giving them precise instructions. She already knew where she would be sent, where Johnny would be sent, and which country her father would keep for himself. He took the hard part, and gave Johnny the easy country. The farmer boy was being brought on carefully, but expected to do a man's work in spite of his years. Her father had been working cattle and horses since he himself was a ten-year-old.

She knew it would be a long day. Her father had shown them a small portion of the east pasture to ride. He'd obviously chosen the easiest part of the ranch to gather first. *He must be planning to hire on some help for the west end.* Her heart skipped a beat. Surely he wouldn't hunt up Jacob for the job. She hoped he'd found a job someplace far away.

By day's end the trio had gathered forty seven cows and forty calves. The other seven were either dry or hadn't bred. She would watch to see which ones her dad would cull this fall when they shipped. It was these little things she knew she had to learn before her dad wasn't able to ride any more. She smiled to herself. *He won't turn this outfit over to anyone until he's completely incapable.*

Pushing these thoughts aside, she deliberately decided to put off learning some of the intricacies of ranching in preference to doing what she loved. Riding the colts and gathering the new calves. No matter how hard the work, she found great pleasure in being horseback, enjoying the wide open spaces above the corral and ranch house. Her wild streak hadn't waned one iota, and she had no desire to rein it in.

Johnny shut gates behind them as they moved the cattle into the pasture above the house. They were already slurping up the meadow grass while their babies curled up on the softer ground for a nap. It had been a hard day for the babies—long trails with lots of rocks and they'd moved along as fast as they could.

"Tomorrow we'll head back to the upper east ground and check for remnants on that side of the ranch." Her father was already giving instructions for the upcoming day. She was tired to the bone and wanted a soft chair and a hot meal.

"I hope Willa went through the day without a nap," she commented to her dad as they unsaddled. "It would be nice to hit the hay early." He laughed in response.

They unsaddled, brushed the horses carefully and hung morrals on their noses while Johnny threw hay into the old wooden troughs. "You go on up to the house." Her dad swatted her gently on the butt with the end of a rein. "We'll finish up here. Your mom might need a little help."

Willa came running through the open front door and stopped at the top of the stairs calling and waving. Opal sat on the steps holding her treasure and looking at a splinter in her finger.

"Ooooo, Papa will have to get that out for you." She spoke gently to her daughter, who responded "No, no. Gamma."

She laughed and gathered her up to move into the kitchen doorway where she asked her mother, "Do you need any help?"

"Nope. You go visit with Willa. She wouldn't nap today at all. She spent most of the day on the porch watching the horses in the corral and calling to them. She did ask for you a few times, though."

"Great! I was hoping we could get to bed early tonight. I'm sore all over, and whipped." Opal smiled and drew the curly hair away from Willa's soft brown eyes. She was so intent on everything! She watched every move made by those she found within her realm, and she already found ways to persuade them to do her bidding. *What a little minx.*

The pair returned to the porch where Willa began her childish garble as fast as her little tongue could work it around. Opal laughed and returned the conversation in short blurts, watching her father out of the corner of her eye. He walked slowly to the porch and reached for a rickety railing, pulling himself up the stairs where he stopped to visit with Willa. Opal made a strong mental note, *I need to get Johnny to fix that railing before he pulls it over on himself.*

Her dad turned and whistled at Johnny, motioning him to the house. He took his meals with the family lately, since he was the only hand left on the ranch. Times were harder than usual, and her dad figured since she was able, she would fill the place of someone who had to be paid. He was right.

They had just settled into supper when she heard the dogs barking and went to the door. Matthew rode up, singing as he came. She smiled and stepped to the top of the stairs, waving. "Put your horse in the corral and come in for dinner."

"Nah, I'm on my way to town again an' I'll eat in there. But I could tie up and come in to say hello to everyone before I head out." He stepped out of the saddle and tied his horse to the rail near the front porch.

She waited for him to reach the top step, then turned to walk into the house as he followed. "What in the world are you goin' back to town for? Seems like you spend an awful lot of time in there lately." He dodged the question and simply addressed the family seated at the table.

"Evenin,' all." Matt was polite as he shook hands with the men folk and reached to give her little mama a hug. "Good to see everyone." He stopped close to Willa to ruffle her curly hair, and pinch the nose above the mouth that smiled up at him.

"No, no!" Willa barked at him. Opal noticed it didn't bother him that her daughter wasn't happy with his actions. He ig-nored her little voice, and visited Maxwell before he reached across the table to retrieve an offered biscuit. Then he said a quick goodbye before she walked to the porch to watch him ride away, waving as he loped up the dirt road. She returned to the house after he disappeared from sight.

"You know," her father offered, "That boy would sure be helpful around here if you'd give him an open gate."

She picked up her fork and began eating rather than answer. It was little things like Matt's indifference to Willa's responses to him that bothered Opal most. It was like she was just a little something on the sidelines to be noticed then set aside. If Opal would ever marry again it was most important to her that Willa be a high priority.

Later she folded Willa into bed and gingerly climbed in beside her. They snuggled and giggled for a bit before both fell asleep to rest weary bones and overactive minds. Opal dreamed again of a gentle face that was fading into a fuzzy place in her memory bank. She could remember the color of his hair, and his gentle eyes. She dreamed of his rough hands and the packets of flowers he would bring to her. Flowers she kept in a box on the shelf that one day, somewhere far into the future, she would unfold and tell little Willa stories about the father she would never know.

***

The following evening the trio rode back into the home ranch as the sun was setting and shadows grew long and deep. It had been a hard day. Even though they were only gathering a few remnants, it was tough going, bringing the five head of cows with two calves out of the mountainous terrain o the holding pasture. As they were pulling saddles and wiping sweat from the backs of weary horses, Opal heard Willa crying. It wasn't the usual cry of want or anger, it was a whimper, coated with fear. Her heart skipped a beat, and she stepped around her horse's shoulder to listen closer. Her dad heard the sound shortly after, and the concern in his voice was evident.

"You better head on up to the house. Johnny and I will finish up here. Go on, girl." Her father's voice held concern, but in his usual stoic manner the instructions were matter of fact.

183

As she opened the door, it bumped against something on the floor, so she squeezed around the edge to find her mother lying on her side, back facing the door. She shut the door, calling her mother's name sharply.

Willa began to cry louder and reach for her mother to pick her up. "No, Willa, be a good girl." Her concern was to find if her mother was unconscious, or worse. Her head was pounding, she couldn't think past her mother's face turned into the floor boards.

Willa screamed. This time it was the desperate tone of voice. Opal heard her dad's feet hit the wooden slats of the porch. She called out. "Stop, Dad! Open the door slowly. Mom's lying on the floor and you'll hit her with the door."

Sliding sideways carefully through the barely cracked open door, he found his way to her side. "What the hell...." he whispered. This time the usual matter of fact voice held fear and concern for his tiny wife, lying still and quiet before him on the floor.

"She's alive, Dad. I don't know what's the matter, but she's breathing and her heart is beating. Better holler at Johnny to catch up a fresh horse and ride for the doctor. No. You take her to the bed and I'll catch Johnny and send him."

It was her tiny mother's stature that made it possible for her aging father to lift her from the floor and carry her to the bed. He staggered a little, even under what little weight she held, so Opal turned back and reached to help him. With one on each side, they made it to their room and set her carefully on the bed. He was straightening her legs and arms as Opal looked back. Leaving the door open she raced to the bunkhouse screaming for Johnny.

"Ride for the doctor, fast as you can get there! Something is wrong with Mother!" Her voice broke as she heard the words.

He was horseback in a matter of minutes, not stopping to saddle a horse, but swung up on the bare back of the mount as it left the yard at a dead gallop.

She raced back to the house, and up the steps to find Willa standing in the doorway sobbing and shaking. Opal lifted her to her shoulder, holding her close and soothing her with soft words.

184

"Gamma's okay, honey. You don't worry none. You're okay now, Mama has you." She sat at the table rocking gently to and fro until the child's cries became little sobbing gasps. She set her in her raised seat and tied her there with a soft strip of cloth her mother used to restrain the busy little body. She gave her a piece of hard bread and a glass of milk, then stepped to the door of her parent's bedroom. "Has she opened her eyes, Dad?"

"No. I can't get her to come around. Nothing we can do until the doctor gets here. 'Cept say a prayer." He bowed his gray head, and Opal noticed his hands were shaking as he folded them in formal position of his usual prayer for blessing the food.

She moved to his shoulder, setting her hand on him in comfort. He stiffened, but accepted her outreached offering. They prayed together and she waited with him until Willa began to call her and whimper. "Gamma . . . Gamma."

Opal took her out of the chair and held her in her lap, comforting the child with soft crooning and singing her songs she herself had learned from her mother. What if her mother died? Her heart chilled and her mind seemed to turn to a white hot flare of light. Shaking her head, she refused to accept that possibility. What would her dad do without this little bit of treasure in his life? What would she do, and worst of all how would Willa survive without her precious grandmother? Her throat closed, and tears burned her eyes, but she blinked fast so Willa wouldn't see her crying.

It was well over two hours before Johnny returned with the town doctor. He had been in the throes of stitching up a seven-year-old, would-be-bronc-rider. The youngster had ripped an arm open on the stob of a nearby tree as he spurred and thrashed himself about frantically in the crotch of an old oak tree.

Opal heard the horses coming up the road and ran to the porch with Willa on her hip. Johnny took the doctor's horse as he dismounted, and the old gent stepped up the stairs as quickly as his old knees would allow. Opal waited in the doorway, watching as the doctor examined her mother. Her father stepped to the foot of the bed and she noticed he looked so very old and tired. For the first time fear gripped her throat and her heart felt like it was swelling in her chest cavity.

She walked away from the doorway to the room her parents had occupied since she was a wee one herself. She sat quietly in a chair by the table holding Willa and feeding her bits of cold biscuit with apple butter smeared liberally. The tired child fell asleep in her lap, completely exhausted and still hiccoughing from what could have been hours of crying as she sat by her grandmother on the floor of their home. Opal lifted her gently, and taking her to their shared bed, laid her head on the pillow without removing her clothing or her little lace-up boots. Hopefully she would sleep until morning.

The doctor was standing near the kitchen door as she returned to the main room of their home and her father was pouring him a cup of lukewarm coffee. She stood near the table listening carefully.

"I don't know for sure, Maxwell. I think she may have fallen and knocked herself out, but she should have come-to by now. Her heart is beating normally, and her breathing is not labored. I find no physical reason for her to remain un-conscious. All we can do is wait. It's one of the aspects of my job that I hate with a passion, but sometimes things happen that we just have no reasoning for, and no solution to. If I knew for sure if she fell, or had pain before she fainted." He looked at Opal with an expression of questioning.

"Willa didn't say anything. She couldn't anyway. She's just cried out for Gamma over and over. I don't know how long the two of them were the way I found them."

She moved to the kitchen and put a stick of wood in the stove, fanning it to increase the flame and the heat. "I'll heat up that coffee for you, Doc."

They waited quietly together, rotating from the doorway of the bedroom watching and hoping for a change in the tiny woman's condition. The moon was rising, and it was hours before she moaned and began to regain consciousness. Her first words were to call for Willa, and Opal fairly leaped from the doorway to the side of her mother's bed.

"Willa is okay, mother. She's asleep, but she's fine. Do you remember what happened?"

The doctor and her father came to the bedside, and the doctor checked her pulse, her heartbeat, and looked at both her eyes carefully. "Do you remember anything, Lily?" he asked.

She lay quietly for a few moments, then responded "No . . . I just remember walking into the big room near the table talking to Willa. Nothing more."

"Do you know when that was?" The doctor seated himself on the bedside.

"Well . . . it had to be shortly after noon meal. I had lifted Willa from her chair and cleaned her up. I remember getting dizzy and seeing flashes of light, then I don't remember much else. I was worried about Willa, I remember that."

Opal gasped. Her child sat with her unconscious mother for hours before she and her father returned. Her mind raced with what could have happened. What if Willa had been able to get out of the house? Then she remembered where she found her mother. It was probable her mother had, in her last conscious minutes, positioned herself so the toddler couldn't get outside easily. She reached for her mother's hand, holding it gently.

"How much food are you eating that has iron in it?" the doctor asked Lily.

"I don't know. I just eat what we have to eat. Why?" responded her mother.

"It's possible you are low on iron, and your blood isn't giving your body what it needs to function properly is all. I have a tonic in my office we'll get you started on, and see if that helps. How much water are you drinking?"

"Oh goodness, doc. I don't keep track of that. I drink when I'm thirsty."

"Well, your skin sticks together when I pinch it up, so I think you're dehydrated and we'll get you drinking a lot more right away. Opal, you go get your mother a couple of large glasses of water and set them here by the bed. Lily, you drink every drop of that, and don't get out of this bed until tomorrow."

"That's fine with me." Lily responded weakly. She closed her eyes and nearly fell asleep before Opal returned with the water. The doctor slapped her hands to wake her and waited for her to sip one glass empty. Then she closed her eyes and fell asleep.

Opal went to the bunkhouse to have Johnny saddle the doctor's horse. Knowing he was riding home in the dark made her nervous. She wondered how many times he'd turned his horse toward town and leaned forward in the saddle to doze his way home.

She told Johnny to saddle a horse for himself and ride into town with Doc. "I think you should ride back into town with him. You can stay overnight and come out early in the morning."

"That's a good idea," the doctor responded. "Then I can send the tonic I want her to take out with him in the morning. You get her to take two tablespoons of that stuff in the morning every day until it's gone then I'll give you some more."

"See you in the morning," he whispered to Opal.

She walked up on the porch, stopping to rub her arms in the brisk night air. "Spring cold," she thought. Then she turned to find her way to her bed where she lay beside her daughter, both fully dressed, and fell asleep in short order. Her dreams were filled with fear and visions of people leaving her and Willa alone in strange places.

***

Maxwell didn't sleep. He rested near his wife, but his troubled mind refused to accept sleep as though it would take him away from her. For the first time in their lives he was facing age and infirmity, and it brought fear to his soul more than any experience of his lifetime. As the sun rose revealing her sweet face in the soft light, his eyes traveled around their room. He saw dust on the surface of the quilt he had laid over her, and wondered if living in dirt ever bothered this little woman.

She never complained, never asked for more than what he had given her. His gaze traveled to the walls, and a faded dresser, then a makeshift closet where a handful of his shirts hung next to three dresses. All were faded, except the dress she saved for church-goin'. That one still held on to a soft blue that danced with the tiniest of white flowers scattered across its shell. He took a moment to say a whispered prayer of thanks to the God she believed in so strongly for bringing her to him.

He heard Willa talking to her mother, and Opal's soft response. He rose carefully, not wanting to disturb his sleeping wife, but her eyes opened to watch him. He smiled gently and spoke softly. "I'd say good morning, but I'm kinda waitin' to see if it really is."

She smiled and reached for his hand. "Maxwell, I love you. You're a good man."

Tears welled up in his eyes, and he tried to respond but words wouldn't come. "I know." He patted her hand and pulled away to move into the kitchen where he stirred ashes until he found some hot coals then got a good fire going and a fresh pot of coffee brewing.

Opal and Willa came to his aid and the pair began to fix breakfast. Willa stood on an old round topped stool and stirred the bowl while Opal dumped flour, soda, sugar and eggs into a pile so the wee one had a purpose. The mess she made flipping flour over the edges of the bowl was quickly wiped up and soon the old cast iron skillet was hot.

Maxwell stood in the doorway sipping coffee, watching Opal make Willa stay on the stool away from the stove. She poured small circles into the skillet where they sizzled over just a dollop of lard. As the bubbles began to stay open she flipped a golden brown miniature cake over. Between flips she made fresh maple syrup with hot water, sugar and a cap full of Mapeline. He chuckled and asked her "Can you make anything besides pancakes?"

"I guess we'll find out." She smiled a crooked little grin.

"Looks like you and Johnny are on your own for a few days. Someone has to stay with Mother until we know she's able to get back on her feet and stay upright."

"I was thinking last night that maybe it's time to hire some help until we get through spring works. There's a lot ahead of us, and I don't want your mother to be here alone with Willa again until the tonic he's sending out takes holt."

"Why don't we see if there's a woman or young girl in town who could come out and stay with Mother and Willa?"

"I know you don't like bein' trapped inside . . . 'specially during spring works. But I got my reasons for goin' this direction, girl. I'll be needing another strong arm to help with the branding soon enough anyway. I know you can work, but I want you with your mother and Willa for a while."

He watched the veins on her neck bulge and her face turn red. She lifted Willa from her stool and set her in the little chair reserved for her at the head of the table. Tying her in with a strip of cloth, she put three tiny little pancakes made just for her in a pile and poured syrup over them. "Hot, baby girl. Hot."

Willa sat quietly watching him, fork in hand, as he prepared his own pile of cakes for eating. Once he started eating, she followed suit and together they consumed breakfast. Willa drank "pearl tea" from a little tea cup her grandmother kept just for her. Canned milk, a touch of sugar and lots of hot   water. Sometimes made with the maple syrup for sugar.

Maxwell was finishing his meal when he heard a rider. Johnny came at a trot so Maxwell rose to greet him at the door. He reached to take the tonic from him as though it surely must be some miracle drug that would cure his wife and bring her back to them, well and able. He passed it off to Opal. "Better get some of that into her as soon as you can."

"Johnny, you get some breakfast down and let's get to work."

Maxwell walked to the room where his wife lay and assured her Opal would bring her some tonic soon. "I'll see you this evening.

Johnny and I have to ride today, but Opal will stay with you and Willa."

Turning quickly he walked to the front door and yanked his hat down. "I'll get the horses out, you can saddle when you get done eatin'."

"Yes, sir. I'll be right out." Johnny wolfed down another quick bite.

"Hold on." Willa said. "You can take a handful of leftover pancakes with you." She set a large stack of cakes in a small tin box with a loop on the end of it. It would be tied to the back of the saddle until retrieved for a quick refreshing stop with a drink of water.

Maxwell snatched them from the counter, patted Willa on the head, and laughing at her syrup covered hands and face, tweaked her nose. He left the house with Johnny hot on his heels stuffing a dry pancake in his mouth as they walked to the barn.

It was only a few minutes until they were saddled up and long-trotting through the pasture. It would be a couple of hours and they'd be working their way through the canyons and valleys to bring in another set of cows and calves. The work would have to be done quickly or the holding pasture would be grazed down and they'd have to feed cattle. That, Maxwell did not want to have happen.

The pair rode home in early afternoon, sweaty and tired. Maxwell walked to the house while Johnny saddled a fresh horse and rode out again, this time toward town.

He entered the house, walking straight to the bedroom where he sat on the edge of the bed talking to his wife. He quietly told her how many cattle they gathered, what a good hand Johnny was making, and of his decision to send him to town for hired help.

"Oh my. Did you tell Opal yet?" She sat up in bed, leaning forward to place a hand on his arm.

"I will." Rising, he moved to the kitchen and gulped down a long glass of water and snitched a left over pancake to snack on.

"Somethin' smells good, girl. Whatcha cookin' up?"

"A roast and a pot of beans. You better get hold of the old Mex in town and have him come out and jerk the rest of that beef hangin' in the root cellar. It won't be long it's going to be too hot to keep even in the cool down there. Where's Johnny going, he could have had him come out tomorrow." She stopped to watch him, and he felt her eyes bearing down on him like a fox over a rabbit hole. "Where did Johnny go anyway?"

"I sent him to town to see if he could find someone to hire on for a couple of months of day work." He chewed as he talked, wiping his mouth with the cuff of his dirty sleeve.

"Mother will be okay in a couple of days and I can get back out there." She replied tersely.

"Nope. I decided you're going to stay here with your young'un and help your mother. She may get up and about soon, but I don't want to take any more chances until we know she's strong again. And that's that, girl." He spoke gruffly and with the authority he knew he had to press into Opal's brain.

She sat down hard in a chair, looking at him with an incredulous expression planted firmly. "You aren't going to make me stay in here through the works are you? Not really?" Fury began to twist her mouth as she spoke.

"I don't know, girl. You'll stay until I am sure your mother can handle things on her own."

"How about I go into town and find someone to stay with her and Willa instead of hiring on a man to do the riding? You can hire someone for a few days to help brand, but there's no need to hire someone to do the riding. I'd rather do that," she argued, and pressed him.

"*Nope.*"

She clenched her fist, and leaned toward him. "Dammit, Dad, you want me to run this outfit then you just push me into the house and go off and hire some man to cover my tracks. It ain't right."

His voice intensified. "*Just stop it, girl.* You owe your mother! She is Willa's grandmother, not her mother. You need to act like a mother for a while, and like a respectful daughter. That's my final word."

He stood, pulled his hat down low, and walked to the barn to await the return of his young hired man.

***

Opal stood at the window stewing. Her face was flush with the heat of anger, and she clenched and unclenched her hands.

She heard her mother calling, but she chose to ignore her and watched her father near the corrals. He paced, like a coyote walking a fence line he couldn't find a hole under. She smoldered.

"Opal, please come help me." The tone of her mother's voice drew her from her anger, replacing it with frustration.

"I'm coming," she snapped. But she wanted to stay instead. Her love for her mother moved her feet when her head was screaming, "This is not fair."

"What is it?" Opal asked abruptly from the door of the bedroom.

"I need to get out of bed again to use the chamber pot. I have trouble lifting myself, it's so low." She raised herself up on the edge of the bed and swung her legs over the side. "Just a little support here is all I need."

Opal stifled her irritation, lending her mother a helping hand, staying nearby until she was finished. She helped her back to the bed, still seething with resentment.

"How long do you think you'll be like this, Mother?" she asked curtly. When she saw the tears in her mother's eyes, and saw her lip quiver, she came to her senses. "I'm sorry, Mother! That came out wrong . . . I truly am sorry." She gently helped her mother lie back on the old, sorry pillow.

"I don't want to be this way, you know how I hate being down. It makes me so angry at myself." Her mother was hurting, and her

193

frustration was evident in the tone of voice that prevailed.

"Shhhhh . . . don't cry. Let me go get Willa and you can read her a story if you feel up to it. She loves it so, and I know you'd like the company."

"Willa . . . Willa, where are you?" she called. There was no answer, but soon a bouncy, curly head and tiny little feet wandered into the room, and straightway climbed up on her grandmother's bed. Opal found an old book that was her primer in school, and handed it to her mother. The pair curled up in the pillows and Opal listened while her mother made up a story and turned the pages that held nothing similar to what was being told. No wonder that little girl loved her gramma so.

She returned to the kitchen to begin a pan of biscuits which she would add to the roast and beans she'd had cooking most of the day. The house was filled with a unique aroma the three produced. Through the window she saw Johnny and a second rider stopping in front of her father to dismount. Something familiar about the way the second man sat in the saddle stopped her dead in her tracks. Her heart pounded harder and she gritted her teeth. *Jacob.* She ceased to think, ceased to reason, just stood with clenched fists and an overwhelming desire to run through the back door and hide in the trees until he left or she fell off the edge of the world. She walked back into her mother's room and tearfully sat on the edge of the bed.

"Opal . . . what is it?" Her mother's voice was soft and inquisitive.

"I could just shoot Dad and Johnny." She spit the words out. "I could really just walk out there and shoot both of them! But first I'd shoot that dam' jackass Johnny brought home with him."

"Dam' atth," her daughter mimicked.

"*Oh, Opal. Stop that!* Just listen to what you've got your daughter saying. You should be ashamed. Where is your charity? He may be a Godsend to your father and you're being such a child about all this."

Opal sat frozen. She couldn't think, she didn't want to reason. She was just mad to the core of her very being. Her life was topside

194

down, and she was spinning out of control. How on earth would she ever be able to face that man and her father?

It wasn't long until she heard the door open and close quietly. She was afraid to move to the front room, she might have to face Jacob again. After everything she'd said to him, how could she?

Her father came to the door of the bedroom, asking softly, "Opal, could we talk out here?"

She rose, and moved to the front room and the long table that served as their eating space. Jacob was not there, much to her relief. Her father motioned her to sit. She obeyed, but her mind raced with words she was already forming to throw at him.

"Opal, Johnny brought someone home to help us out for a while. He says he looked all over town, but there wasn't anyone around who was looking for work, except . . . well . . . except the one he brought home." He stood over her with his hands on the back of a chair. "I know you won't like this, girl, but you're going to have to find a way to accept it. Your mother needs help, and I won't have some stranger in my home tendin' to her and the baby."

"No, but you'll let some stranger ride my horses and peddle himself all over our ranch." The second those words left her mouth the expression on her father's face changed, and as was the case when that expression found its way to his countenance, her heart stopped and she felt shame flush her face.

"I'm sorry," she stuttered. "I shouldn't have said that."

When will I ever learn to keep my trap shut?

"You're right. You shouldn't have said that and you better not let it come out of your mouth again, you hear me?" Her father was struggling to contain his anger, his face red and the veins on his neck bulged. "If you don't like the way I run this outfit, you can toddle your little butt to town and get a job as a waitress, or whatever else suits you. When I die it will be yours, but until them I AM THE BOSS . . . do you get that?"

"Yes, sir." She had to hold onto her feelings, and bring her thoughts back to some common sense. She could find herself and

Willa looking for a home if she didn't get her head straight, and she knew she'd pushed her father past his limitations.

"You get that supper on the table and there will be two hands to feed tonight. I'll talk to Johnny about fixing meals at the bunkhouse later, but tonight you're doing it." He rose to pick his hat up off the table, turned back and forming just a hint of a smile, added, "Supper smells good." He left the door open as he returned to the barn.

She followed him slowly to the door and watched as he spoke with Johnny and Jacob. They had unsaddled and were moving horses into the corral. Johnny filled the morrals and threw hay into the bins as the three stood and talked. Her father pointed, and all three shifted from foot to foot as they discussed something that was only to be imagined. For now, she didn't really want to know.

She moved to the kitchen and gathered up plates and eating utensils to spread them on the table. When the biscuits were brown and crispy around the edges, she pulled them out and set butter alongside the pan on the table, then hollered out the window to her father, "It's ready, come and get it."

She spooned up a bowl of beans for her mother and set a buttered biscuit on a saucer, taking it carefully to her mother's room. "Willa, you come in the kitchen and we'll eat." The toddler must have been hungry, she jumped off the bed and climbed up in her chair at the head of the table. Opal tied her in place, then handed her a biscuit.

The men washed up in the pan near the front door. She felt herself blushing as she set the rest of the evening meal on the table. They entered, hung their hats on the rack provided, and settled around the table. She brought the pan of beans with a ladle and set it on the old wooden slats, then returned for the large iron skillet filled with thick slices of roasted beef.

Jacob stood. "Here, let me help you with that." Taking it from her he set it carefully in the center of the table. She wanted desperately to tell him she didn't need his help, but she caught herself and simply said, "Thanks." Her father was already serving up bread and beans to Willa, so she returned to the kitchen to fuss with cleaning up her mess. She was NOT going to sit down to eat with that man!

She cleaned up most of the counter and set a pan of water to heat, took down the big round galvanized tin wash tub. Setting it away from the stove, she found a drying towel in preparation for Willa's bi-weekly bath. Then she took a small tea cup, filled it with hot water and shards of steeping dried tea, with just about a half a teaspoon of sugar stirred in carefully. Giving wide berth to the men and the table, she delivered the tea to her mother, and stayed to visit until her father called out, "Willa says she's done."

Cleaning up the mess surrounding her little girl, she gathered her up and they went to the kitchen to enjoy a warm bath and a good scrubbing. By the time she finished, the men had left the table and moved out to the porch. She carried the towel-wrapped little bundle back to her mother's room to dry her off and comb her hair, slipping her into a soft night gown. "You stay here with Gamma while I go do the dishes."

Willa curled up in the crook of her grandmother's arm with tiny little wrinkled feet sticking out from under the hemmed edge of her night shirt. It was only a matter of moments before both were sound asleep in each other's arms.

Opal finished the dishes, wiped the table, and dared to step out on the porch hoping the hired hands were gone to the bunkhouse. They weren't. She started to return inside, but stopped as Jacob said, "Opal, could we talk, please?"

Oh good grief! What could he possibly have to say that would interest me in the least? She turned to stand in the door with a dish towel in her hands, and resisted the temptation to begin wringing it. And wringing it. And wringing it.

"Could you sit down for a few minutes?" he asked quietly. She already resented that "fatherly" tone in his voice that reeked of "lecture time."

"I can hear you fine from here." She tried to be polite but let him know he wasn't her boss.

"Please?" he asked again as her father and Johnny stood to his feet quickly, and nearly trotted to the corrals to hide out until this obvious confrontation was over.

She walked to her father's chair and carefully, deliberately, positioned herself in what was considered to be his favorite place to survey his kingdom.

Jacob removed his hat and holding it carefully, turned it over and over in his hands. His head was lowered as he said softly to her, "I know you ain't happy about this arrangement, and I'll do my best to stay outa your way." He looked up at her, but she couldn't tell if he was sad or just pompous. "It's gonna be tough on you and me and everyone around us if you keep treating me like I have some kind of horrid disease you don't want to catch."

"I understand," she replied curtly, biting her lip.

"Do you? Do you understand that I ain't here to hurt you or anyone in your family? I just want to help your dad get through this tough time and get what needs be done around here finished up, then I'll be on my way." His voice was deep, and resonate with concern.

That won't be soon enough to suit me. But she didn't let the thought become spoken words. "I understand," she repeated. She felt her mouth tighten into a sneer, and she did nothing to hide it.

He rose and pulled his hat down over sweaty hair that apparently hadn't been washed for several days. His shirt was dirty, and his pants had spots from the knees down. She wondered what they were from.

"Evenin' ma'am." He spoke stiffly, walked off the porch and straight to the bunkhouse. The light burst through the open door, then disappeared as he closed it behind him.

She sat quietly waiting for her father to return. He came up the stairs, glanced at her, then moved through the door and went directly to his wife's side.

Opal waited for a while before she moved into the house and began turning off lanterns. Her father walked out of his room with

Willa draped over his shoulder, took her to her bed, and gently laid her on the pillow.

She stopped, and watched through the open door as he paused for just a moment to brush the toddler's hair away from her face, and smiled just the faintest of smiles before he left her there and returned to his wife's bedside to prepare to join her for sleep.

Opal turned off all but one of the lanterns, and walked with it to her room, where she set it on the side table and put her nightgown on. She sat gazing at her miniature re-creation of Will, covered her with their quilt, turned out the light and slid into bed.

***

She fell asleep thinking about her mother, her father, and little Willa. When might be a turning point for them to return to some kind of normal existence?

The sun was barely bringing light to the world when Opal heard her father's voice in her doorway. "Opal, Opal, I think your mother is gone." His voice was low, and quivering.

"Where would she go in the middle of the night?" She tried to focus on his shadowy figure.

"I tried to wake her . . . she won't wake up." His voice was breaking now. Fear coated the words like an icy shroud. Opal tried to understand what he was saying, but her brain couldn't quite absorb what he was telling her.

It hit her with a breathtaking jolt of reality. She raised up, struggling to put her feet on the floor, but she felt numb, her legs wouldn't move. It took a moment for the adrenalin to kick in, then she leaped past him and ran to her mother's bed. Shaking her, calling her name, Opal pulled the covers back and rolled her mother over where she could see her face. It was blue, cold and waxen. She released her hold on the empty shell that lay before her, turned to her father who had followed her, and now stood watching like an onyx statue, frigid and hard.

Her hands flew to cover her mouth to stifle a scream. She couldn't frighten Willa. She walked toward her father, reached out a hand for his arm but he did not respond. She drew back and began to sob quietly, her body shaking more from trying to hold back the sobs than from the pain in her inner most parts.

He turned and walked to the front door of their home, quietly put his hat on and walked outside. He left the door open, so she could see him walk straight to the bunkhouse. It was seconds until Johnny ran to the corral, threw a bridle on a horse and flinging himself on the bare back of a mount, flew down the road. Obviously her father sent him to fetch the doctor.

Opal sat down at the table, stifling sobs and wiping tears on the sleeve of her gown. *I have to get dressed. The house will be full of people in a short time.* She moved quietly in her room, not wanting to wake up little Willa until she had to. Looking at the tiny face she sucked in a breath hard . . . held it . . . then turned her face to the wall and leaned against it for support. *This child will not know what to do without her gramma. How can I tell her that special woman is gone.* Her thoughts stopped, held in some vacuum of numbness, while she wiped tears and tried not to think about anything. She didn't want to step back into reality. *Gone . . . how can she be gone?* The word resounded, over and over like the gong of a huge bell off in the distance.

Her father and Jacob were walking toward the house, so she pushed her bedroom door closed and finished dressing. Willa stirred and turned over, but fell back into peaceful sleep. Opal finished all but her boots, and holding those in her hand with socks stuffed in the top she moved from the room and gently closed the door. She didn't speak to either of the men, but moved to the kitchen and began to stoke the fire and build a pot of coffee.

They walked to the bedroom, but she couldn't imagine why. It was very obvious what was there. She wanted to make them leave, push them away from her mother's still body, drive them from the house. She softened, and tears began again. Her father would be lost without this woman . . . his little Lily of the valley. How could they go on without her? How could God let this happen to them? Her thoughts raged, and her hands moved quickly about her chores to keep from feeling lost and helpless.

Jacob came out of the bedroom, walked to the kitchen quietly and stepped to her side. "You all right, girl?" he asked softly.

"I'm fine." She stiffened and moved away from him.

Stepping back he said, "Your dad's in with your mother . . . you wanna go in there?"

"No. He don't need me around to watch what he's feelin'. He needs his quiet time with her I reckon."

"Do you need your quiet time with her, too?"

"Not now. Not now." Her shoulders began to shake. *When then? When ever again will I have quiet time with my mother? When will we stand in this kitchen and make a meal, or sew a quilt, or laugh with Willa?* She started to lean forward to support herself on something, then realized she was standing by the stove, but had already leaned past the point of no return. She was going to fall against the hot wall of the old iron. She felt Jacob's strong arms catch her, draw her away from the heat, and hold her. Not close, not with a strong touch, but gently and just a little away from his own sweaty shirt.

"Here now, you best go sit down and let me finish this coffee." He released her before she pulled away. She mumbled "thank you" and moved to the table where she waited for the doctor to arrive or her father to leave her mother's side, or the baby to awake. None of those things happened for a long time. She sat numb and quiet until Jacob set a cup of hot coffee in front of her, and took a cup in to her father. She stared at him, incredulous at his kindness, then dismissed it willfully.

The doctor arrived, quickly finishing his time with her mother. Opal sat waiting, watching her father's face as the pronouncement came.

The doctor was to the point. "She just fell asleep and didn't wake up. She wasn't in pain, she died very peacefully from what I can tell. There must have been something wrong inside, where we couldn't find it. I wish there was something I could have done, but there's just too much we don't know. Even as an educated man I struggle with how much knowledge evades us." He stopped and sipped coffee offered him by Jacob, who stayed in the house.

Opal had begun to see Jacob as a vulture hanging over the edge of the house waiting and watching. She kept looking for reasons to dislike him, to wish him gone. But deeper than her pain, deeper than her thoughts, there was a heartfelt gratitude that he was there. It was all very confusing.

The doctor and her father were brief as they planned the burial. The doctor would stop on the way to town and see if the preacher was around, and fill him in on what they wanted. Carefully, oh so very carefully the three men placed her mother's body in the back of the buckboard, wrapped in blankets and placed on a pad of more blankets. She stood watching, feeling hopeless and helpless, turning away frequently to sob and wipe the tears away. As the doctor drove away, her father moved back into the house and closed the door.

Willa came from the bedroom rolling her little fists around her eyes trying to make them open. She moved to her mother and lifted her arms up, wanting to be held and hugged and coddled. She could not know it was with a broken heart that Opal gave her what she needed.

After a light breakfast, prepared by Jacob and served up kindly, Willa began to move toward the bedroom where she sometimes found her gramma. Calling to her, she went to the room and checked the bedding, then came back to Opal asking "Gamma?" Opal gathered her up, and took her to the corral in her little soft nighty where she gently told her daughter that gramma was gone away and would not be able to come home.

***

Nearly a week passed before life returned to something less than a fast trot going somewhere hard. Willa and Opal were both cried out and exhausted. Friends had come and gone for days, bringing food and good wishes. The preacher had been by twice, the doctor stopped her on the street in town to tell her again how sorry he was he couldn't help.

Her life was restricted to the confines of the house. She was dedicated to Willa, and to filling the shoes of her mother as they had worn a path from the kitchen to the dining table. She began to ease up with her resentment and anger, with trying to blame her father, the doctor, and whoever else she could, including God.

She had fallen into a productive pattern of rising with the first crack of dawn, feeding her father and his hired help, sending lunches, cleaning house, playing with Willa, cooking suppers, doing wash and feeding those blasted chickens her mother so treasured. Every time she cracked an egg for pancakes she thought of the nasty smelling waste she had to clean up day after day and wondered how her mother had found such peace in that stinking shed with a rickety fence around it. How many times had she seen her mother with an apron full of cracked corn and barley, talking to her chickens and singing her way through the cleaning up of all they left behind.

Her resentment came in like a tidal wave at times, ebbed when she worked, and her emotions rocked her from anger to broken-ness. Without Willa, she would have been able to hate this changed life, and she yearned for days that passed quickly only a few weeks before. She took Willa on long walks to the barn, the corral, out into the pasture to see the new calves. It wasn't long until the spring flowers on the east side of the house and barn began to peek up. She made time to show them carefully to Willa, allowing her to pick only a few at a time, leaving most to grow and fill the yard with color and sweetness.

A few times Opal had saddled a horse. Setting Willa on the top rail, she would ride alongside and gather her up to hold tightly in front of her. They would take short rides as the child laughed and clapped her hands with pleasure that flung itself from her heart.

This then, was also the child of her mother—the one that had a deep and abiding love for horses and what they brought to her life.

She was folding clothes and placing them in drawers one evening when she fumbled across the stack of tobacco papers with dried flowers, tied with a torn piece of cloth from the sleeve of Will's worn cotton shirt. Holding them carefully, she sat on the bedside, her mind filled with visions and memories. Oh, so carefully she unfolded each paper, touching the flowers he had wrapped so carefully, keeping in his shirt pocket until he could present them to her. Always with his silly little "flourish" and doffing of his hat.

Tears ran freely across her face, her chest hurt deep inside, and her mind began to explode in short bursts of love and pain. They alternated so quickly it all seemed to have the same singular impact on her heart, and on her mind. It was hard to discern one from the other, and all her emotions homogenized into a great bubble that was nearly to burst.

Shoving the flowers back in the drawer, and her emotions into the back of her soul, she moved quickly to the porch where Willa stood looking over the rail. She pointing to the meadow where a trio of men rode. Cattle stood watching, switching tails and chewing cud.

Opal squatted down beside her daughter and they identified each rider with a carefully enunciated name.

"Grraaampapa."

"Jawnnnneee."

"Jaaacuub."

She took Willa by the hand and moved to the kitchen to prepare for the men's return to the house and an expected meal. Willa climbed up on her little stool as she often did to find a spoon and a bowl. Pretending to help her mother, she began to sing. Opal stopped, listened carefully, as only a few recognizable words came forth. The melody was one she'd heard her mother singing as she bustled around the kitchen, and here it was pouring forth from this child. Here in this child, was more than a daughter, there was a continuing flow of what was once her mother's spirit. Here, in this child she would find Will, and her mother, and who knows who else.

It crept up on her slowly, steady. She first felt the sensation near the hollow beneath her collar bone, and it swept up her neck and warmed her face. For the first time in her life, she came to realize the gift she had been given. The importance of nurturing what lay within that little curl covered head that was singing with no music, and few recognizable words, but from her heart she was pouring forth what she had already learned. *Joy in the moment.* A way to find a joyful response to the fear and sorrow that had moved into their lives. *So, so like Lily.*

Opal found herself singing with her daughter as they put together a meal of hash and beans and the steadfast supply of biscuits. She hated setting out yeast bread to rise and punch down and let rise again then punch down to form loaves and let rise again before she could smell the sweetness of warm yeast bread. Biscuits were easier. Quicker.

The trio of men were stomping on the front porch and she heard them laughing as they washed up in the pan of water she supplied. When finished, they came to the table where she had placed empty pottery cups and an old pitcher of water. She was setting food on the table as they entered, and Willa ran quickly to her grandfather, holding up her arms calling, "Papa," over and over. Opal saw his face soften, and he lifted her with a smile and a kiss on her cheek.

She could not remember her father ever kissing her. Perhaps when she was little, but to her remembrance she had never touched that crinkled old face with her lips. Nor had she any recollection of his cracked, chapped lips ever once leaving a little love on her own face.

They sat together and she helped Willa fill her plate and preside over the evening meal. She prattled and laughed at Johnny as he played peek-a-boo with her from behind a banged up hand with swollen knuckles. "Owee," she said, and pointed to his scabbed rough hand.

"Mmmm, oweee." He nodded.

"You need some ointment for that?" Opal asked.

"Maybe later if you got some handy." He waved off her concern and continued to shovel food into his hungry mouth.

"Where did you ride today?" she asked her father quietly, somewhat tentatively. She almost didn't want to know, didn't want to hear the stories about the range, the cattle, the ride and especially about the horses.

Her father spoke, but she didn't hear what he said. Fight-ing back tears, she moved to the kitchen and returned with a coffee pot. Pouring each cup full she half-heartedly heard the stories he relayed, wondering, *how did mother do this her whole life and not think she was missing something?*

Jacob was unusually quiet, and she caught him looking at her for long periods of time as they finished the meal. He rose after supper and moved to the porch, lit a roll-your-own and watched the sun set with a calm demeanor, thoughtful, not talking. He and Johnny went to the corral, fed the stock, then entered the bunk-house, and the world became a dusk-filled embrace of quiet. The only thing she could hear was the calling of the night birds and a soft blowing from one of the horses. Her father had gone to bed early.

She and Willa cleaned the kitchen then found their way to their room where Opal held a book in her hands and made up a story for the bright little girl until she fell asleep, both curled up in a little nested indentation in the old mattress.

***

With the morning light, she was in the kitchen when Jacob knocked and entered. "You got a minute?" he asked.

"Yeah. Why?"

"I want to show you something." He motioned for her to follow him, and he led her to the barn where he pointed to an old saddle that had been cut and molded and shaped and re-arranged until there before her was a throne for little Willa.

"Do you think she could ride with you for short rides?" he asked with a twinkle in his eyes.

Her heart leapt! "I don't know. I've only taken her in front of me on my saddle, she's never ridden alone without me walking beside her." Here could be the key to opening her cell door! Would her father allow it? Even if she couldn't ride with them for long rides, she and Willa could begin working together and spending time horseback. She looked at Jacob, speechless, wanting to thank him but not knowing how to express what she was feeling. No one else had even sensed her longing to be again on a horse's back, her desire to return to the outdoor work of the ranch.

"Thank you, Jacob. I don't know what to say."

"Well, I don't think little Willa is ready to hit the hills yet, but with time she'll be riding beside you and your dad and will find her place here." He stopped to reach for a little yellow string with the white circle on the end of it in his pocket.

"I gotta go get breakfast ready. Thanks again, Jacob. This was . . . well, it was something I never would have expected. But I am grateful." She moved toward the house, wanting to take the saddle to the corral and try it on one of the horses. Turning back she asked, "Which of the horses will it fit?"

"Any of them. But I have one in mind that I think will take good care of Willa. We'll try it after breakfast." He lit his cigarette as she turned and walked to the house. Her heart was lighter, her hopes for the day brighter, and she actually leaped over two steps as she reached the porch and fairly skipped into the house.

She set breakfast out, and tied Willa to her elevated chair. "We have a *r-e-a-l-l-y great surprise* for Willa after breakfast," she told her daughter with a little giggle. While Willa may not have understood everything she said, she fully believed this toddler was very smart and knew enough to put puzzle pieces together in a conversation. She was bright for her age, and responsive to words and people. She was already trying hard to speak words that she didn't understand, but putting sentences together didn't seem to be a great challenge for her. She just didn't use the right words.

Willa pushed her half empty plate away and squirmed to be free of the binds that tied her into the chair. Reaching for her mother she whimpered.

"You finish your breakfast first, baby girl," Opal commanded. "Outside, later." She herself could hardly wait to set Willa in that little saddle, place her feet in the shortened stirrups and hand her the reins of a gentle horse. She remembered her own first ride like it was yesterday! She wanted the same experience for Willa.

Jacob finished before the rest and placed his dishes in the pan in the sink. "I'll go catch up a horse for her."

It wasn't long until the entire family walked to the barn with the excited child riding on Opal's hip.

"Horse!" Willa called out clearly.

"His name is Rowdy," explained Opal.

Jacob placed the little saddle and cinched it up. Willa became very quiet, her eyes widened, and her little fist gripped her mother's shirt at the collar like a vise. She gazed at the little saddle seated on the back of a very large speckled horse.

"Mine?"

She put her chubby little hand on her mother's cheeks and turned Opal's face toward her own. "Mine?" Willa asked again.

"Yes, baby girl . . . yours." Opal smiled.

Willa became very quiet and still as she watched Jacob finish getting the older horse ready.

"Can you say Rowdy?" Opal asked.

"Owdee," replied Willa. "Owdee."

Opal smiled and handed the little girl to Jacob, watching as he set her on the saddle, placed her feet in the stirrups and handed her a set of reins knotted just right. Willa didn't need coaching, she gathered the reins and kicked Rowdy, pushing him forward with her hands tightly around the reins.

Jacob stayed in the corral with her, watching and walking within an arm's reach of the little horseback girl. They took several laps around the corral with Willa kicking hard and yelling "Hahh! Haahh!" Jacob laughed at her as they made their way, but Opal stood by the fence with tears in her eyes.

This wasn't just freedom and training for Willa, it was her key back to the life she loved. Now that this little girl had experienced the freedom of being on the back of a horse, she would want to be there all the time, just as Opal did. Her heart was swollen inside her chest, beating harder than usual, but she felt like she wanted to let out a whoop to stop the stars.

When it came time for Willa to be taken off the back of this giant of a friend, she refused. Jacob wouldn't force her to come into his arms, so Opal had to be the one to remove her from this new-found excitement. She screamed "No, no, Mama! No, no!" "You come down for now, we'll ride tomorrow as long as you like." *As long as you like, and I hope it's all day little one.*

***

Jacob stood near the corral gate after he let Willa and Opal pass through. The old horse stood with his head near Jacob's shoulder and nudged him lightly as if to remind him he was still saddled. He rubbed the horse's ears and whispered softly to him while he uncinched and removed the little saddle. Hanging it on the fence with the blanket, he turned and rubbed down the horse and wiped him shoulder to rump.

"You'll have an easy life now, you old crowbait. No more long hard days work for you, you're going to be carrying the prize possession of this outfit, so keep that in mind." He slipped the bit from Rowdy's mouth and walked him to a back gate and let him into the pasture. Gathering up the saddle and blanket he placed everything strategically beside the door of the saddle house and pulled his own saddle from its rack. Johnny was waiting for him, mounted already, having seen the experiment from the sidelines. "I tied your horse to the fence back of the saddle house, Jacob. I'm ready to go when you are."

"Soon as the boss man gets here, we'll move out." Jacob responded as he saddled a younger version of the Rowdy horse.

"This colt any relation to Rowdy?" he asked Johnny.

"I don't know, but he sure could be . . . colored a lot like him, and he's got the same temperament. They been raisin' horses around here long enough for them to be from the same dam and sire."

They continue to discuss horseflesh and breeding until Maxwell came from the house with long strides and a determined look on his face. "Well, we've used up a good part of the morning playin' patty fingers with the girls, so let's get mounted and get gone. You saddle my horse up, Johnny?"

"Yes, sir. He's tied around side of the saddle house to the fence. I didn't want them to get ol' Rowdy stirred up while Willa was checkin' things out."

Maxwell *harumphed* like a bullfrog, and pulled his reins loose. Then led his horse around the front of the saddle house and used his familiar stump to get himself mounted. They started out the road at a fast trot in spite of Johnny finding his mount had a hump in his back and did a little crow-hopping before he lined out. It was several hours before Maxwell pulled up and began pointing Jacob and Johnny in different directions, issuing orders of where to ride and how to gather the new pasture.

"Jacob, you head up Cantle Canyon to the west, and bring every-thing you find off that side into the creek bed. It's dry, but they'll follow some of those trails out of there. Johnny, you git the east side same way and I'll head up Bull Canyon where it feeds into Cantle and bring what I find up there in to you. We'll run out of daylight if we don't hustle."

Jacob nodded, turned his horse and moved out easy as he gave his horse a bit of a breather before he started climbing. Watching for a trail upward he scanned the brush until he saw where a light trail poked its way through a stand of manzanita and pushed his way through to find his way up the side of the canyon.

He looked back to see Johnny moving toward the crest of his side of the canyon moving easy. Maxwell was pushing his horse hard, too hard, Jacob thought. *That old man gets somethin' in his head an' there ain't no turnin' it. Better keep an eye out for him today, if he keeps pushin' he's gonna run out of horseflesh before we finish.*

The day wore hard on the trio, but they gathered a good size bunch of cattle and pushed them into the creek bed in the bottom of the canyon by mid-afternoon. Cattle had come down Bull Canyon, but Jacob hadn't see Maxwell follow them out, nor had he heard the familiar "whoop" from the old man that was his way when he was pushing cattle. By the time he and Johnny were within sight of each other, moving what they had gathered into one bunch to move them out of the mouth of the canyon, neither could find or see Maxwell.

"Can you take this bunch on down into the meadow below while I go look for the old man?" Jacob quizzed his young counterpart.

"Sure, I'll move slow, so you have time to catch up and help me get them through that gate below." Johnny pointed and nodded.

Jacob followed the fresh turned dirt left by the hooves of the gathered bunch until he reached the mouth of Bull Canyon where it fed into Cantle. He whistled long and loud, waited and listened for an answer. He urged his horse into a trot and continued to follow the freshly turned sod of the closest trail, stopping every quarter of a mile or so to whistle again. After about three miles of traveling upward on a hard trail he began hollering after each long whistle. Then his mount nickered, his head in the air, and Maxwell's horse returned the greeting. As Jacob rounded a bend in the trail, he caught site of Maxwell leaning back against a large boulder with his hat in his lap.

"You okay?" Jacob rode up and dismounted.

Maxwell looked up at him as though he wasn't sure who he was. "What's that?" he asked.

211

"I asked if you are okay." Jacob knelt down beside the old man, taking his hat from his hands. "You get bucked off or what?"

"I don't know. I can't remember so I musta' whacked my head on somethin'."

Jacob leaned over and looked carefully for signs of a bruise, bump or skinned spot. There was nothing within his sight, so he suggested, "Let's see if we can get you up. Think anything is broken?"

Maxwell grabbed his hand and pulled himself up, then staggered a little before he found his footing and reached for his hat. "I'm all right. Where's the cattle I had ahead of me?"

"Johnny's got 'em headed to the meadow, but he'll need help getting them through the gate, so if you can get aboard we best head that way."

"Hell yes, I can get aboard!" Maxwell fairly spit at him.

Jacob pulled in behind the old man and followed him out to catch up with the young cowboy. The trio pushed fifty-six head of cows with calves in tow through the gate and waited as the cows found their way to water.

Johnny looked at him with a question in his eyes, but Jacob only shook his head "no," and they continued toward the house. The sun was far behind the hills and the light was nearly gone when they rode in and unsaddled. Supper was ready, so they ate quickly and quietly, then he and Johnny moved on to the bunk-house. He decided to wait until morning to talk to Opal about the incident with her father, and see how he was doing in the morning.

"How old you think the old man is?" he asked Johnny as they readied for sleep.

"I don't know. I heard he was long toward his late eighties, but sometimes I think he's older than that, depending on the day and the work. He amazes me that at his age he's still going strong and works as hard as any man I know."

"Keep an eye on him, Johnny. I don't know what happened out

there today, but he wasn't himself when I got to him." He rolled over and closed his eyes hoping to catch up with sleep pretty quick.

***

For weeks the men rode daily, Maxwell in the lead, pointing, commanding, instructing. He surveyed his kingdom from his porch evenings as cattle milled in the holding pasture around the house. He marked it off in his mind before he went to bed every night.

With cattle gathered from the hills, they began branding, castrating and doctoring the herd. Then, returned them to their feeding ground in the high country to fatten and grow until fall. In a few weeks, the focus again turned to the horses, and Opal had taken back her territory as the head of the horse herd. Well, nearly. It seemed that her daughter was determined to share in that honor. Since Jacob had planted her little butt in her own little saddle the child was never far from the corrals and the horse herd.

Jacob watched with pleasure as this fearless child learned quickly and demanded her own way constantly. But in the demanding, her hands were gentle, and she never jerked her horse around or hit him. Now and then he would find his way to the corral or the pasture where Opal worked her horses and give hints and instruction to the curly-haired little moppet. She remembered everything Jacob told her, and within a few months Opal was able to let her be her own little master of ceremonies. And a ceremony it was for her, every morning, to saddle and ride.

Jacob wondered how long it would be till he'd be handed his walkin' papers. Spring works were drawing to a close, Johnny was riding the hills every day watching the cattle, checking for predators, making sure waters were full and cattle were moving where there was plenty of feed. Summer days were hot and full of flies and mosquitoes. Evenings were soft and filled with hours of pleasure taking meals and porch time with this family he had grown to love. Surely Maxwell wouldn't need him much longer.

He was glad, in a way. He'd become too attached to Willa for his own good. It was already going to be hard to ride away with that sweetness waving goodbye from the porch. Just thinking about it made him tear up and his throat get dry.

Then there was Opal. That, too, had become more than just "hired hand concern". He had come to a place of wanting to help her, not just work for her dad. He saw her pain, her lonliness, and each passing day it was more obvious that Maxwell wouldn't be able to do what he'd always done. Opal wasn't going to be able to do what she'd always done, either.

Somehow was there a way he could help her find a way around the cold love that was evident for all but the little child of her heart? She would never respond to him with more than acceptance, and even that was slight. Only since his gift to Willa had she begun to be polite and considerate. He watched her constantly, concerned for her safety and well being. Always from afar, never close enough to be pushed away and rejected. *Hell, I'm an old fool. She'll marry some day to someone like Matt Baker and I'll be standing around watching. I gotta get out'a here before that happens!*

That evening on the porch, as the sun disappeared to its nesting place, he broached the subject with Maxwell. "How much longer you figgerin' on keepin' me around?" he bluntly asked his boss.

"I don't know. I guess it depends on how long you're willing to work for what we been payin' you. It ain't much, that's for sure and certain." The reply was curt.

"But the food's sure good!" replied Jacob with a grin. Maxwell grunted a response.

They sat quietly, Maxwell seemed to forget what they were talking about, so Jacob brought it back around. "I can stay for what you're paying me as long as you need me, sir. But I don't want to take advantage of the situation either, and I reckon I better start figgerin' out where my next layover will end up."

"You just settle in at that bunkhouse. I'll tell you when I think you need to leave." Maxwell was in his usual "I'll run this outfit" mode. He rocked softly as they listened to the night birds and the soft voices of Opal and Willa singing through the evening household chores.

"Wonder how that girl finally got her head screwed around straight and decided to be a mother." Maxwell's gruff voice spoke of recognition in the changes that had come about.

"I think she was always a mother . . . and a good one at that." Jacob responded. "She just loves horses and bein' outdoors a hell of a lot more than bein' inside where she feels trapped. She was lookin' for a hole in the barn and bein' able to take Willa with her seemed to give her back that freedom."

"Yeah, I know," came the old man's response. "You're the king of the world since you had that little brainstorm." A hint of jealousy and resentment rose in his tone, and Jacob glanced to see what expression was holding his face.

Maxwell continued, "I would have bought her a saddle sooner or later, and a nice one at that. But not until she was about five." His voice held on to that strange note, and Jacob wasn't sure exactly how to respond. He made a mental note not to ride over his boss where the little one was concerned. *But hells bells, that old man don't seem to see much more than his cattle and this ranch. Maybe the horses. He don't seem to have much sense about what that little one might need beyond bed and board and her mother.*

He rose from his perch, looked into the eyes of the old rancher. "You can still buy her that saddle, but I'd make it sooner were I you." Jacob smiled, pinched the fire off the end of his cigarette, and made his way to the bunkhouse.

"I'll let you know when I'm ready for you to leave." Maxwell hollered after him.

Jacob smiled as he closed the door behind him. Finding an old, falling-apart book of poetry, he sat on his bed and read the lines in the light of a dirty lamp before he folded himself into bed.

It seemed the night was short-lived when the sun brought light to the world. When he set his feet on the floor he heard a buzzing sound that made him jerk his feet back up on the bed.

"Hey, Johnny!" he hollered. The younger cowboy mumbled, "What?"

"Hey Johnny! There's a dam' rattler in the house somewhere. You see him yet?"

Johnny came-to pretty fast with those words and grabbed for a pistol lying on his bedside table. "I can't see him . . . too dark yet.

Where you hear him at?" His voice became slightly high pitched.

"Not sure yet, he quit buzzin' when I pulled my feet back up on the bed. He sounded close though." Jacob began to bounce on his bunk hoping to stir up the critter again. The buzzing resumed and leaning to the edge of the bed he hollered across the room, "He's right here near the head of my bed . . . hell . . . how long you suppose he's been there? I been sleepin' right over the top of a dam' rattler all night." He hated snakes with a passion, and here was one less than a leap away from him.

"I'll get him!" Johnny squeaked as he came across the room, bent over, peering under the bed from a safe distance.

"What are you doin'?" asked Jacob. About that time Johnny aimed his gun and moved the barrel around aiming directly under the bed. "HEY, what the hell you doin'?" hollered Jacob.

BLAM! BLAM! Johnny shot off two shots so fast Jacob couldn't blink. The room filled with smoke, his ears rang and his eyes burned.

"GOT HIM!" yelled Johnny triumphantly. "I got the sneaky little sum'bich."

"I hope so after all that!" Jacob yelled back, reaching for his pants as he set his feet on the floor. "Now you take him out of here with that broom over in the corner and stay away from his head when you do."

"Hell, he ain't got not head no more!" Johnny laughed.

"Well get him out of here, no matter." Jacob finished dressing. "Then you can fix the holes you drilled in the floor or we'll have mice and all kinds of critters in here with us." He wanted out of the smoke filled room as fast as he could dress.

As he stepped out the door, he saw Maxwell headed from the main house as fast as his bowed and crippled up old body would carry him. "It's all right! Johnny just killed a rattler."

"In the house?" asked Maxwell as he walked up to Jacob.

"W-e-l-l-l . . . yeah." Jacob responded slowly, a grin making its way to his face. "I guess you could say that. He blew holes in the bugger that's for sure."

They watched Johnny leave the bunkhouse with a snake draped over the end of an old wispy broom. He was still in his socks, and had the broom stuck out as far away from him as it could possible get. Laugher rolled from the lips of both men, and for the first time since his wife passed, old Maxwell Redding laughed until his sides hurt.

Jacob turned to see tears rolling down the face of his old boss. He seemed to have released a dam of emotions that wouldn't stop rolling over the crest of the barrier that had built up for weeks. It really wasn't all that funny, but once the laughter started it seemed like it just kept coming all on its own.

Jacob put his hand on the old man's shoulder and laughed with him, until the flood of emotion eased off and they shook their heads at each other.

Johnny came back around the edge of the bunkhouse in his stocking feet. "What's so dam' funny? That bugger was nearly four feet long."

Maxwell took a deep breath and wiped his eyes. "You boys get cleaned up and come on up to the house. I bet Opal's got breakfast goin' by now." He turned and moved back toward his home, leaving his hired men to feed his horses. Age softened him, at least when it came to work load.

As Maxwell walked away, Jacob noticed he was a little un-steady on his pegs. Just before he reached the house, he stopped, wavered, then sat right down in the dirt.

Jacob ran to him, squatted down beside him. "What happened to you?"

Maxwell reached for his hand. "Help me up. I think I just got a little lop-sided is all."

Moving to the porch, carefully, Jacob sat the old man down in his chair. "You wait here and I'll get you some water." He moved into the kitchen where Opal was making coffee. "Your dad just sorta' fell down real easy like. I think he's okay now, but you better come take a look."

They moved quickly to the porch, he handed Maxwell the water, and Opal knelt beside his chair. "Dad, what happened? You okay?" She patted his hand.

"Stop poundin' on my hand!" He pulled away, stared at her for a moment, then drank the water slowly. When it was gone, he handed the glass to her and stared as though trying to figure out who she was. Jacob took the glass from her, and stepped back to lean against the porch railing, watching Maxwell carefully. It took quite a while for him to talk to Opal as though he remembered her. She helped him rise and suggested he might go to his room and rest for a while.

They walked together to the door of his room, and she watched his strange movements, like he was confused as to where he was. She turned toward Jacob with a question on her lips. He didn't respond, but walked to the kitchen and placed the glass on the edge of the counter. Picking up an empty cup he poured luke-warm coffee and moved to the table to find a seat. Opal sat across from him.

"What happened?" she asked cautiously. Her hands were fidgeting with a spoon she pulled out of the sugar bowl. Willa toddled out of the bedroom and climbed into her mother's lap, softly croon-ing, "J-a-a-a-a-cub."

He smiled at Willa, but responded to Opal. "I don't know for sure.

We were havin' a good laugh over Johnny killin' a snake in the bunkhouse and he was headed for the house. He didn't really fall, just kinda set himself down easy like. I think he's just really tired from the push to get works over and he's already fussing about fall works."

"A snake?" Opal shivered hard. "I hate those things somethin' awful."

"He's done for. Johnny made short work of him. Do you want me to go for the doctor, or send Johnny?"

"I'll ride into town later and talk to Doc. No sense makin' him ride out here. I think Dad's better but we'll see when he wakes up."

Her father slept well into two hours. It was rare that he would be found in bed while the sun was up. Jacob hitched up the buckboard and loaded Opal and Willa onto the seat and whacked the horses on the butt to see her off to town. He checked on Maxwell several times, but the old man wouldn't eat breakfast or dinner. He seemed to want to sit on the porch, and his gaze was locked onto the meadow below the house.

Opal returned sometime before noon, with Willa in her lap holding the reins and talking to the horses as though they could understand every word she said. She seemed content with her ability to control what was happening in her world, but responded quickly to Jacob's offer to help her down. He began unhitching the team, but Johnny came and motioned for him to go on up to the house. He finished the job then walked to the porch to wait with the others for a report from Opal.

She sat fidgeting with her gloves, then began the explanation. "The doctor wasn't very helpful, just came up with another excuse and explanation that even with all his education there were times he had no answers. Best explanation was what was called a 'stroke' of some kind or maybe Dad's heart was givin' him trouble." She bit her lip. "If he'll come to town soon, Doc will check him over better, meanwhile the facts are he's just getting old and things in his body are bound to be changing."

Johnny waited. Jacob stood quietly. Maxwell sneered.

"Just like a dam' sawbones. They don't know nothin' until we tell 'em somethin'. I'll go by and see him next time in town." He looked at Jacob, raised his finger in the air and pointed to the meadow. "You and Johnny ride out and check cattle in the lower pastures with what's left of the day. I think I'll sit here and enjoy the breeze. I might take a ride later today with Willa."

Opal shook her head and smiled. The pair moved toward the corrals where they took their time saddling up. They groomed carefully, swept out the floor of the saddle house and re-arranged the walls. They had no intention of trying to ride the lower pasture in what was left of the day, but they'd check cattle that were close.

***

Opal moved quickly around the kitchen, made some peanut butter sandwiches with left over pancakes, and threw a can of peaches in a separate canvas bag, then took them to the barn and handed them off to Johnny, watching while he tied them to the back of his saddle. "See you boys tonight."

Returning to the house she told Willa to read her Papa a story, then moved to the kitchen to start a yeast bread rising.

She stood at the window for a few moments as Jacob and Johnny long-trotted off through the meadow, headed in the direction of the lower pasture. She knew they weren't riding far.

She stirred the yeast and warm water, sugar, and eggs until smooth, then began working the soft brown wheat flour into the mix a cup at a time. Soon it was so sticky she had to pour it out of the bowl into a bed of more flour and continued working it and kneading it until it was spongy. She returned it to the bowl after wiping it with a heavy coat of lard then set the whole thing in the sun on the window sill, covering it with a damp piece of toweling.

A couple of hours would pass before she'd punch it down and let it rise again, then shape it and put it in the oven for supper.

Checking on Willa and her dad she swept the floors and wiped the dust off the top of things around the house. She kept herself busy, watching him carefully through the day. Willa tired of reading him a story and began making mud-pies in the front yard. The sun was setting when Jacob and Johnny returned and she called Willa inside, put her in the galvanized tub with about three inches of warm water and told her, "You wash off all that mud before you can eat supper."

Meanwhile she sliced left over roast into chunks and diced potatoes, throwing them into a sizzling skillet of bacon grease. She put the two loaves of bread she'd formed earlier into the oven, and made coffee. Jacob and Johnny came to the porch and sat to visit with her father until called to the table. It was a quiet meal, only a few sentences passed among the five.

It was early evening when she finished cleaning up, and her dad going to bed as soon as he finished eating surprised her. She tried to get Willa to bed, but she wasn't havin' any part of it. Opal found herself on the porch making up a story to the pages of the old primer when Jacob meandered back to the house from the corral.

"Your dad doing okay?" he asked softly. He leaned against the pillar that held the rickety porch roof, deftly rolling a Bull Durham in his fingers. The match lit up his face as she and Willa gazed up at the denim clad figure hovering over them.

"He seems better tonight. I'll try to get him to town in the next few days and have Doc look him over, but you know how easy that'll be." They both chuckled.

Jacob set himself down on the top step and said "Go on with your reading. Maybe Willa girl will fall asleep." He sat quietly smoking, listening to her story. When Willa did fall asleep, he lifted her gently and took her to her bed. Opal remained on the porch, her mind filled with mixed thoughts about this man she had once hated so deeply, and was coming to find such a god-send to her family. He was a handsome man, of that she was well aware. He set a horse like he was born there, and that was definitely a plus.

221

But he was so blasted bossy and opinionated, and he had to be at least ten years older than she.

Jacob walked past her to the top step, turned and smiled that crooked little grin. "See you in the morning." He stepped off the porch, and made his way to the bunkhouse. She watched him until the door closed behind him, then moved to her own room to carefully undress her sweet daughter and slide under a light cover. She slept.

***

The sun created a halo around the curly locks of her sweet child as it found a crack in the curtains. Opal lay watching her for a few moments before she rose to prepare breakfast. She rolled over and looked at a tattered calendar on the door of her little closet and realized it was first Sunday. The shepherd would be at the church today tending his little flock. She couldn't remember when she last made the effort to be in that number, but today she would take Willa and visit the old building that had served as her school and church for as long as she could remember. She thought of the night she "went forward" in that old church and prayed with an old circuit riding preacher, accepted Christ and settled where she would spend eternity. Now her mother was there, waiting. She realized she missed the singing, the reading of the Word, and found she was looking forward to the morning.

They swiftly consumed breakfast, and she bustled about with a purpose. She asked Johnny to hitch up the wagon for her, announcing she and Willa were going to church if anyone would like to come along. Waiting to see if there were any takers, she glanced sideways at her father. In years past he would have been anxious to accompany her. She remembered him as a praying man, a devout man, and one who frequently had conversations with his Lord. Since her mother passed that had become pretty hit and miss.

"How about you, Dad?" she asked. "You haven't been for a while, and there really isn't anything to do the boys can't handle."

He sat quietly, apparently mulling over his options. "Well, yes, I guess that would be a good idea. I'll help Johnny hitch and you and Willa get ready. Will you bring my Bible from the stand?"

"Gladly," she replied. She and Willa scooted off to their little room to prepare for the short trip to town. Willa laughed and clapped her chubby little hands knowing they were going to do something exciting.

Maxwell drove the wagon to the front of the house and hollered just as she was picking up his Bible from the desk in the corner. When she lifted it, she revealed a smaller one, lighter of color and more worn and frayed than that of her father's. She picked it up carefully . . . gently holding it as she lifted the cover. "Ophelia Redding" was scrawled across the first page. This was her grandmother's Bible. Why had she never seen it before? Laying it gently back on the desk she caught up with Willa who was on her way to the seat of the buckboard next to her Papa.

As they rumbled along the road Willa brought to their attention the appearance of every bird, rabbit, deer and critter. She talked about the clouds, the trees, and her own version of why the wind was blowing. Her vocabulary had grown rapidly once she discovered how to put together a sentence of sorts. Maxwell chuckled as she filled his morning with her childish wisdom and understanding.

"Dad, I noticed Gramma Redding's Bible on the desk this morning. I've never seen it before, didn't know you had it."

"Your mother kept it in her little box under the bed. I found it a few days ago and thought maybe Willa would like to have it some day. It's pretty old, and it won't last long with good use, but later on maybe she'd like to keep it."

His face seemed relaxed, softer. His words were loud enough to be heard over the creaking and rumblings of the wagon wheels, but still softly spoken.

"I think she'd like that, some day. Tell me about her?" The rest of the journey was taken up with family history that Opal had heard bits and pieces for years, but for some reason this morning it took on new meaning. Perhaps because now her own family history was being built around her father's memories as days passed too quickly. The conversation made for a short trip to the little church near the edge of town, and once there it was fun to catch up with local gossip and listen to their pastor's words of encouragement and hope. It seemed too soon they were on their way home in the heat of the day.

They were not far out of town when a rider loped along side and hailed the trio. "Howdy, Redding family!" called out a familiar voice. Opal recognized it before she turned to see his face.

"Morning, Matthew!" she called back.

Willa chimed in, "Hullo, Mattie."

She realized she hadn't seen her friend of old for weeks. She'd missed his smiling face and boyish ways. "You headed home or got time to come by the house for dinner?"

"Hey . . . that sounds great! Haven't seen you in a while, so it'll be good to have some time with you all. Willa . . . you wanna ride with me?" He reached for her to join him.

"No . . . I like Rowdy." She replied peeking around her mother's shoulder.

"Who's Rowdy?" he asked.

"My horse." She proudly announced with a flourish of her hand to her heart. She laughed and waved as he fell behind the wagon and followed them the remaining miles to their home. Now and then Opal would observe Willa glancing backward to wave at him again. He'd tip his hat and wave back, flirting with her like a kid. Opal had to laugh at the two, thinking how boyish Matthew remained after all these years.

They rumbled into the yard where her dad whoa'd the horses to let her and Willa out of the wagon. She quickly moved Willa out of the way and into the house where she began putting together a light lunch for six.

The meal was enjoyed over lively discussion about the neighbors and who was working for who this year. Which of the hands from Mr. Mitchell's ranch were still hired on and who had moved to greener pastures for the summer. How many bones had been broken during the spring works and who had been bucked off and busted up. Opal loved this kind of a visit, and she devoured his words like honey on a warm slice of yeast bread. Hours passed, they moved from the house to the porch and enjoyed Willa making her famous mud pies to serve up on wood planks with sticks for forks and sprigs of leaves for garnish.

As much as Opal enjoyed Matt's visit, she noticed he still was not willing to interact with Willa much beyond being a bit flirtatious. When she brought him his mud pies he waved them off and made a face. His focus was on her rather than Willa, which made her feel appreciated, but to love her had to be all inclusive with love for her daughter. Matt's kind of love was still full of his own existence more than that of her family. *He hasn't grown up much, in spite of the months gone by.* But it was good to laugh with him and hear his crazy stories.

He and Johnny shared the same interests, many of the same friends, and Johnny was very interested in the tales of triumph during spring works. The Redding household was pretty simple, and the work was done with little "cowboy panache." Her father worked hard to keep their horses from bucking, while these young cowboys liked to brag about the ones that did. Her father worked his cattle easy and carefully, the young ones liked the dash of the chase and the adrenalin rush of "roping a wild one."

Maxwell and Jacob had wandered down to the corrals and stood at the gate into the horse pasture, talking. Her interest shifted to their stance, and she wondered what they were discussing. She gathered up Willa and moved their way, leaving the two young cowboys to discuss their fearless deeds. Willa ran ahead and Opal's heart swelled as Jacob turned to greet the little scamp and lifted her to the top rail of the fence, and began to chat with her.

They talked about the color of the horses, how many cows had horns, and especially where Rowdy was this evening. Opal stood next to her father listening to the child's prattle and Jacob's kindly responses. Again, she found herself with conflicted emotions where this man was concerned.

Her father leaned against the corral fence a little heavier than usual, and seemed to be drifting in his portion of the conversation. She watched him, listened to his voice, and quickly realized he was not "tracking" through the visit. "Dad, would you like to go back up to the house?" she asked gently.

"No. I'm fine right here, girl. You go to the house if you want to." His voice was terse and his not-so-subtle way demanded her departure.

"Come Willa, let's go have a snack." She reached for her daughter who immediately responded with a resounding "NO."

"Yes, ma'am, you little scamp!" Jacob took the little girl off the fence. He set her on the ground and patting her on the bottom, scooted her homeward. "Go on now."

Bedtime was always a bit of a chore, Willa never wanted to turn in unless she was just so tired her little legs wouldn't mo-tate another step. By the time they reached the porch, she was more interested in chatting with Matt and Johnny, who were still swapping stories about their prowess on the range. Opal sat to listen, but tired quickly of the braggadocio that was getting knee deep. She tried to change the subject, but both younger men were deeply engrossed in impressing one another, so she moved inside to her father's desk and began shuffling papers and receipts.

She hadn't spent much time trying to understand much about the business end of ranching, but now she was trying to learn. Her father's frequent confusion and propensity to drift off in his thoughts at strange times was bothering her. If he was indeed losing his faculties and ability to connect his thoughts and function as the leader of the outfit, she had to figure it out quickly.

She wished she'd paid more attention to the intricacies of the business rather than believe she could spend her life riding horses and helping with cattle now and then. She lit a lamp and set it on the table before her as the light waned and the shadows filled the corners of this long room she had grown up in. Well, she wouldn't worry about it any more tonight.

She moved to the porch to find Willa had wandered away. "Where is Willa?" she asked Matt and Johnny. She quickly stepped to the edge of the porch, scanning the immediate area.

"Don't know," responded both boys at the same time. "She was here a while ago."

Opal's heart was racing as she ran down the steps, moving quickly to the corral. "You two search around the house," she hollered back at the pair on the porch. If Willa had any opportunities to visit the horses that would be her first choice. She hollered at her dad and Jacob, "Is Willa down there with you?"

Both men immediately turned and seeing what was unfolding they split up and went separate ways in search of the wandering waif. Matt and Johnny joined the search by moving around the house in two directions. Opal's heart pounded in her ears, a million places Willa could get into trouble flashed before her eyes, each one bringing more concern.

"She's here!" shouted Jacob. Sure enough, she had found her way back to the corral and wormed her way through the fence to the holding pasture where she was scratching Rowdy's legs and the bottom of his belly. "I have her," he called to Opal.

She waited near the gate as the older cowboy made his way through the grass with Willa in tow. Here, again, was this gratitude and appreciation rising up within her when she really wanted to dislike this man. It was getting harder.

"You little stinker!" She gathered the little one into her arms. "You scared me. You cannot go to the barn without me, do you understand?"

Willa did not respond, but peeked at Jacob over her mother's shoulder, waving goodbye as they moved back to the house.

Johnny had taken this event to heart and was headed for the bunkhouse, passing her on his way. "Sorry about that, Opal." His face was red and he ducked his head, unable to look her in the eyes. She shook her head and walked on.

Matt was unimpressed at the occurrence, and followed her inside as she began to ready the child for bed. He followed her from place to place as she washed Willa's hands and face, then her little feet. She pulled her night shirt on while he chatted on about things she was tired of hearing. Willa asked him to read her a story, but he had no idea how to use the primer as a lead-in for making up stories for the child. He was reading line-by-line the reading lessons held in the pages of the old book, and she tired of that quickly. It wasn't long before her little eyes closed in sleep and he slipped her into her room and pulled the door behind him.

Opal moved onto the porch, watching for her father who was seated on an old bench by the door of the barn. She sat in a rickety chair to keep an eye on him. Matt moved a chair for himself quite close to her arm and leaning forward began to talk to her in a manner she was surprised to find quiet offensive.

"Opal, when are you going to give me a chance to come courting? I've been patient and tried to give you time to forget Will."

"I will never forget Will." Her voice took on a tone of irritation, and she leaned to the other side of her chair, trying to buy some space between them. *You are such an idiot . . . how could I ever forget the father of my child, the man I loved and married.*

"You know what I mean . . . I'll never forget Will either, but I'm talking about letting another man into your life. Willa's near two years old, and your dad doesn't seem to be holding his own too well. You're going to have more than you can handle here before long." He leaned back in his chair.

"Willa's closer to three, Matt, and we're doing fine with what help we have." She tried to be polite, but her anger was rising at his purely selfish words. She began to drum her fingers on the arm of the chair.

"What? That old grub line rider and Johnny? Why, neither one of them can hold a candle what I can do for you. You know I've got the goods when it comes to cattle and horses."

"I know you think you do! Criminy, Matt, you're pretty high on yourself these days." Her disgust was evident in her voice and she leaned forward to put her hands on her knees. "I'm going down to get Dad."

228

"I'll go with you. I guess I better get my horse and head for Mitchells. You know there's talk he's going to move me to the foreman's position before long."

"Good for you." She wanted him to leave sooner, so she started down the old steps off the porch. She was surprised when he placed himself directly in front of her, just below. He reached up and caught her in his arms, pulling her toward him. There was no tenderness, no gentle touch or soft words . . . he just tried to kiss her lips in his rough, unyielding manner. She pushed him away, hard, and he stumbled backwards down the steps to teeter as his boots hit the dirt.

"Hey, hold on, Opal . . . what'ja do that for?" His expression was one of great surprise, as though he simply could not believe she wasn't thrilled at his advances. She nearly laughed, but caught herself quickly. She didn't want to hurt his feelings, she just wanted him to leave.

"Aw Matt, you know I ain't ready for that kinda stuff." She forced a laugh and bounced down the steps past him and they moved to the barn together. He saddled a horse as she convinced her father he should retire to the house since Jacob and Johnny had gone to the bunkhouse. Leading his horse Matt walked beside them to the hitching post where he very politely told her good-bye.

She went inside, watching as he stood at the rail for a long time after they left him. Was he actually waiting and watching to see if she would return? He mounted and headed home as the shadows lengthened and the big yellow moon began to rise over the horizon lending him the light he needed to ride by.

"Goober should have left a long time ago," she said out loud. Why couldn't she find it in her heart to love this childhood friend? He was a great guy! She thought he probably loved her in his own way, and he'd certainly tried to convince her of that many times. *But he's still such a child . . . so full of himself.* Yet it was more than that.

She watched as the light in the bunkhouse window faded and darkness filled the earth except for the light of that big old moon. "Hope he gets home all right," she mumbled as she lifted her own lamp and moved to the door of her father's room to be sure he was in bed. He was snoring softly.

She sat for a long time on top of the quilt that covered her curly-haired little tot, reading by lamplight through the pages of her old worn Bible. Her eyes were tired, so she turned out the lamp and lay next to her daughter. She had been so frightened when she realized the little scamp had dis-appeared. She fell asleep thinking she must keep a closer watch on the toddler.

*****

Jacob lay quiet on his bunk long after the lamp faded. A plain face with dark brown eyes and mud colored hair filled his mind making him restless. Along with hers, came the sweetness of a very small face framed in light brown hair with even lighter wisps strewn throughout the curls that were surely there naturally. The pair seemed to dance through the air above him, catching his attention then alternately disappearing in their laughter. Sometimes it seemed to mock him, others it was a soft, gentle smile with wanton eyes. He fell asleep to dream of holding the older one in his arms as he had the younger at times. But she would turn to a wisp of wind and be gone before he could touch her hair with his lips.

He woke unrested to the morning light drifting through a dirty bunkhouse window. Lying still, he tried to digest his dream and decide why he was bold enough to have those thoughts. Dust fragments floated through the air like white stars finding their way to earth.

"Dammit." He expounded as he threw back the covers and planted both feet on the ground.

"Johnny! Johnny, get up, you lazy bum! This bunkhouse is filthy . . . don't you go to bed tonight until it's clean, mopped and dusted, you hear me?"

"Uh huh . . . mmmmm . . ." Johnny responded sleepily. "What's in your craw this morning? Why don't you clean it yourself?"

"I have things to do and won't be here at all today. You won't be riding this morning, so get it done." Jacob pulled his pants on, stepped out the back door and walked to the little shed on the far end of the corrals, then returned to complete his ablutions and readied himself to be somewhere all day where he would not have to see those faces again. "Tell the boss I'm going to town and will be back sometime before dark. You keep an eye on things and don't let that baby girl out of your sight, understand? She's gonna' get in trouble if she gets a chance."

"You're a bossy bugger this morning!" Johnny threw back at him making a mock-angry face.

Leaving the bunkhouse he made his way to the corrals to morral the horses and throw hay out. He stood watching them shake the contents around while he took a small white sheet of thin paper from the side pocket of his Bull Durham sack. He shaped it into a long cup, then pulled the gathered top of the pouch, opened it and poured a line of tobacco into the trough. He placed the orange string between his teeth and pulled the drawstring tight, slipping the pouch back in the left pocket of his denim shirt. Rolling the paper around the trough of tobacco, he licked it from top to bottom, and sealed it with his fingers. Pinching off one end, he placed the other in his lips and struck a match on the leg of his pants with one swift, strong motion, lighting his cigarette and taking a deep breath. He realized that was the first deep breath he'd taken since he woke up. Blowing the blue smoke through his nostrils and narrowly opened lips he took a few moments to enjoy the pleasure of what was unfolding.

When the horses were nearly finished, he carefully chose one who'd been rested for a few days and led him to the saddle house. He wiped him down well with the edge of a used up shoeing rasp, then a piece of old saddle blanket. He removed the morral, placed the bridle, saddled, turned him around a few times. Gathering his reins in his left hand he set his foot in the stirrup, pulled himself up in one smooth motion, settled in the seat to see if the horse would hump. He stood quiet.

Jacob watched the window near the kitchen of the house above the barn, waiting for a quick glance at a shaggy little head moving around. Shaking himself, he turned and after walking a short distance, broke into a trot, and eventually a lope as he headed for town. The swinging doors on a certain saloon were calling his name. He'd have breakfast at the little café, pick up some things at the mercantile, then find someone to talk to that would fill his mind with something other than visions from his dreams. Maybe he'd stop by and gab with the doctor for a spell and see if he could pick up information about Maxwell's condition before returning late this evening.

The day moved slowly, dragging the minutes across the hands of a clock like a sore leg. A soft storm was moving into the valley, heady and sweet with the fragrance of grass and trees growing wet with a cool breeze fanning drops of heavenly dew blowing into place. He found the doctor at home not long after he finished breakfast in the small café and began to quiz him, explaining what was happening to the old rancher.

"Just old age, I reckon," was the short answer. The longer version was that he would probably become more and more forgetful as the days passed and the progression of his mental state could cause him to have long periods of time lapse. He could begin to forget where he was.

Jacob ate a slab of bread and bowl of soup for dinner before he made his way to the saloon. He spent some time visiting with the sheriff over a beer and a shot glass, but most of the day was taken up watching young Matt Baker drink too much and brag too hard as he leaned on the bar for most of an afternoon. Jacob wondered if this kid would ever grow up enough to become the man Opal needed.

From where he was sitting, he wasn't much of a man to settle into raising a family. He might be able to pull off the cattle end of the ranch, but he sure wasn't going to be able to do much to help Opal with the horses. But the worst part was he didn't seem to care much about little Willa.

Jacob rode up to the hitching rail near the barn as the sun was lowering itself over the tree tops on the mesa. Still too much daylight to hit the hay, but he sure wasn't wanting to go to the house and watch Opal fixing supper. He could hear Willa singing and chattering to her mother through the open kitchen window. *Should'a stayed in town a while longer.*

Johnny was gone . . . no tellin' where he was off to, but Opal would know. He reluctantly walked to the house and knocked. He heard Willa's little boots tapping on the floor as she ran to open the door. He waited to see her little face peek through the opening.

"J-a-a-a-c-u-b." She spoke his name lovingly, and the word left her mouth with a laugh that stopped his heart for a full second. *How the hell am I ever gonna' leave this place?*

He stepped inside, removed his hat and waited for Opal's face to appear in the kitchen doorway. When it did, he held his breath for a moment.

"Hey . . . where you been all day?" she queried. Willa made her way into her grandfather's bedroom and began playing with an old chess set he kept in a drawer.

"I didn't realize your dad played chess," he commented.

"He hasn't for years. Not many people do these days. You play?"

"No. Never learned. I've been in town. I had some things needed doin' and I wanted to talk to the doctor. I been worried about your dad. Where is he?" He fiddled with the brim of his hat while he spoke.

"He and Johnny rode out this morning not long after you left. I didn't think they were riding today, but he had something on his mind. Didn't take lunch and didn't say where they were going either."

"Dammit." He looked at her face for signs of worry, and found them quickly. "We need to talk about your dad and what the doc told me, when you get time."

"I got time. I can't do more for supper until they ride in. Let's sit on the porch. Willa, you come with Mama and Jacob."

"I playing here," she responded.

233

Opal smiled at her and stepped out on the porch where she leaned against the wall of the building. Leaning her head back on the log behind her she took a deep breath, closed her eyes and stood quietly as though the day had been far too long.

The rain had moved up the valley, drizzling across the meadow, dripping off the edge of the porch in un-frozen   icicles. Her face softened, an ease moved across her features in a way he'd never seen before . . . calm, for the first time. She breathed in deep, held her breath and a smile brushed her lips.

He watched her face change, soften, and didn't have the heart to speak of her father. It was a needed time for her, a moment in her life to breathe and be still. She needed more time like this one, less of the sorrow and strife. He couldn't bring himself to speak . . . he wanted to see her like this forever.

The urge came over him like a wave of heat, and without realizing fully what he was doing, before he could stop himself, he moved as close to her as he dared. He stood over her, looking down onto that common face that he had come to love so secretly. She opened her eyes, startled at first, then questioning his as though silently asking, *What?*

Reaching out, he put his arms around her waist and pulled her gently to him. Moving one hand to her face he pushed the damp curls away from her eyes and tucked then behind her ear. The expression on her face changed, for just a second she looked like a startled deer about to break and run, but that melted away, and for just a moment he was sure she leaned into his chest.

He pulled her face to him, and as if to taste something forbidden and sweet he set his lips on hers and began to savor what he had only imagined for months. She melted into him, and he felt her warm body pressed against his, stirring emotions he wasn't used to dealing with. He wanted to pull away, but just as strongly as the desire had pushed him to her, it held him there, wanting more. He felt her longing, tenderly reaching out to engulf him, pull him closer than he dared to dream possible and hold him with a wisp of breath. Her breath smelled sweet, her hair soft, her body next to his set him on fire with wanting her. He jerked away suddenly, knowing if he didn't stop, he never could.

234

It was now going to be impossible for either of them to turn back to the way things were. Life would never be the same for either of them. He drew back a full step away, watching her gaze into his eyes, questioning him. What was she asking? What had he done? *Oh God, what have I done? What now?*

His eyes remained downcast as he spoke. "I'd say I'm sorry, but I can't, Opal. I've thought of nothing else for weeks. I ain't got words to say how I've come to love you and that baby girl in there, more than I've ever cared about anything or anyone in my life. I know you could never love me, never want me to be part of your life, but I had to do that, once. Just once." He turned and leaped down the steps as though he was running from his own heartbeat.

He heard her voice calling him, but he found his way back to the corrals, to his horse, to his saddle, and rode hard away from the haunting cry of her voice in the wind. Was it real? Did he only hear her call his name because he wanted to so badly? He hit his horse on the rump with his reins and kept going . . . going . . . with no purpose but to get as far away as he could.

Opal's heart raced as Jacob released her. She couldn't hear what he was saying for the ringing in her ears and the pounding of her heart. She stood looking up at this man speaking to her with tears in his eyes. He'd kissed her . . . and she'd kissed him back. Her neck was still warm with the flush of her thoughts as she relived the feeling of him pressed against her. She was reaching to draw him close again when he turned and vaulted down the stairs. What had he said to her? She called his name, hollered at him to come back.

Frightened with her mother's raised voice, Willa cried out for her to come. She turned halfway to look toward her daughter, then realized she had no choice. *I'll go talk to him later.* She went inside to calm Willa and they moved to the kitchen to prepare the evening meal.

She saw Jacob through the window that faced the barn. He was riding away, but surely he would return. She had trouble thinking . . . what went into biscuits? Had she added the baking powder or the salt? She was shaky, and her heart beat faster than usual.

Jacob did not return for dinner, nor did he ride in before they all retired. She lay in bed thinking about his touch, but more the expression on his face when he had pulled away. It was like he was scared she was going to let him have a piece of her mind. He couldn't have known all she wanted was more. Why had he kept going when she called after him? Sleep was meager, and she rose tired and worn in the morning hours. She watched from the window as Johnny fed the horses, but there was no sign of Jacob.

It was hours later, and dark had settled on the land with only a light from the moon to help Jacob find his way back to the ranch. He quietly found his way through the woods and across the pasture. He located the familiar hitching rail near the saddle house, tied his horse and moved into the bunkhouse. He opened the door slowly so as not to wake Johnny. He rolled his bedroll, winding up clean shirts and clothes, his possibles and his few belongings.

"Where you goin'?" came the voice from the dark. Johnny raised up on his elbow and waited for an answer.

Jacob leaned forward on his hands, allowing the bed to support his weight. "I don't know. I just have to leave this place."

"Yeah, I figured it wouldn't be much longer. She gets a hold of your heart pretty quick, doesn't she?"

Jacob turned and smiled in the dark, knowing Johnny was saying in his own way that he, too, was taken by the sweetness and spice that lingered in this family.

"She's dam' irritating," went on the voice in the dark. "But she gets under your skin in a sweet way too, huh? So, where will you go from here?"

"I don't know. I'll send word somehow. Keep in touch, let me know how things go for them. And for hell's sake keep an eye on the old man. He's fading, and she'll need you."

"Aw, I'm way too young, and nothin' she'd wanna take up with. Maybe Matt will win her over sometime." The voice was sad now.

"Hell . . . that could take years. You stay on here and be the man you know you can be. Just be her friend and watch over them if

236

you can." Jacob gathered his belongings and sneaked back out the door. His throat was tight, and his chest hurt. Was he doing the right thing? *How the hell could I ever face her again after what I done?*

***

Jacob rode in the moonlight toward town and found a place to tether his horse near the stables. Making his way inside, he pushed a pile of straw together and lay on his back staring at the board walls. He did not sleep.

Morning found him already up, his horse fed and moved into the stable. He walked to the little café and waited on a bench in the sunlight for the door to open. Coffee and breakfast were what he needed for now. Later he walked for what seemed like hours, up and down the streets, only to find it wasn't near noon when he stopped back in for another cup of coffee.

"Back already?" the waitress asked politely.

"Yeah . . . that okay with you?" he asked curtly.

"Sorry, just asking." She poured the coffee and left abruptly.

"Bring me a piece of that pie on the shelf when you come back," he instructed as she made her way to the stove.

"Sure thing." Without waiting, she placed the pie carefully on a small saucer and returned to the table to drop it unceremoniously in front of him. "Let me know when you need more coffee."

"Hey . . . I'm sorry. I didn't mean to be rude. It's just been a short night."

"No need to . . . well . . . enjoy your pie. Like I said, let me know when you need more coffee."

He finished quickly, left more than enough to pay for the food, and

237

placing his hat on his head and retreated to the saloon across the street. To his concern, he found young Matt leaning on the bar holding court again.

Jacob ordered a beer across the counter, paid and lifted it to carry to a table in the corner where the light didn't often find its way. Quietly, he watched and listened to the brass of the young man who seemed to be completely oblivious to his presence. It wasn't long until his conversation turned to a certain young widow.

Jacob sat up and leaned forward on the table, setting his empty beer mug in front of him. He ran his finger around and around the glass circle that surrounded what was only a scum of foam. He played with the handle trying to control his irritation at the young cowboy discussing his personal relationship with Opal in a place like this.

"Well, sometime soon I'm going to hold her feet to the fire and make her decide if I'm going to be livin' out there takin' Will's place or if she's just gonna be a lonely widow for the rest of her life." He pulled his hat off his head, then set it back cocked to one side. "She keeps bein' snooty to me and she'll end up buryin' her dad and losing that whole outfit." His words were slurred, loud and brash.

Jacob stood to his feet, then stepped back against the wall, trying to control the rage rising in his guts. He didn't hear what followed. The voice either became lower or the ringing in his ears was too loud. He was just about to find the door and leave before he did something he would regret when the words became loud and clear.

"That old man they hired on better load up his gear and head out pronto. He's been there long enough, and when I'm bossin' that outfit, him and that Johnny kid are going to be down the road at my say-so that's for sure." Matt swigged down a shot glass of whiskey and followed it with beer.

As Jacob walked slowly up behind him, the expressions changed drastically on the face of the younger men looking his direction. They backed away from Matthew, who slowly turned toward Jacob with a shocked expression on his face.

"Didn't you see me sit down over there when I came in?" Jacob asked him low and menacingly.

"Hell no . . . what do I care what you do?" replied Matthew.

"I think the two of us need to step outside. I have a few things I'd like to say to you, but this isn't the place to have that discussion."

"I got nothin' to say to you except it's about time you pack-ed up and got the hell off the Redding place," Matt countered. He leaned forward, his voice came up, and his eyes squinted nearly closed. "You got no reason to be out there anymore, and when I get right with Opal you're gonna' be gone any-way, so may as well make it today."

Jacob grabbed him by the forearm, twisting it behind his back so fast Matthew didn't know what happened. "HEY! Let go a me!" he hollered.

"OUTSIDE," commanded Jacob as he shoved the him to the door with his free arm flailing about, moving him toward the back entrance.

Once they'd left the building, he released Matt who spun to face him with a snarl, and vulgarity spewing from his lips ending with, "Who the hell you think you are?"

"I'll tell you who I ain't. I ain't your patsy and you better shut up and listen to what I have to say." Jacob spoke low, but with a stern resolve that should have given Matt warning, but he did not take heed. Instead, he came at Jacob swinging like a lopsided windmill. Jacob warded the blows easily, pushing him away.

"Stop it, Matt. *Listen to me.*"

But the younger man kept coming at him over and over until he finally connected a glancing blow to the chin, causing Jacob to lurch backward. As he struggled to pull himself upright, Matt hit him in the midsection with his head and smashed him into the wall behind.

A ball of fire blew up between Jacob's ears, and within seconds he'd popped Matt several times in the jaw and across his left ear hard enough to cause him to stagger backwards and fall to the ground. Matt reached for a gun that wasn't there. "I'll kill you, you old son-of-a ... " He realized his nose was gushing blood, wiped his mouth with the back of his hand.

Jacob walked to him, placing a foot on either side of Matt's knees. He stood above him like a towering volcano about to explode. "Shut up and listen, you little jackass. I left yesterday, but if you keep acting like an overgrown kid with no brains you'll never win her. She's more woman than you'll ever deserve, but if you go at it like you should, you just might get where you want to be out there."

He took two steps back, pointing a finger at the bleeding, filthy young man before him.

"I'm tellin' you it's time to be more concerned about what's happening to her and that baby than what's going on in your mealy little brain." He paused, looked down at the young cowboy then stepped back. "Hell . . . you ain't got it in you, you sorry little dip-wad."

He turned and strode to the stables where he saddled his horse, and rode out of town headed south at a fast trot. He didn't slow down except to breathe his horse until he was well on his way toward the next town.

***

Persistently Opal asked about the missing face at the table.

Johnny sat eating breakfast, trying hard to ignore her questions. "I don't know where he went, he pulled out in the middle of the night, but took his own horse and all his possibles." He continued to eat as though he was avoiding her questions.

"Did he say if he was coming back?" she asked. She sat perfectly still, staring at Johnny, afraid of what he was about to say.

"He didn't tell me. But sounded to me like he was pullin' stakes and I wouldn't be lookin' fer him to ride up to the porch any time soon."

She rose quickly and walked to the kitchen counter, placing her plate and cup in the wash bin of cooling water. She felt strangely lonesome. Would he really leave her now? Could he walk away from what had happened between them and leave her to deal with her father, Willa, the ranch, and all that was ahead of them now? Then again, why should he stay? She had never even been more than polite to him, and certainly had been rude and unkind more than once. But hadn't he noticed she was softening, she didn't avoid him, that she had been staying closer to him as he moved around the ranch?

"I have to ride into town, Johnny. If I leave Willa here with you and Dad will you promise to keep an eye on her and not let her get away from you?"

"What if your dad wants me to do something?" he asked through a mouth full of food.

"Tell him I said you have to stay with Willa. If he pushes, just take her for a walk and he'll forget what he told you before long. I'll be home as soon as I can."

She grabbed her hat and gloves on the way out the door and paused on the porch. Maybe she could still catch him if she hurried.

Her father yelled at her from his room. "HEY . . . you come back here. Johnny and I have work to do and you ain't leavin' Willa here with us."

"Dad, I have to ride to town. Please stay here with her until I get home. I'll hurry, I promise."

"Nope. Johnny you go saddle up. We got two sick cows up below the rim and they won't wait. Gotta get to them before it gets too hot. You can go to town when we get back." He pushed her out of the doorway, and planting his hat, he walked to the barn where he caught up two horses and saddled his own. He hollered at Johnny to hurry.

241

She wanted to scream. Slamming her gloves on the table, she watched Johnny shove what was left of his pancakes in his mouth and moved to put his plate in the wash pan. Willa was cleaning up her meal and prattled at her mother.

"Go outside. Ride Rowdy." Willa told her mother around what was left of her morning pancakes.

"Maybe later, baby girl." She could saddle up their mounts and take Willa with her. That might be best anyway . . . she did hold some sway with Jacob.

She finished cleaning up, dressed Willa in long pants and tie shoes and put her little boots on a shelf in the bedroom. Suddenly she wasn't in such a hurry. What would she say to Jacob if she did find him in town? Would she beg him to come home? Would he feel it was home if she was able to talk with him? Maybe she should wait for him to return, then see what happened.

She paced the porch like a kitten in a cage looking for a way out. They did the household chores, gathered the eggs and fed the livestock. She glanced toward the road constantly, searching the distance for the familiar seat of the rider.

Johnny and her father rode in mid-afternoon, and she cornered Johnny as he made his way to the bunkhouse. "I have to ride in to town to see if I can find him," she begged. "Please stay with Willa and I'll ride fast as I can."

"Go ahead . . . I don't think you'll find him, but you prob'ly gotta try." He shook his head at her and walked to the house where he gathered Willa by the hand, and they began a walk around the barn and toward the pastures.

She threw a saddle on one of her young horses, walked him to the house to find her hat and gloves, and tied the colt to the rail. She didn't say anything to her father as she pulled her hat down and left the house. She mounted and rode out at an easy lope. She wasn't far out of town when she saw Matthew riding up the road toward her. He pulled up then turned off the road and rode out through the trees. *That's strange. What gives with him?* She shrugged it off, knowing he had been acting strange for quite some time. *I wonder if he's ever going to grow up.*

It was hours before she found someone who told her Jacob had ridden out earlier in the day, after he and Matthew had it out behind the saloon. They wouldn't tell her the why of it, just that Jacob left early and Matt had ridden out not long before she arrived in town. Frustration set in, and some anger that her father hadn't been cooperative in letting her ride in earlier.

There was no sense riding after Jacob, he could be miles away by now. She would have to wait and hope he would return. The trip home was filled with regrets and wishes she had been kinder, more hospitable at the very least. He might never return. She faced her fears with heartfelt sorrow. She was riding a wave of emotions, knowing she loved this old rider, and if he never returned it would be a great loss to her family.

The days that followed were filled with the rise and fall of her emotions, Willa's questions about where Jacob was, and her father's anger over losing his hired help. He frequently chided her for being the cause of his worries. A deep sadness settled on her, much like the weeks that followed the loss of Will. Her heart ached deep within her chest and tears found their way to her eyes in spite of her desire to keep them at bay.

Summer seemed longer to her than ever in her life. She watched the mail for a letter, and frequently found her heart beating faster when anyone rode to the house. She raged with jealousy when Johnny received a letter from Jacob in late July. "Where is he?" she asked.

"There's no return address, he just says for me to take good care of you an' the baby, and keep an eye on your dad."

Her heart ached for the sight of him, yet she suffered pangs of anger at his leaving when she needed him so. It was nothing new for her to play mental ping-pong with emotions of anger, fear, resentment, love, passionate need, and some she had no name for. It was no surprise, their relationship had been that way for months.

End of summer meant more work, and her dad finally admitted it was time for him to turn the fall works over to her. They hired a second rider and Johnny was of great value to her in those days.

As far as she was concerned, he could stay forever . . . and she told him so.

Maxwell stayed at the house with Willa, and they hired an old Mexican woman to come during the day and cook and clean. Opal could have accomplished both ends of the duty roster, but she was happy to have someone else doing the house-work, and they needed someone with Willa and her grandfather.

The toddler stayed mad at her mother through most of the fall works, standing on the porch every morning when they left, screaming she wanted to go too. Opal let her ride with them when they worked pastures close to the ranch house, but the little one was not satisfied with anything less than being horseback with her mother.

When they went to town, Maxwell drove the buckboard with Willa and Opal following horseback. Willa would accept nothing less. She was becoming very obstinate and single minded, and Opal had no idea in the world how to alter that course.

Maxwell said, "She needs a good whuppin'. That's all she needs." But Opal didn't have the heart to be the one to do it, nor did Maxwell.

Winter set in early, and snow covered the hills with a thick blanket of all that was precious to the land and the water supply. At the advice of older ranchers, and her father when he was lucid, Opal sold most of the cattle, culling all the ancient ones her dad had kept because they still had a calf every year.

Calves were fat, most of the cows were holding their own, and she had a buyer who was willing to pay the best price they'd ever been offered. She kept the younger cows, and had planned to buy good heifers, but now was glad she waited. They had to bring everything out of the high country to keep them from being buried in the gigantic snow drifts that filled the canyons. Keeping them in lower meadows meant they would eat off the grass, and could lose weight this winter when the feed was low or maybe even gone.

The bulls her father was so very proud of stayed on, even though she knew she would have to sell them within a few years. They were tough, used to the rough terrain, and managed to cover the cows well. But they were getting old, and she wanted to replace them when the time came.

Johnny had asked for some time off when the works were over, and was gone visiting relatives somewhere a train would take him. It was lonely without him, and early morning chores were cold and miserable. Willa was restless and cranky when she wasn't allowed to go outside. Opal took her along to do evening chores, but the bitter cold of morning was too much for the toddler.

November came softly, quietly, and Opal began to think about Christmas. She wanted this year to be special for Willa. Things were so different this year from last. Gramma was gone, Jacob was gone, her grandfather was not himself. What could she do that would set this year apart? This was new territory for her, something her mother would have planned and taken care of. This would require her to reach into her past and recall things her mother had done for her. Hand-made dolls she'd left out in the yard, dresses she wouldn't wear, ribbons for her hair that were still in a pile in the top drawer of her dresser. That wouldn't do for Willa . . . so what now?

The snow melted during daylight hours, the roads became nearly impassible with mud. She and Willa rode to town more often, leaving the buckboard to avoid pulling through the muck. But early December meant the buckboard had to go in as they were low on supplies, and she hoped there would be something at the mercantile that she could tuck away for Willa's "under the tree" gift.

Johnny was home, settled back in the bunkhouse and had taken over the chores that had to be accomplished in the freezing wind and blowing snow. She was thankful beyond words for this young man who was turning into such a blessed help.

They had finished up breakfast one of those cold mornings when she instructed him, "Would you hitch up the team for me this morning? I really have to get into town, and if we go in on the freeze and get home before noon we might not have so much trouble getting the wagon through the mud. I'd like it if you'd drive all of us in this morning, as I don't want Willa horseback in the mud coming home, either."

They bounced along the frozen ruts when Matthew loped up behind them and pulled along-side the wagon. "Mornin' to you!" he jovially called out. "Can I ride along with you this morning?"

Willa waved and hollered, "Mattie . . . hey, Mattie" Her smile covered her face and her voice was full of the pleasure of seeing this friend and neighbor.

"Haven't seen much of you lately," Opal responded. "Been busy over at Mitchell's place?"

"Yeah . . . we've lost some cattle this winter to the high country snows. We should'a moved them earlier than we did, but Mitchell knew the meadow wouldn't feed all the ones we kept after fall works, so we were hoping for a mild winter. But we pulled everything down as soon as we could, and he's counting the loss on his fingers at supper every night now instead of fingers and toes every morning."

Everyone chuckled, and the group fell into the comfort of old friendships. Questions flowed briskly as they journeyed along the familiar roadway. As they pulled into town, Matt spoke directly to Opal, "I'd like to ride along home with you this evening if that would be all right?"

She smiled to herself, thinking *Why would we be in town all day, Mattie?*

"We'll be leaving as soon as we can get what we come for and head back. I want to get home before the road mucks up again. But if you've got time on your way back, stop by and we'll eat an early supper so you can get home before dark."

"Thanks . . . I think I will. Maybe I'll be done early and catch you on the way out of town anyway." He waved and planted his horse in front of the saloon.

She shook her head. "Stupid kid may never grow up," she commented to Johnny who was helping Willa to the boardwalk. He had no comment, but walked into the store with a little hand holding his tightly.

246

She handed a list of food and household items to the chunky woman behind the counter, stopping to talk only a few minutes before she began perusing the shelves. Was there any special item she might find that would fulfill her need for an "under the tree" present for Willa? She might not be back to town again before Christmas.

Willa found her own gift! There near the front door, a little wooden bowl sat on the shelf, and tucked inside it were a small wooden spoon and a very small apron. "Look Mama," called Willa. "It's my size!"

"Uh huh . . . it sure is," responded Opal. Now to divert her attention so she could let the owner know she wanted that added to the order. "Look, Willa . . . books."

"Ohhhhh ... look, Mama! It's a my size book," she called out again. Her voice peaked with excitement, and again Opal pointed to a children's book as she got the attention of the woman at the counter. "This one too," she mouthed to the lady, pointing to the book from behind Willa's back.

"Let's get you a candy stick." She again diverted Willa and talked her into helping load the wagon with smaller parcels she could carry. She added a handful of hard candies to the stash for the stocking she would hang. Johnny packed the wrapped parcel with the little bowl and a children's book himself, and hid the packet under the other items to retrieve when they got home. She would ask him to hide it in the bunkhouse for Christmas morning.

The trip home was full of delightful conversation. Willa sucked on her candy stick and talked about all the wonderful things she had seen at the store. Opal was as excited for   Christmas to arrive as she had been when she was a child. She'd found a small gift for Johnny, and a new book for her father. They would kill a fat chicken and break out the spiced canned peaches put up in August by the old Mexican lady. There were sweet yams in the buckboard, even though they had little shoots breaking forth in their eyes, but they would be just fine as a sweet addition to the dinner. She would make a pie with the apples in the root cellar, and there was a crock of apple cider making on the shelf.

Matthew never showed up for supper. *Maybe he'll come Christmas.* She'd like that. It would be lonely without Old Tom and her mother. She was overcome with the feeling of loneliness, and sincerely considered her feelings toward her friend of childhood years. *He's fun to be around. He has a good heart.* She brought herself up short. *He's a dam' overgrown selfish kid.* But . . . there weren't many to choose from in these parts and she sure wasn't up for a "mail order bride groom."

***

Two days before Christmas, Johnny rode up a short canyon and cut a shapely piñon tree about three feet tall and packed it home on a mule. He managed to nail a couple of boards to the trunk that would hold it upright, and placed it in the corner of the big room in the main house. Willa and Opal strung popcorn and cranberries with a few beads from her mother's sewing stash and draped the tree with a grand flourish and abundant ceremony. Some paper stars and snowflakes, cut carefully with tiny hands, filled in the empty branches of the tree.

As Christmas Eve crept upon them, her father did as he had always done with the reading of what folks thought of as "The Christmas Story" from his worn Bible. Willa clapped her hands with the lines about the animals near the baby's bed.

"He was a happy baby," she added to the story lines.

Johnny kept a fire going in the wood stove in the kitchen, and it kept the rest of the house warm. Clothes and sweaters, heavy socks and long sleeved flannel shirts were the chosen dress for the evening.

Willa was nodding off to sleep when a gentle knock came at the door. She jumped and ran to answer. "Must be Matthew," Opal commented to her father. "Can't believe he rode over in the dark!" She followed Willa, but let the tyke open the door, knowing she would have a hug for him.

When she saw the face in the doorway, she gasped, and nearly went to her knees.

"*Jaaaacub!*" screamed Willa. She ran to him and threw her arms up.

He lifted her to his shoulders, hugging her back and burying his face in her curly hair, tears streaming down his cheeks. "Hello, little one," he spoke through broken quivers in his voice.

"J-a-a-c-u-b," she continued to coo as she pulled back to look at his face, and her little pudgy hands stroked his leathery cheek. "Don't cry," she whispered. She pushed his hat back on his head as she wiped his tears.

Opal found herself wiping tears as she waited until Willa was finished with her hugging and cooing.

"Come see Johnny." Willa motioned to him, but held on with one arm around his neck, refusing to be set down on the floor.

Perching her over one arm, Jacob moved into the room, shaking hands with Johnny then with Maxwell, who rose politely, but growled instead of a welcome.

Opal knew there would be words formed in her father's mind that would certainly be released at some opportune moment.

When Jacob turned to look at her, he smiled sheepishly, pulling his hat from his dark hair. "Hey, Opal, it's good to see you." His voice was soft, apprehensive.

She simply nodded in response, unable to form words that would leave her lips without a sob. "You, too," she finally pushed through. "Can I get you something to eat, or a warm drink?" Her voice quivered, and she turned away to hide what she knew must be obvious to everyone in the room.

"Coffee or something hot would be good. I didn't get done in town as quick as I thought and it got dark on me. Had to try to remember how the road lay to find my way here, and a couple of times I wasn't sure I was still on the road at all."

She moved to the kitchen and pulled the coffee pot from the stove. She dumped the grounds and added fresh water and dry coffee, irritated that her hands were shaking so bad she nearly missed the opening on the pot with the scoop of coffee. She tried to reason why he was here, but her mind raced and filled with the memory of his kiss. She blushed, and tried to push it away, but again it surfaced, causing her to flush and shake. She wanted to send everyone away and have him all to herself, but if she did what would happen?

She set the coffee to make, and moved to a chair at the table. Seated, she watched as Jacob laughed and talked to Willa, who remained in his lap with her arm around his neck. He answered questions from Johnny, and tried to converse with Maxwell, who seemed to warm up to him. She knew he had always liked Jacob, in spite of his resentment when the cowboy simply rode away in the night with no farewell and no explanation. Opal had never mentioned what happened between the two of them the night he left.

The coffee boiled over before she could get to it, but she moved it to the side of the stove and poured a cup of cool water over the top, settling the grounds before she poured Jacob a cup. She stopped at the table on her way to deliver it and put about a half a teaspoon of sugar in, stirred it gently, remembering that when it was available he liked a little sweetness in his coffee. When she handed it to him, his fingers touched hers, and his eyes reached in search of something she couldn't identify. It made her insides shaky and she was glad to hand off the coffee before she spilled it.

It wasn't long until little miss Willa nodded off to sleep with her head on his shoulder. She had tried so very hard to keep her eyes open. She yawned and wiggled trying to stay awake, until Jacob lifted her gently and carried her to her bed. He sat beside her, stroked her hair and talked softly to her until she fell asleep, clutching his finger with her own little hand, unwilling to let go.

Opal stood in the doorway until he rose and moved toward her. She turned and walked back to the table where she stood behind a chair. She noticed her father had gone to his room, the door was closed, and Johnny had stealthily left the room and was obviously on his way to the bunkhouse.

She stood quiet as he glanced around the room and commented, "Looks like we're alone, girl. I have something on the porch for Willa if it's okay to bring it in?"

"Sure." She answered softly, afraid to say anything more for fear the bubble in her chest would burst and she would begin to gush words that would make no sense right now.

He stepped out the door, the cold wind blew it open farther and she ran to hold it and close it behind him. He brought in a parcel that had been waiting in the seat of her father's chair to be moved inside after Willa had gone to sleep. He laid it on the table, motioning her to open it. "We can put it under the tree if you like."

She unwrapped a hand-made doll, dressed in a gingham dress with a blue bonnet. "It's so sweet. Willa will love it. I never would have thought to get her a doll . . . but I know she will love this one. Simply because you brought it for her." Opal stroked the doll's dress gently, avoiding eye contact again.

She set it down on top of the wrapping paper, and turning to him asked the question that had formed itself in her mind a million times. But all she could utter was, "Why, Jacob? Why did you leave? Didn't you hear me calling you?" Her voice broke as the last words left her quivering lips.

"I couldn't face you after what I did. I shouldn't have done that, I had no right." He stopped speaking, breathing hard. "But I missed you all so much I had to come back, even if it's only for a day or so. I hope you aren't mad at me for this. I just couldn't face Christmas without seeing Willa."

"Just Willa?" she asked so soft it was almost a whisper.

"And you . . . and you." He looked straight into her eyes, still searching for some hint of feelings to betray her.

"Oh Jacob . . ." she reached for his arm, stepping close and lifting her face to his. "I have watched for you, waited for you to ride up to this house for months. I can't bear it if you leave again." Tears trickled from the corners of her eyes, and found their way into her hair.

"Are you saying what I think you are?" Jacob whispered.   He reached to draw her into the fold of his arms, waiting and watching every expression on her face.

"If you're thinking I want you to be right here, right now, then yes, I am."

She stood on her tiptoes, reached up to kiss him gently on the cheek, holding him close. Her heart was warm, and contentment filled her soul. She didn't dare anything more, at least not for the moment.

He reached to place his hands on her shoulders, moving her away to see her face. "I can't stay, Opal, unless I know that what you want and what I want is to be together till the end of our days. I can't find the right words to tell you how much I love you . . . it's been on me since the day I helped you set   little Willa in her saddle. I guess I'm crazy in love with you. But I couldn't stay here unless I know you could find it in your heart to love me back even just a little."

"A little?" Her eyes filled again with tears and her mouth went dry.

"I know you didn't like me much for a long time, and I know I make you mad *all the time*. But I'm hoping you have come to care enough that I could hope for something to grow between us. I have been miserable without you in my life, and I've been sick over losing Willa." His voice filled with concern and apprehendsion.

She tried to form sentences in her mind that would reveal her love for him. But it had come as such a surprise, even to her! How could she express what had so carefully entwined itself into every fiber of her being over months of emotional confusion.

Instinctively, she knew there were no words. She moved against him, reached up to enfold him in the circle of her arms around his neck. She pulled his leathery face to hers where she met his lips in a kiss that quickly became desire, drawing him into her very being. He responded with a passion she had never experienced before, one that was nearly overwhelming with a need to absolutely absorb her.

Suddenly, he struggled to draw away, to look her in the eyes again, to take her face in his hands and kiss her tears away.

He lovingly brushed her hair aside to make a place for soft kisses planted all over her face. They laughed, and cried, until they folded themselves into a chair, her on his lap with her head resting quietly on his shoulder.

"Well . . . this sure isn't how I figured this night would end." He spoke softly into her ear.

"Me either." She lifted her head to search his eyes. Her hands found his cheeks, and she caressed him gently, kissing his face until he closed his eyes, then she kissed his closed eyes before she found his lips with hers again. "I'll never let you leave this place, do you hear me?"

"Yes, ma'am . . . I hear you." Then he smiled that impish grin and added, "But not cuz you said so. Just cuz I couldn't bear to ever leave again."

They moved to a comfortable chair, and remained wrapped in each other's arms until she fell asleep on his shoulder. His leg went numb under her weight, so that he wanted to move her, but he couldn't bear to shift her away from his grasp. He felt her breath on his neck, smelled the scent of her soap, and carefully moved her hair away from his face where it tickled him as his own breath moved it gently to and fro. His toes had begun to feel like needles were poking him when the sun broke through the clouds on the horizon.

Willa and Maxwell both woke about the same time, and Willa danced her way into the room, squealing loudly when she saw

Jacob still there. She hugged him tightly, until she saw that beneath her tree were little bundles wrapped carefully and she whispered, "For me?"

"For you," both Jacob and Opal responded.

It was indeed the most special Christmas she could have imagined, and Opal sat quietly throughout the day, watching Jacob and Willa. Chores were done morning and night, Johnny came to join them for meals and gift exchanges. Maxwell warmed up to Jacob, but did comment that he thought he was pretty friendly with Opal considering he'd been gone for a long time.

It was evening when Jacob sat quietly in front of Maxwell and mustered enough inner strength to look him squarely in the eyes. Clearing his throat, he spoke clearly, "Maxwell, I'm askin' if you would allow me to marry Opal?"

"Do you love her?" Maxwell asked gruffly, completely oblivious to what should have been a well known fact.

"More than I can say." Jacob answered as Opal came to stand nearby.

"And you . . . girl . . . you love him? I thought you could barely stand to have him here."

She flinched. "I know, Dad. It took a while for me to realize that in truth I love him as deep and strong as anyone in my life I ever have. I will marry him, even if you say no, and Willa and I will be with him regardless of your decision."

She was still that rebellious little girl who stood her ground with him from the time she was old enough to know what she wanted.

Maxwell laughed. "Well gal, as if I didn't know you would do what you want to. You two look to me like you already made up your minds, but I'll get used to it."

She moved to his side, placed her hand on his shoulder, and for the first time she could remember, wrapped his shaggy old head in her arms and hugged him with a grateful heart. Yes, he would get used to things this way. And, he had cared for Jacob before he'd left that night. He would come 'round, she was certain.

***

They simply stood before the preacher one early morning not long after Christmas. Only Johnny, Willa and Maxwell attended the ceremony, which lasted less than five minutes, prayer, vows and all. Then they gathered themselves back into the buckboard with Willa at the reins and everyone fussing about her hitting too many ruts and bumps. She cared not one whit for their coaching, and completely focused on her job. She clucked and laughed her way to the home ranch, chatting with whoever would listen about everything she saw along the way.

Opal sat tucked firmly into Jacob's shoulder, leaning against his back with her own arm entwined through his. *How has this come to pass? I never thought I could be this happy again.* She seemed to feel her mother smiling from somewhere far away. She wiped a few tears away as her heart hurt that her mother wasn't here to see this unfold. *I wonder if Will is watching, smiling, is he okay with all this?* She remembered the voice so many months ago telling her to love again, to be happy.

Surely this would meet with his approval even though she still knew nothing could or would ever replace that part of her heart reserved and tucked away only for him. Would Jacob bring her flowers, she wondered.

That evening, Opal watched nearby as Maxwell sat on his porch, presiding over all in his domain. She knew his thoughts were on an oh-so-special little woman who had been by his side for so many years. That was surely what he would be thinking of, for there was a gentle smile on his lips, and a look of soft contentment on his ancient, wrinkled face.

45760858R00144

Made in the USA
San Bernardino, CA
31 July 2019